BEST
WOMEN'S EROTICA
OF THE YEAR

VOLUME FOUR

BEST WOMEN'S EROTICA OF THE YEAR

VOLUME FOUR

Edited by
RACHEL KRAMER BUSSEL

Copyright © 2018 by Rachel Kramer Bussel.

All rights reserved. Except for brief passages quoted in newspaper, magazine, radio, television or online reviews, no part of this book may be reproduced in any form or by any means, electronic or mechanical, including photocopying, recording, or information storage or retrieval system, without permission in writing from the Publisher.

Published in the United States by Cleis Press, an imprint of Start Midnight, LLC, 101 Hudson Street, 37th Floor, Suite 3705, Jersey City, New Jersey 07302.

Printed in the United States.
Cover design: Allyson Fields
Cover photograph: iStock
Text design: Frank Wiedemann
First Edition.
10 9 8 7 6 5 4 3 2 1

Trade paper ISBN: 978-1-62778-248-7
E-book ISBN: 978-1-62778-249-4

CONTENTS

- vii   Introduction: The Sexual Allure of Outsiders Who Take Risks
- 1   Take the Shot • MICA KENNEDY
- 17   The Dressing Room • ALESSANDRA TORRE
- 23   Mark • ROSIE BETH RANDALL
- 37   O Captain! My Captain! • CALLIOPE BLOOM
- 49   The Jump • REBECCA CHASE
- 65   On Display • LOUISE LAGRIS
- 74   The Pick-Me-Up • SULEIKHA SNYDER
- 88   Belonging • TAMSEN PARKER
- 102   With Honors • SOFIA QUINTERO
- 114   Breathe • PATRICIA ELZIE
- 124   Aftershock • JO HENNY WOLF
- 137   Her Invisible Prison • JOCELYN DEX
- 147   The Invitation • REGINA KAMMER
- 163   Protest of Passion • ELIZA DAVID
- 173   Words with Benefits • TAMARA LUSH
- 189   Essential Qualities • ALYSSA COLE
- 202   Eight Seconds • MADELINE MOORE
- 215   Seven Sweets and Seven Sours • MEGAN HART
- 224   Baby Doll • SIENNA SAINT-CYR
- 238   Beautiful Dirty Wonderful • R. M. WOOD

- 251   About the Authors
- 255   About the Editor

INTRODUCTION:
THE SEXUAL ALLURE OF
OUTSIDERS WHO TAKE RISKS

The first three volumes of *Best Women's Erotica of the Year* didn't have official themes, but when I was compiling *Volume 4*, I decided I wanted stories on the themes of Outsiders and Risk. While on the surface those may seem incongruous, both spoke to me regarding current events and seemed urgently relevant. At a time when outsiders of many kinds are being ostracized, discriminated against, and shunned, I wanted to explore what being an outsider feels like on a deeply personal level. I always want the authors I publish to turn readers on, but this time, I also want to make you think.

The outsiders you'll read about here sometimes grapple with navigating a new culture, as in "Aftershock," by Jo Henny Wolf, or the constraints of their own culture, such as the tender, heartbreaking longing in "Seven Sweets and Seven Sours," by Megan Hart. In Eliza David's "Protest of Passion," a community organizer finds herself swept away by a different kind of passion than the one motivating her lover.

INTRODUCTION

I left it to my authors to define what exactly an outsider means to them, and their characters. All of us have likely been outsiders at one time or another, depending on the circumstances. Outsiders may be able to learn something about themselves via insiders, and in the process enjoy some hot sex, as happens in "The Pick-Me-Up," by Suleikha Snyder. Sometimes it's hard to say who the outsider is, such as in Alyssa Cole's sexy science fiction tale, "Essential Qualities." The bisexual protagonist of Calliope Bloom's "O Captain! My Captain!" ventures into unknown territory with her new lovers, going from outsider to insider as she takes a risk that pays off.

Taking risks in the face of fear has certainly cropped up in past volumes, but the risks the characters take in these stories are heightened. Sometimes these risks are erotic in nature, like trying something new for the first time, for instance posing for an erotic calendar, as the heroine of "Take the Shot," by Mica Kennedy, does, or starring in a gang bang, like Julie in "Beautiful Dirty Wonderful," by R. M. Wood. Sometimes the risk itself is a turn-on, such as the illicit but utterly arousing behavior of the naughty narrator in "The Dressing Room," by Alessandra Torre.

Sometimes these risks, while sexual in nature, involve confronting aspects of these characters' core selves that require a great amount of bravery. In "Her Invisible Prison," by Jocelyn Dex, Eden faces a battle between her desire and her agoraphobia. Her steps out of that "prison" are hard fought and all the more exciting. And lest you think a story involving mental health can't be scorching hot, Dex will surely prove you wrong. Similarly, in "Baby Doll," by Sienna Saint-Cyr, Heather pursues her fetish only with the very careful reassurance of her lover.

Many of these stories involve finding community of one sort or another, whether that's the world of rodeo bull riders in "Eight Seconds," by Madeline Moore, or kink club BDSM as in "Belonging," by Tamsen Parker. While passion and desire are at the heart of these tales, there's more happening than simple arousal.

There's a little something for everyone, I'd like to think, within these pages, from the woman going back to school who gets an education beyond the books in "With Honors," by Sofia Quintero, to a divorced woman getting seduced by a learned man in "Words with Benefits," by Tamara Lush. You'll travel back in time with "The Invitation," by Regina Kammer, get kinky with "Mark" by Rosie Beth Randall, explore a penchant for tickling in "Breathe," by Patricia Elzie, and attend an orgy in "On Display," by Louise Lagris.

You can find out more about the series at bweoftheyear.com and follow our books and authors @BWEoftheyear on Twitter and bestwomenserotica on Instagram. You can always reach me at bweoftheyear@gmail.com to share what you want to see more of in future volumes.

I hope, at least in some small way, this book entertains you and gives you inspiration to take the kinds of risks these characters do.

Rachel Kramer Bussel
Atlantic City, New Jersey

TAKE THE SHOT

Mica Kennedy

I could always run away.

Though my hand's already on the studio door, I'm sorely tempted.

No. You promised. Woman up. You are not a chicken.

The quiver in my stomach says otherwise. But it's understandable. It isn't every day your little sister asks you to pose for a sex calendar—or that you agree to it. What was I thinking?

Truthfully, I wasn't. I was trying to sleep in now that the university's spring semester was over. Naturally, this meant a phone call came at the asscrack of dawn. Only one person would dare.

"Somebody better be dead, Caroline," I mumbled.

"How much do you love me?" my sister asked.

"Oh crap. That never bodes well."

"You don't even know what it is!"

"But I know you. Spill."

"I need you to come model on this photo shoot," she said. "Candace got stomach flu."

"What did you do to my goddaughter?"

"It wasn't me. I told her not to do dollar wing night."

"Poor kiddo." I made a note to call her later. "So what, exactly, do you need?"

"I need you to pose for a few tasteful, sensual pictures with another model."

I made a noncommittal noise.

"Please, Nina," she begged. "My editor's after me like I owe her rent money."

"Define sensual. Not nudity?"

"No, Prudence," she mocked. "You'll be covered. With makeup, no one'll recognize you."

"I'm not a prude."

"Not since you dumped You-Know-Who, anyway."

"Don't start." My ex's failings were her favorite topic.

"That asshole spent five years treating you like a prop. *You* can be mature about it; *I* will hate him forever."

"He was just—uptight—"

"Uptight? The man has a tree-sized stick up his ass—and not in the good way!"

"Carly, please. I don't want to think about my ex or his ass. It's been a year. Let it go."

"I'm just saying. He'd absolutely hate this."

She was right. The man was a stickler for propriety. He *would* hate this.

Damn. Now I had to do it.

I breathe deeply and enter the studio. The jumble of lights, stacked backdrops, and enormous umbrella lights in the loft overwhelms me. Carly, however, is calm amid the chaos. Lens checks, shifting furniture, and screechy metal playing in the background. Nothing fazes her.

When she sees me, I get a huge smile. My baby sis is practically my clone. We share enormous topaz-brown eyes, toothy grins, even the same curvy body (we Johnson girls are particularly blessed in the booty department). Even with our contrasting skin tones—mine deep brown, hers lighter tan—people assume we're twins.

"Nina, thank heaven." She hugs me like it's been years. "Thank *you*."

"Like I'd let you down," I scoff. Never mind my momentary freak-out.

"Going from professor to video vixen is a big step."

"What is this video vixen business?" I give her serious side eye. "I agreed to 'tasteful, sensual pictures.' That's a direct quote."

"'Tasteful' and 'sensual' don't make you blush like that."

"If you want to see blush, get me some makeup. Stop embarrassing me."

"You're no fun." She sticks her tongue out at me. I give her my sternest teacher face but she just laughs. My students claim I'm tough; my sister doesn't even pretend to believe it.

She leads me to the improvised dressing room at the back of the studio. It's basically a curtain and rope, but it'll do.

"I have to do test shots on set," Carly says. She hands me a garment bag. "Put this on. Syd will do your face in a few minutes."

I draw the curtain shut as best I can. I kick off my shoes, then quickly strip off my yoga pants and sweater. My bra takes longer, of course; when your size involves more numbers than a locker combination, keeping your breasts where you want them involves engineering like the Sistine Chapel. The mass of hooks and underwires takes careful attention.

Finally, I slip it off and slide into a bustier of deep-green leather attached to a fluttery, translucent mesh skirt. I don't know how, but the thing pushes my breasts to heights they haven't seen since the nineties. The cups barely manage to cover my areolae. This can't be the whole outfit.

I check the bag. All that's left are a tiny scrap of a thong and a pair of open-toed stilettos. I put them on, grumbling. Carly and I clearly differ on the definition of *covered*.

Deep breaths. I can do this.

Syd knocks on the curtain. She nods at the outfit.

"That's perfect," she says. "Let's get you dolled up."

I spend an hour in the makeup chair. Between the soft brushes and Syd's gentle hands, I nearly fall asleep. But when she twirls me around to see the effect, I am stunned.

The woman in the mirror is alternate universe me. Not a forty-something teacher with under-eye bags like carry-on luggage. She's a goddess with cheekbones sharp enough to cut glass, sunset-painted eyes, and a mouth drenched in burgundy velvet.

Syd coats my skin in shimmery lotion that makes me glow. She even weaves a golden coronet and flowers into my hair. I've become a buxom woodland nymph. I adore it.

Syd steps back and nods decisively. "That's hot."

"Not just hot," Carly agrees. "Bangable." I snort.

The set has been transformed into a forest. Tree stumps draped with moss, vines overhead, blue and purple lights. Carly's plan finally clicks.

"You're doing *A Midsummer Night's Dream*," I say. "Why didn't you tell me?"

"Because I'm doing dirty *Midsummer*," she replies. "You know how you get." She gestures at the prop table. It's covered in BDSM gear.

Holy cat-o'-nine-tails, Batman.

Carly's smirk merely reinforces my resolve.

"I'm not the prude you think I am," I say in my most bored tone. "This is fine."

"All right, Titania," she says dryly. "I'm holding you to that."

"So. Where's my Oberon?"

Carly looks over my shoulder. "Behind you."

I'm smiling as I turn, eager to meet my partner in this mad adventure.

Instead, my face drops as I recognize my teaching assistant, Josh Medina.

Shit.

I've been obsessively imagining him half-dressed for the last year. The reality is far better than any of my fantasies.

His golden-brown limbs and chiseled chest could make a sculptor cry. And those raven-dark eyes rimmed with lashes so lush you'd swear he was wearing makeup. He's the perfect Oberon.

His eyes light up when he sees me, and his slow smile turns my knees to butter. I pull my sister aside.

"Carly, I can't do this."

"Why not? Weren't you just bragging about how much of a prude you aren't?"

"This is different. I'm his boss." I want to shake her, but I'm too busy covering my boobs with my arms. I'd kill for a robe right about now. "How'd you even find him?"

"That day I helped you move into your office," she replies. "We were talking, and you glanced over my shoulder. You got this goofy look on your face, like all your dreams had come true at once."

I remember that day instantly. We were carting boxes up the three flights of stairs, getting completely sweaty and gross, when Josh strolled by my open door. He'd been wearing that tight blue Henley and jeans that made his ass look like a perfectly ripe peach. I wanted to bite it.

He'd waved and smiled, polite as always. Something had to be wrong with me if even basic manners made me want to do unspeakably filthy things to him. I thought I'd kept my cool, but Carly had seen right through me.

"I had to see who could put that expression on your face," she says. "When I did . . . how could I not cast him? He's so striking."

Striking doesn't come close. Hot as balls, my goddaughter would say. My twenty-two-year-old goddaughter who, I remind myself, is much closer to his age than I am.

"You're both adults," Carly says. "He's not in your class, neither of you is pressuring the other, and it has nothing to do with your work. I fail to see the problem."

"Of course you don't see it. But this is my job. How can I maintain my authority when my TA has examined my T&A all up close and personal?"

"Um, Professor Johnson?" Josh's soft voice catches my attention. I turn to him.

"Yes, Mr. Medina?" I say, slipping into my professional register. A little lower and firmer than my usual tone. It's probably ineffective, since I'm standing here with all my worldly goods on display, but it makes me feel calmer.

He swallows hard, stands up straighter. I appreciate the chance to take in every glorious, sculpted inch of him.

"Wow," he finally says. "You look . . . amazing."

"Thank you," I say. I deliberately don't return the sentiment. I don't trust what might come out of my mouth.

"You're the last person I expected to see here," he says. "I wouldn't think this was your scene."

"Spent a lot of time thinking about that, have you?" I ask, arching an eyebrow. He blushes. It's adorable.

"Nah, I just—I mean—not a lot." He laughs, in that it's-a-joke-but-not-really way. Oh god. What if it isn't? Is he flirting? I don't know what to do with that.

"Caroline—Carly—is my sister. She needed a model, so I'm here."

"Cool. That's sweet of you."

"Foolish, more like, but I'll take sweet."

"Nah. It's badass." His face turns serious. "I overheard you and your sister talking. I know this is a little weird, but I'm okay with it. If you are."

"You work for me, Joshua. It wouldn't be right."

"But I don't. Not anymore," he says quickly. "I found a job in my department."

He'd been admitted too late to get a TA position in the physics lab, but we'd been thrilled to have him. We needed someone who could help our ESL students with scientific jargon.

"That's great," I tell him. "Our loss, but congratulations. I'm sure you'll be brilliant over there."

"I'll still volunteer sometimes, when I can," he says. "But since I don't officially work for you anymore, this is okay, right?"

"Really? You don't think it's weird, taking sexy pictures with me? I mean, I don't normally do this, but I've heard it can be . . . intense."

"I am all for intensity," he says, with another devastating smile. "There's no one else I'd want here."

Eek. Definitely flirting. My head's spinning a little.

Try to focus. Carly needs me here. Josh wants me here. And I? I want to be brave.

He holds out a hand. Trembling, I take it.

"All right," I tell him. "Let's make some magic."

The photo shoot is a blur. The heat from the lights, the awkwardness of holding poses, of being watched—none of it matters. I'm captivated by how beautiful he looks bound to that tree, ropes taut against his pecs, ball gag in his mouth.

I lean against him, eyes closed, bejeweled hands lifting my breasts as if offering them up. His breath grazes my lips, hot and fast. I want to close the gap and devour him.

Then he's on his knees, jeweled collar around his neck. Holding the lead in one hand and a whip in the other is intoxicating. It's too easy to imagine this is real, that he's mine to do with as I please.

When Carly seats me on an ornate chaise lounge, one hand taut in his hair, one stiletto-clad foot draped over his shoulder, I am instantly wet and throbbing. Josh leans back, nestles his head between my breasts. It's all I can do to stop myself from reaching for his cock.

Somehow, I make it through the rest of the shoot without embarrassing myself. In the dressing room, I don my street clothes again, carefully rehanging the bustier and skirt. I tuck the soaked thong into my purse. When I emerge, Josh and Syd are watching Carly download the images.

"Wow," Josh says.

I have to agree. The pictures are perfect. The fairy

queen as Dominatrix, her trickster king tamed, in her thrall. It's hot as hell.

"Mercy," Carly tells me. "I should have made you my model ages ago. Sister, you are really fucking hot."

"Hush," I say, very carefully not looking at Josh. My ears are hot.

Syd agrees. "If I didn't know better about you two . . . "

She doesn't finish the thought. Josh and I share an awkward laugh. Whatever magic existed between us, the spell's broken now. I don't examine why that saddens me.

He was just playing a part, I remind myself. Stop obsessing. He's gorgeous but off-limits. There should be nothing more than a distant friendship between us.

"Your editor will be glad, I'm sure," I say. "Does the calendar have a title yet?"

"*Fat Girls Who Like to Fuck.*"

"Carly!"

"Oh, calm down," she says, flicking through the images. "It'll be fine."

"Really?"

She shrugs. "We're substituting an asterisk for the *u*."

I shake my head. Only my sister.

A post-performance high has me restless. Or maybe it's having been half dazed with lust for the last six hours. Either way, I'm not ready to go home. I ask Syd if she's up for a drink, but she's helping Carly select the final shots. I leave them to their edits.

Outside, a breeze off the lake soothes me. It'll make for a pleasant ride home. Halfway to the parking lot, I hear Josh's voice.

"Professor!" He's breathing heavily, like he ran to catch up.

"I think you ought to call me Nina by now, considering?"

"Okay. Nina." He blushes again. "Do you still want to get that drink?"

I look up at him. Even in the twilight, his darkly lashed eyes and sharp cheekbones stand out. His face is . . . sweet. Fresh. Far too young. I can't do this.

"I don't think so." His face falls. A twinge of regret lances through me. I crush it.

"That's too bad. I thought—I hoped you wanted company. My company, specifically."

"You sweet, sweet boy. You have no idea what I want."

I turn away but he grabs my hand. His thumb strokes lazy figure eights across my palm, reigniting the fire in my core. I watch our joined hands, mesmerized. He tips my chin up so that I'm forced to meet his eyes.

"Show me," he whispers. "Please?"

It's his *please* that gets to me. So full of longing and need. The heat I see blazing in his eyes burns away any hesitation I feel.

My lips are on his almost before I know it. He leans in, threads his hands through my locks, and pulls me so close that every part of him is touching every part of me.

We kiss each other, slowly, thoroughly, lips and tongues dancing together so perfectly it feels like we must have done this before. In another time, or another life, maybe. I don't know. The only thing I'm sure of is that I never want to stop.

When we come up for air, we're both shaking. I take a few deep breaths, but my pulse is still racing.

"Nina," he whispers into my skin. "Beautiful, beautiful Nina. I've wanted to do that for so long."

"Hush," I say. "It's just the rush from the shoot. We were in a very . . . stimulating situation. That energy just spilled over."

"You haven't ever thought about this?" His tongue flicks that spot just below my earlobe. I moan. "Thought about us?"

"It would have been completely inappropriate, Josh."

"But you felt something, right?" He looks me in the eye. I nod.

"Shit. If I'd known that, I'd have quit months ago."

"No, no," I argue. "I wouldn't have wanted that. I liked seeing you every day."

"Are you willing to see me now?" he asks between kisses. "Is that something you want?"

"Right this moment?" I laugh, though his lips on my neck give me shivers. "I want you to be about five years older, and me to be about ten younger. So we could meet in the middle."

"Do you really care about that?" He rests his forehead on mine. "'Cause I don't. All I care about is that the most amazing woman I know is letting me kiss her, and I can't believe how damn lucky I am."

This man and his silver tongue will be the death of me. I can't wait.

We kiss some more, tangling together until we bump against the side of an ancient Dodge van. It's white, with thin burgundy stripes—a '70s classic.

"We should be careful of the van," I say, reluctantly breaking away. "The owner might not like it."

"The owner likes it very much," he says, dangling the keys.

"Oh, my lord. Who sold you a shaggin' wagon?" I laugh.

"I bought it from—wait, hold on, what did you call it?"

"A shaggin' wagon. A van that you—you know, you—" I'm intrigued. "You mean you've never—?"

"Never what?"

"Give me the keys."

"Why?"

"Because you asked me what I wanted," I say boldly. "Right now, I want you to get in this van and fuck me senseless."

He hands over the keys at once, and we climb in. It's dark, but the streetlights over the lot are just enough. He pulls the curtains separating the front seats from the rest of the interior, and we're in shadow again. I take his hand, and we sit down on the wine-colored carpet.

His lips graze mine. I'm already addicted to his sweetness, the faint hint of cinnamon on his breath. When my nails scrape his back, something fierce ignites between us. Then it's all popping buttons and sliding belt buckles and shoes that end up who knows where until I'm writhing on the floor in just my bra, aching for his touch.

"Wait, wait," Josh says.

"Seriously?" I'm groaning in frustration.

"I know, I know," he says, soothing me with another kiss. "I don't want to rush this. Let me take my time, hmm?"

I pout; he kisses it away, sucking and nibbling at my bottom lip. The sensation goes straight to my clit. He is so careful not to touch me as he removes my bra.

"Beautiful," he repeats. He stares at me with heat and tenderness in his eyes. I'm desperate to get his hands on me.

Finally, he trails a cool fingertip across my collarbone. I

suck in a breath when he follows it with his tongue. I need this so much. He continues, swirling cool and hot across one breast then the other. I can't hold back a moan when he flicks my nipples.

"Ah," he says, satisfied, as if he solved a puzzle. "You like that."

The needy noises I make encourage him. He does it again and again until I think I might come from this alone.

"Can—can I touch you back?"

"Soon," he promises. "Right now I need to concentrate."

His hands and mouth glide over my belly, hips, thighs. Between the licks and touches I'm almost out of my mind. I prop myself up on my elbows, watch him part my knees with strong, sure hands. He strokes slowly, so slowly, making his way toward my aching pussy.

His mouth follows his hands. My breaths come so fast, I'm almost dizzy when he licks the juncture of my thighs.

He looks up, his gorgeous eyes shining in the filtered light. "Can I . . . ?"

"Oh, please," I reply, and his tongue is on me, inside me in a flash. He alternates long, slow strokes with quick flicks against my clit until I'm gripping his hair and arching off the carpet like I'm electrified.

I'm close, so close. When he eases my clit into his mouth and gives it the tiniest suck, my brain short-circuits. I come so hard I see stars.

Josh murmurs sweet words in my ear as I return to earth. He kisses me, and the taste of us on his lips makes me even hotter than before.

"Tell me you have a condom," I growl.

He laughs. "So serious, Nina."

I flip over and straddle him. Grinding against the hard length of his cock. Now it's his turn to suck in a breath.

"Damn right I'm serious. Condom. Now."

Miracle of miracles, he produces one. Greedily, I snatch it from his grasp. He laughs again at my eagerness.

"I thought you wanted to—" he starts, but it turns into a hiss when I slide the condom on him with my mouth. His cock is thick and perfect, and I can't help lingering over it, eagerly slurping him into my mouth again and again, until he pulls me back up with a growl of his own.

"Woman," he breathes, "you're killing me."

"Is there a better way to go?" I tease. He doesn't answer, just smiles and sets me back on his lap.

I lift up, hovering over him for a moment before I slowly take him inside me. Sweet mercy. Inch by delicious inch, he fills me up until I'm stretched and breathless.

"You good?" he asks.

"Mmm. Oh, yes."

I ride him at a slow, easy pace, adjusting to the feel of him. He rolls my nipples between thumbs and fingertips, pinching them just enough that lightning zooms through me. I'm halfway to a second orgasm when he grabs my hips and takes over. He goes deeper, harder, fucking me so thoroughly that I can only whisper "*Yes*" and "*More*" and "*Oh my god*" and "*Yes fuck fuck yes*" as I come.

His orgasm is moments behind mine, and the wild abandon on his face when he comes is the most magnificent thing I've ever seen.

We kiss again, sweet and languid. He turns away to deal with the condom, then I'm nestled on his chest soon after. I will this moment of peace to last. Listen to his heart. Wonder what this means for my own.

I want to stay in this bubble, but the real world's already on my mind. He no longer works for me, but there are a thousand reasons this night can only be a lovely memory.

"Where did you go, just now?" Joshua asks me.

"I'm here," I say. His face tells me he knows better.

"I'm serious about seeing each other. This isn't casual for me. You know that, right?"

"I don't know anything, really," I say. We scrounge around for clothes, dressing as fast as we'd undressed. We step out of the van, and I'm tongue-tied. I want to say everything and nothing at once.

"So. I have a speech. Want to hear it?"

"A speech?"

"I'm in communications," he shrugs. "We always have a speech."

"What about physics?"

"Double major."

"I didn't know that." I sigh. "I should know that."

"I'll tell you all about me. Next time."

He wants a next time. My breath races at the thought.

"Short version," he says, "you're scared of this. Of us."

"Terrified."

"If today hadn't happened, would you have said anything?"

I shake my head.

"So we'd have kept wanting each other. Being too scared to admit it." He strokes my cheek. "I'm done being scared, Nina. I hope you are, too."

I don't understand how he's this brave. I'm terrified.

But I also wasted years being what someone else wanted, and it made me miserable. I might be the teacher, but clearly, I still have something to learn.

"We have to go slow," I say.
"Like snails," he replies.
"That is utterly unsexy."
"Come here then. I'll show you sexy."
I do, and he does. Over and over and over again.

THE DRESSING ROOM

Alessandra Torre

I am halfway into the dress when I get stuck. The sort of stuck where your arms are up, hands flailing through the sleeves, bodice tight around your face, and there just isn't enough room to get your elbows past your ears and through the armholes. I need to abort this, ASAP. I blow out a frustrated breath, a wave of claustrophobia swelling as the hot wool sucks into my mouth. I lean forward and try to wiggle out. Thank god no one is in here with me. No one to see this spectacle of uncoordinated proportions. Then again, had someone been in here with me, they could be helping to yank this thing off me. I lean against the thin changing room divider and slide sideways, hoping the dress will snag on its hook and work its way over my head. I am about to succeed when I hear the noise. I pause, my wool-covered head bumping painfully against the hook, and stifle a squeal of pain.

The sound comes again, and I lean closer to the wall, pressing my ear against it. A moan. I think it was a *moan*.

My change in position helps, and the dress slides over my head, my response to the fresh air and its cool greeting almost orgasmic. And . . . speaking of orgasmic . . . I press my ear to the wall, its fabric-covered surface scratchy against my lobe.

"Yeah. Right there." A woman's voice, thick with arousal. I hold my breath and can barely hear the soft sound of panting, her controlled bursts of air.

"Look at me." The man's voice is rugged, his words an order, delivered with the hint of an accent. I need more of his words, need to follow his directive and see him. I crouch, as quickly as I can, and peek underneath the divider.

A foot of access, but it's all I need to paint the picture. Her feet bare, toes painted a bright teal that is chipped along the edges. Her feet are strong and shoulder-width apart, not the delicate feet of a model but the sort that belong to a girl like me. It gives me hope, makes me think that I could be in there, could be looking at him, could be merrily panting my way toward an orgasm. At a right angle to her, he stands. New tennis shoes, dark jeans. I take pleasure in examining the neat tie of his laces, the clean surface of his shoes. This man takes care of himself. He probably picks his clothes up off the floor, flosses before bed, and pays his bills on time.

The heel of one of her feet lifts, her toes splaying, and she groans, a long, sweet sound of pure, unadulterated pleasure. The way they are standing, he must be next to her, his hand in between her legs, his fingers busy. There is the slick sound of flesh, and my own fingers inch toward my panties, the cotton boy shorts the only thing standing between me and pure nudity.

"Jesus, you're wet." He growls out the words, and I close my eyes, pushing to my feet, and pretend that he's speaking to me. The thick catch of the words . . . he must be staring into her eyes, his fingers sliding in and out, the palm of his hand tapping out a metronome of pleasure against her clit. I sit on the chair, my thighs parting, and work my panties over my hips, my own hand sliding in between my legs, two fingers pushing inside of me. He's right. *I am wet.* I picture his face, and he is handsome, his features rugged like his voice, his jaw covered in a faint beard, his eyes drifting down my naked body, drawn to my open legs. I spread my fingers, opening up the slick lips of my body, and then push the fingers back inside.

The woman moans, and I risk a small moan of my own, letting my eyes half close, wanting nothing more than to have him before me, those dark jeans moving closer, their stiff fabric brushing against my bare legs.

I roll my fingers over my clit and picture him pushing my hand aside, his replacing my own. His fingers are thicker than mine, slightly rough, and when they push in between my folds, his eyes darken.

Jesus, you're wet. His voice had scraped over the words, the memory of it causing my thighs to tighten and my hips to buck.

Fingers quickening, my clit coming to life under my touch—my body tightening, pleasure building.

She pants, he whispers something, and there is the scrape of hangers against their metal rod. I envision her hands wildly sweeping out, scrambling for balance, her legs weakening from the pleasure.

I straighten my own legs, my socks sliding across the linoleum floor, and picture him kneeling between my knees, his fingers working in and out, his eyes flitting up to meet mine.

"Oh my god, you're so hard." She can barely get the words out, her voice louder than before, and I wonder where the dressing room attendant is, how many others are hearing this. I keep one ear tuned for the sound of the buzzer—the *ding-dong* that indicates someone's entrance into the dressing room. Nothing. No footsteps, no rustles of fabric, no words of indignation. Just me and them. *Me.* My fingers now deep inside of me, curved and pressing on my G-spot, my eyes clenched shut, my fantasies running wild. *Them.* Her thighs trembling, his cock hanging out, his fingers busy, wet from her juices, his eyes tight on her face.

She moans, and a curl of pleasure unfurls inside of me.

"Wrap your hand around it," he growls, and I groan in response, hoping the sound is covered by her whimper. I imagine the stiff feel of him, my palm wrapping around his shaft, the hiss of his voice as I grip him tightly, sliding my hand along his length. I bet he's gorgeous—a thick, meaty stick of arousal and possibilities. I picture the head of him, swollen and stiff, jutting out from his hand, and lined up to me, the press of it against my opening, the look on his face as he pushes inside of me.

I'd want it quickly—one hard thrust that takes away my recent bouts of loneliness. One hard thrust that cracks open my pleasure, almost painful in its strength, almost rough in its invasion. I want him to grip my shoulders, pin me back against the wall and thrust those hips forward, his cock into me, his knees shifting against the floor, my gasps silenced by his mouth, by his deep kiss that tastes of hard work and security, his thrusts shallower as our kiss deepens. I increase the tease of my clit, my legs straightening out, toes flexing.

"I'm close," she pants out. *Me too.*

"Don't stop jacking me off," he grits. "Keep going."

If I were her, I wouldn't stop. I would prolong my own pleasure and focus on him, dropping to my knees and working my hand up and down his shaft. I'd look up into his face and watch his eyes grow hooded, his jaw clench, his features tighten as he gets close. He would groan my name, reach down and cup my face, would watch me with need as I tease him with my tongue before taking him into my mouth.

It's been so long since I experienced the full press of a cock against my tongue—since I felt the flex, the twitch, the swell. I miss hands tugging my hair, thighs flexing under my hands, the control and power of reducing a grown man to his barest animal needs.

I picture it, picture me before him, his mouth dropping open, a calloused hand reaching down to grip at my breast, his thumb brushing over my nipple.

"Oh, fuck," he growls, and I come undone, my back curling, thigh trembling, my fingers slick and quick, the orgasm sharp and intense. I come and listen to her do the same, his words gruff and soft, urging her on, urging *me* on, each filthy word stretching out my pleasure, my body limp and languid by the time the intensity ebbs.

My legs are lazy when I reach for my jeans, slowly pulling them on as I listen to the muffled rattle of a belt buckle in its clasp. I reach down for my tennis shoes and see her knees against the floor, her body shifting as she takes care of him. I listen for the sound of slurps and gags but don't hear them. She must be using her hand. I pull on my bra, then my shirt, and abandon the wool dress, leaving it off its hanger, trying—rather unsuccessfully—to sneak by their stall without my tennis shoes slapping along the floor. When I reach the entrance to the dressing area, I flee, moving through the almost-empty store, my cheeks burning, my body still tingling with postorgasmic joy.

I can't believe I did that. Can't believe I eavesdropped on them, pulled down my panties, and brought myself to orgasm. I can't believe I pictured his cock, wanted his touch, and spread my legs open in that tiny little stall. What if they heard me? What if they did hear me?

I yank open the car door and step in, stuffing my purse onto the floorboard and reaching for the seat belt, suddenly filled with the panicked thought of them coming outside, seeing me, and somehow *knowing* everything.

"Well, that took forever." My husband fumbles with the bottom of his seat, the back of it slowly rising, his mouth stretching into a yawn. "You didn't find anything?"

I shake my head. "No. Nothing that fit."

"Well, that sucks." He reaches for his own belt. *Sucks.* I think of my lips wrapped around the stranger's cock, the taste of him, the sounds rumbling from his throat. "Talk about a waste of a trip."

I swallow a smile. "Seriously."

I sit back, my head resting against the seat, and close my eyes, my body fully relaxed for the first time in weeks. As he shifts the car into drive, I cross my legs, enjoying the damp feel of my panties, my clit still tender from the attention.

A waste of a trip? Well. *Not exactly . . .*

MARK

Rosie Beth Randall

Before letting go of our good-bye, he pulled me close one last time and inhaled deeply. With his nose in my hair, he dropped his voice so only I could hear and said, "If I ever catch you doing that again, Diana, there will be consequences."

It was dark where we were standing, out of reach from the amber streetlamps. The wintry night was cloaked in a smooth layer of fresh snow, but his breath was warm against my ear. The woody smell of his cologne mixed with the power in his words made me want him right then and there, up against the wall beside my building's stoop. It had been so long since I'd felt free enough to want anything like that—since I'd felt desired enough to let myself want that—but being with Mark had changed me, helped me come out of the shell I'd kept around myself all those years. He didn't mind the four-inch scar across the right side of my face, like everyone else seemed to. If anything, he'd taught me to accept it.

MARK

I slipped my hand inside his open coat and went straight for his cock, unable to resist.

"Catch me doing *what?*" I whipped my voice to a taunt at the end just to fuck with him, hoping it would rile him up enough to be unable to resist me too. Our contract plainly stated he had to initiate activity like this; public sex was a rare occasion for Mark. He only wanted it for certain reasons, when it really meant something—but I figured a bit of goading was worth a try. I just wanted to taste his mouth against my own once more, with his cock pushed into me at the same time.

I palmed the zipper of his trousers and curled my fingers around his balls, trying to lure him with a squeeze. But Mark caught me by the wrist and backed away.

"Lawrence will pick you up tomorrow morning at eleven." He released my arm and turned toward the curb, where his car and driver, Lawrence, were both waiting. "Wear jeans and that blouse I like."

When Mark climbed into the backseat without so much as a hint of a smirk, my mouth was watering. His foreplay—detached yet still totally dominant—never failed. He did it so well. Even when he was trying to hide how hard he already was.

The next morning, I emerged from my apartment promptly at eleven. Lawrence was waiting right where he had been the night before, as if he'd never disappeared. Mark wasn't there, but he'd left me a package in his stead. Wrapped in thick matte burgundy paper, with a black velvet ribbon tied around it, the box was about the size one would use for a pair of high-heeled shoes. Dangling from the edge of its many-looped bow was a cream-colored card, Mark's blocky printing on the backside: *Open carefully.*

I knew he had a camera hidden somewhere in that Maybach, so I did as I was told.

Swelling with sudden anticipation, my insides almost couldn't handle my excited breath as I untied the bow. I had no idea what to expect, but the thought of Mark sitting in his office, watching me from afar, thrilled me more than any gift he could've gotten me. I rolled my lips against each other, taking my time as I eased the ribbon off the box and spun it into a tidy spiral. I could feel myself panting—when I set the lush coil on the empty seat beside me, the fresh leather scent of the upholstery was riding in and out of my nose faster than my hands were moving—but I made myself go slowly. I wanted to savor every facet of this moment, this representation of his desire, for as long as possible. Not only for myself, but for him too as he watched.

I was so focused I didn't realize the car was moving until Lawrence stopped at the first red light. I noticed my cunt tingling, already wet against my black lace thong. Smirking, I shifted side to side against the sturdy seam in my jeans, amplifying the sensation. Then I tucked my thumb under the sticky flap of wrapping paper and nudged it open. Throbbing all over with a giddy curiosity, I peeled back the paper with both hands, the way Mark often spread my legs with both of his.

The box's lid was simple, covered in a black twill fabric. It was elegant but didn't have any traces of origin. No designer name or symbol embossed, no clue whatsoever as to what might be inside. It was mysterious, like Mark. We'd been together more than a year, and I had yet to fully figure him out. As far as I was concerned, the man was the total embodiment of the word surprise.

I lifted the lid from its bottom.

And found another cream-colored card atop the burgundy tissue paper inside.

> *If you are reading this, you have twenty minutes left before you'll reach your destination. In that time, I want you to undo your top, take off your panties, put your fingers in your mouth to wet them, and then I expect you to touch yourself (pinching and squeezing your tits while stroking your clit, like I do) until you are ready to be penetrated. Then you may open the rest of this gift.*

I felt my eyes widening. I had to read it several times, because my heart kept leaping into my throat, shaking my vision. I wondered where he was taking me, what he had planned for when I arrived. I wanted to know what he'd wrapped in that tissue; the layers were so crisp and pristine they didn't indicate even an outline of the shape they were holding.

My mouth grew hot and slick with wanting.

Whatever previous inclination I'd had toward protraction disappeared altogether.

The partition was closed and curtained, so as long as I kept sort of quiet . . . I placed the open box on the armrest beside me, thrust my hips upward, ripped the button from the loop in my jeans, and tore down the zipper. After shimmying my waistband and panties off my hips in one go, I swatted away each lapel of my wool coat. Raced through half the buttons down the front of my silk blouse. Yanked each of my breasts from the lace bra that matched my panties. Sat my bare ass back in the seat, opened my legs, closed my eyes, and didn't even pause to take a breath before diving into my own depths.

My juices were already dripping down my thigh, but I plunged my right middle and ring fingers into my mouth anyway, extending my tongue beyond my lips to lap against them because Mark loved when I did that. Teasing myself, I walked my fingers down my warm abdomen, prolonging the buildup before the first touch on my clit. Then I drove my other thumb and forefinger into my mouth, stuck out my tongue against them too, and with the same tempting pressure Mark always used, lowered them to my bite-sized nipples, twisting each, one at a time. I flashed back to the night before. Mark had led me by the hand into his room. Pointing to the white king-size bed, where two lengthy black restraints awaited me, he'd said, "I want you facedown, with your ass up and your hands out in front of you in the cuffs."

I pressed harder into my clit, circling the pads of my fingers clockwise, pinching my left nipple as I imagined Mark's tongue licking across my skin, his spit trickling down the center of my exposed ass. A bead of sweat dripped over the back of my neck when I remembered how hot we'd looked in the mirror beside his bed. Mark had stopped tonguing my cunt and turned to me in the reflection when he'd felt my gaze tracing around his moves. Eyeing me with his soulful brown eyes, he'd spanked my ass hard and said, "I didn't say you could watch yet." He'd pushed his fingers deep inside me after that, demanding, "Close your eyes, until I tell you to open them."

I pushed my middle and ring fingers inside myself, wishing they were his.

A waft of his lingering cologne drifted into my nose, revitalized beneath my body's heat against the seat. Mark usually sat on this side of the car. I felt myself searching for him behind my closed lids, longing for his touch, his physical presence.

"I didn't say you could come, Diana . . . "

At first, I thought I'd imagined it. But Mark's voice really was reaching out from the speaker beside my headrest, tickling the edge of my ear.

A startled gasp fled my gaping mouth.

Raising my top lashes, I looked around, shocked.

Then Mark spoke to me again. "Open your package. You're almost to your destination."

I heard a click. As if he'd disconnected a call, maybe hung up a phone.

I'd been so consumed thus far by the note's instructions I hadn't kept track of the time or where my ride was going. I peered out the tinted window to my left, my heartbeat raging against my ribs. We were in Midtown, headed toward the West Village, but I didn't know what it meant. Still had no idea where Mark was leading me.

Worried I should hurry, I brought the box to my naked lap. Dipped my hands into the folds of rustling paper. Wondered if Mark was bringing me to his office instead of taking me to lunch, like I'd assumed. Then, as soon as I lifted the top layer of tissue from the rest, I felt my burning nipples shrink with an unexpected chill. The feeling coursed through my breasts, down the center of my half-bare stomach, landing deep in my core, expanding outward as the next incendiary drip of wetness my cunt couldn't bear to hold inside me any longer trickled onto my thigh.

I could tell what the gift was now, without even seeing it.

But I continued taking my time with the rest of the unwrapping.

Even if he punished me for it later, I wanted to make Mark wait.

Mark was the only man I'd ever known who actually understood that my submission was the ultimate gift—without it, without my permission and participation, he wouldn't have anyone to dominate, he couldn't achieve his own satisfaction. My husband, before Mark, knew me better than anyone in the world, and even he couldn't wrap his head around that. I'd missed Frank every day since the day I lost him; I would never stop missing him. But sharing moments like this with Mark enlivened me again. I didn't have to explain anything to him. He always seemed able to just intuit what I wanted. None of my friends understood it. They thought Mark was pretentious. His reserved demeanor intimidated them. But deep down I knew; every time I stood by his side I felt more and more liberated from my past. His presence, our connection alone made it easier to breathe, to let go and simply exist.

I pulled back the last piece of tissue, marveling at what he'd given me.

A custom-crafted pair of panties.

With a long shining black dildo standing up from the crotch.

And a matching plug a few inches behind, shaped like the dildo's perfect miniature twin.

Both were already turned inward and securely sewn to the gusset, so I could walk around wearing them, packed into my ass and cunt—without anyone else knowing.

MARK

The tingling through my insides rose to an unmistakable throbbing, causing a flush to overtake my neck and face. I wished Mark could be there to guide both toys into me.

As if he'd known I might think that, he'd left one last note in the bottom of the box.

> *When you're ready, change out of your panties and into these. I want you to picture my dick when you put this dildo into your pussy, and I want you to be steady and gentle when you insert the plug into your ass, like I always am. Then I want you to put your clothes back on . . . When you get out of the car, I expect you to look as composed as you did when you first got in it.*
>
> *PS: There's lube in the refrigerator.*

Smiling, I kicked off my heels and scurried to get my legs out of my jeans and thong. I opened the fridge behind my armrest, grabbed the small cold bottle of lube, and squirted a glossy dab onto the plug. I was plenty wet enough for the dildo—just thinking about it was giving me goose bumps—but even though I was new to ass play, I knew I would need lube no matter how excited I was.

Picturing Mark as I slid the dildo inside me, its girth felt almost as good to me as his cock. I moved on to novel territory with the other toy. Wherever the camera was, I hoped he was enjoying the view of me pushing the plug's rounded point between my hungry cheeks. "Mmm . . . " I gave him a naughty grin as I flattened the waist of the new panties across my hips.

Making sure the leg holes were smooth around my thighs, slowly, I carefully eased down into the seat once more. I'd never felt so full on my own.

Every inch of my body between my belly button and thighs was thumping with the strongest longing I'd ever felt for Mark. For anyone, really. "I wish you were here with me," I whispered, trying to relax my pulsing muscles around their newfound toys. I knew, when I leaned down to get my jeans and heels, it would be a challenge. Especially if Lawrence went over a bump in the road. But after a few breaths to prepare, I was ready.

And it was so delicious I stayed hunched down the whole time I dressed.

After separating my thong from the denim, I folded that pair of panties, wrapped them in the leftover tissue, and put everything neatly back in the box. Creaming at the thought of Mark finding it all later, I grew breathless and overheated as I bent down farther to get my jeans. Once I'd put my feet into the holes, I almost couldn't take having to rock my hips to meet the waistband. I kept clenching the denim as if that could somehow relieve the tension and aching. But it didn't.

I wasn't sure I actually wanted that relief yet anyway.

Really, I wanted to wait for Mark to fuck me himself. Hopefully soon.

Lawrence rolled to a stop. Outside Barneys.

The brakes sprung the car backward, and I gasped again, struggling to catch my breath. Apart from my jeans being on, I was still in disarray. Rushing, I gathered the notes, shoved them into my coat pocket, then slammed the lid onto the box. Zipped and buttoned my pants. Tucked my breasts into place. Flew through my blouse's buttons, closing them quicker than I'd shredded them open. Slipped back into my heels. Gave my hair a single swipe on both sides. And had time for one more try at a deep breath, before Lawrence knocked on the window.

"Ms. Wilson?"

I cracked the door, signaling he could open it. "Yep!" My face flushed again when I took the old man's white-gloved hand. I was clinging to him harder than I ever had, but with the snow turning to slush on the ground and my insides so occupied . . . I didn't want to fall. "Thank you." I couldn't meet his gaze when I let go, but I could finally breathe. Sort of. The morning air was frigid in my lungs.

"Mr. McAllister gave this to me, to give to you." Lawrence manifested a cream-colored envelope from his blazer's inner pocket and passed it across the space between us.

"Oh . . . " I wobbled, unsure whether I could take any more than I already had. "Right . . . " I knew better than to ask any questions, though—Mark only told Lawrence what he absolutely needed to know.

When I accepted the envelope, the man tipped his hat like always, returned to the car, and drove off.

I want you to walk into Barneys. Take the stairs to the fourth floor. No elevator. Give each step its due. You need to think about what a privilege it is to have me inside you. Stop when you get to personal shopping. Your appointment is at 11:30.

I checked my watch. I had seven minutes to tackle the giant, winding white staircase.

By the end, when the sixty-something sprite of a stylist greeted me, I had zero interest in shopping at all. I wanted nothing more than to collapse into the nearest tufted chair. But I could admit, I did want to know what Mark had up his sleeve.

"Diana?" The chic, petite woman beamed at me.

I nodded, trying not to wince. At that point, there was no way I could talk. It was all I could do not to paw at my sweating brow right in front of her.

"I thought that might be you. Mark told me you were pretty."

I blushed. Instinct drove my hand to my right cheekbone, as if I had an itch under my eye, but I told myself this woman couldn't have seen my scar from where she was.

"I have several options for you in the dressing room." She motioned to a hall about fifty yards away. "Let's see if any work, and we'll go from there?"

I nodded again, almost dreading the walk.

"Great. This way, please." She stopped at the hallway's entrance. "I'll leave you here. Yours is the last one on the right. Ring if you need anything."

When I opened my dressing room door, Mark was there.

Waiting, beside the only chair in the space.

"Don't speak." His voice was low under his breath. "Step forward and shut the door." He was standing with his arms folded over his chest.

My stomach dropped. I was in trouble. I could see it in his eyes.

My soaking cunt tingled.

"I said step forward. And shut the door." When I did, he pointed to the floor in front of the chair. "Kneel. Facing the mirrors."

I did my best to mask my hobbling.

Once down, I peeked at Mark through the center of our triptych reflection. Feeling my desire hammering from my chest, quaking my every bone. I was dripping all over my new panties, and my ass was so tired I almost couldn't breathe.

"I didn't say you could look at me."

I dropped my eyes to the carpet.

"Do you remember what I put on the line to be with you?" Mark walked forward, between my heels and the silver velvet chair behind me. "I asked you a question." He sat down.

The memory constricted my throat.

After I lost Frank, I couldn't fathom going back to my college teaching job. The idea of so many students gawking at me with this massive slash on my face was unbearable. But the idea of staying inside, in the home Frank and I built, without Frank there anymore, was even more unbearable. I needed something to busy my hands, that got me outside and didn't require too much of me mentally. I took a job in construction, helping to rehabilitate and landscape some of the parks in Manhattan, thinking no one there would bother me or care about my face. One day, however, Mark, one of the investors in the project, walked across the site just to talk to me. He introduced himself and said, "I don't normally do this, but I feel like I need to know you, and I've decided I would like to get to know you . . . Will you have dinner with me?" At the end of that date, he told me he'd wondered about me every day since the first morning he saw me, that he'd watched me during his on-site visits for years.

"Of course I remember," I whispered.

"Am I the type of person who would risk losing my

success, ruining my reputation, if my attraction to you wasn't real?" Mark tilted forward, reached around my waistband, and opened my jeans.

"Of course not."

"Could I even *be* attracted to you, if I didn't find you beautiful?" He slid his fingers inside my new panties, stopping when he'd found my clit. "I'm waiting."

"No . . . " I noticed my voice had gotten small.

"That's right. The answer is *no*." He curled his other hand around the base of the plug in my ass, pushing it in deeper, like he wanted me to moan.

So I did. Because it hurt, but I liked it, and even though he'd caught me by surprise with all of this, I liked that too.

"Look at me in the mirror."

I wanted to keep staring at the floor, but I knew better. I couldn't take anything more anywhere in my body. I could barely take what he was doing already.

"I need you to see what I see." Mark increased his pressure on my clit, going faster and harder, the way that always made me come. He took his other hand off the plug and used it to turn my chin toward our reflection, bringing my scar into the light. "I said look at the mirror. I need you to see how lucky you are to be mine."

Tears brimmed in my eyes and I didn't want to be crying, but I gave in. I didn't understand how I could feel so many sensations at once. When Mark said the word "lucky," I couldn't help flashing back to the weeks after the accident. Frank had died before I'd woken up from my coma; I had this permanent gash on my face, and every doctor around me was saying, "You're so lucky the windshield missed your eye." "You're lucky you were wearing your seat belt." "You're so lucky," over and over.

A tear crept forth, sliding down my cheek. I didn't feel lucky whatsoever, until Mark came over to me that afternoon and asked me to dinner.

I couldn't comprehend how I could orgasm inside Barneys in that moment. In so many ways I was still heartbroken about so many things. All I could see was how raw my wounds had remained, but something about the look in Mark's eyes made me feel safe. The safest I had in years. Maybe ever. And with his arms around me, when he whispered in my ear, "Come for me, baby. Let go . . . " I couldn't resist.

I closed my eyes and let out a noise I'd been striving to swallow for more than a decade.

Mark moved his hand over my mouth to hold it for me. Protecting me, until it passed.

Then he lowered his palm to my chest, calming me.

"It set my teeth on edge when you joked last night about how you *used* to be pretty, implying that you aren't anymore." He studied my reflection, unleashing a burdened sigh of his own. "I can't be with you, Diana, if you continually refuse to see what I see . . . " He zeroed in on my softening eyes. "If you ever discount your beauty again, I will leave."

"I don't want that," I whispered.

"I don't either." Mark brushed the side of my cheek, wiping my tears. He slowly stroked his last finger over my scar, as if it hurt him more than it hurt me. "But I mean it."

I closed my eyes and leaned my weight into him, nodding, listening to his ragged heartbeat, howling in tandem with mine.

O CAPTAIN! MY CAPTAIN!

Calliope Bloom

It was a clear, starry Halloween night, and when Sophia opened the door to her apartment, her Maid Marian costume made my breath catch in my throat. She was wearing a pale silver-green dress in a shimmery fabric that clung to her hips, with a deep plunging neckline and a tight bodice that pushed up her small breasts. She and I had gone out together every Halloween since we were in college, and over the years, I had watched her go home at the end of the night with a succession of men—sometimes boyfriends, sometimes one-night stands. But I always secretly wished she would come home with me. Tonight, I wished more than ever that I had the nerve to tell her how I felt.

"Hey you," she said affectionately, giving me a quick hug. I could smell the citrus of her shampoo as her long dark hair brushed my cheek. She sized up my costume and laughed. "Nice. You make a cute unicorn." I was wearing pink short-shorts with a fuzzy tail pinned on, a pink camisole, pink high-top Chucks, retro leg warmers, and a headband with a sparkly unicorn horn and pink ears. It was the most pink I'd ever worn. I stepped into Sophia's living room, took off my jacket, and leaned my cane against the wall.

"I figured I'd give in to the stereotype," I said. "Most of the people I meet on dating apps seem to be looking for a unicorn—a bi woman who'll sleep with straight couples, basically as a novelty for them. It's so original when you encounter it for the millionth time." I rolled my eyes.

"Ugh," she said. "I haven't been there, but I sympathize. You want to sit down? Kai's almost ready." I sat down on her couch and tried not to let my eyes stray to her cleavage, which was now directly in my line of sight. *I don't want to objectify my friend,* I thought to myself sternly. But I couldn't stop myself from thinking about unlacing her bodice, then kissing my way down her throat to her breasts. I had never wanted to jeopardize our friendship. I tried to keep reminding myself of that.

I fixed my eyes instead on the Art Nouveau poster on her wall. I said, "And then if I click enough with someone to go on a first date, they see me walk up with a cane and get so weird about it, as if they just saw me grow a third eye but are trying *really* hard not to mention it."

Sophia shook her head and frowned. She sat down on the couch next to me and bent to put on her boots. "A lot of people are idiots," she said. "I'm sorry, Angie."

Her boyfriend, Kai, came down the hallway from the bathroom, drying his curly black hair with a towel. Kai had a lean, muscular build and deep-brown eyes that were almost black. He made Sophia laugh and he respected her, but I was still a little wary—he struck me as someone who was too accustomed to getting everything he wanted.

"Hi there," he said to me. He kissed Sophia lightly on the lips and laid his hand on her waist, and my chest ached imagining what that might feel like.

Kai was dressed as Robin Hood in a deep-green tunic, a short cloak, and dark jeans underneath. I had to admit, he looked rakishly handsome. He hung the towel over a chair and put on his shoes, then picked up a bow and quiver of arrows from the side table. "Ready?" he said, handing Sophia her jacket. "After you, fair maidens." He gestured toward the door with a flourish.

We went to a party hosted by one of Sophia's friends at a place near the harbor. But when we got there, the apartment was crowded shoulder-to-shoulder, the heat of so many bodies was stifling, and we couldn't hear anyone well enough to talk over the music. We hadn't been there for long when Sophia motioned furtively to me, took Kai by the elbow, and we ducked out early.

The three of us walked down to the pier and stood there looking out over the dark water. "What now?" Kai asked.

Sophia looked at me. She knew my legs ached if I walked too far. "What are you up for?" she asked. "An adventure?"

Sophia had always been the more adventurous of the two of us. In college, she sneaked into the pool to go skinny-dipping late one night. I was too afraid of getting in trouble to sneak in with her. But we weren't college students anymore, hadn't been for years. I looked at her in that dress and took a deep breath. "I'm up for anything," I said.

Sophia smiled and pointed at a huge yacht moored farther down the pier. Light poured from its windows, silhouettes of people milled on the upper deck, and the heavy bass of music drifted from inside. "Let's go check it out," she said.

"A party this fancy must have a bouncer," I said nervously as we strolled along the pier, trying to look casual. But as we came closer, we saw that the gangway leading from the pier to the boat's deck was deserted.

Sophia nudged me with her elbow and whispered, "See?"

Down at the end of a shadowy dock a little distance away, I saw what looked like the bouncer, a broad-shouldered man in a white uniform, locked in a passionate kiss with a handsome Han Solo. They were fumbling to undo the buttons of each other's pants.

"Now's our chance," Kai said. Sophia walked across the gangway confidently and Kai followed.

"I'm not sure about this," I whispered.

"It's up to you," Sophia said softly as I stood on the edge of the pier.

She and I looked at each other silently for a long moment. The bouncer and Han Solo were still keeping each other busy. I squared my shoulders, held my head high like I belonged there, and walked across the gangway onto the boat.

We made our way along the deck to one of the doors leading into the spacious cabin. Inside, there was dance music playing. We blended in with groups of other partygoers in costume—other than the fact that everyone else's costumes looked like they cost ten times as much as ours.

"We could rob from the rich and give to the poor," Kai said with a grin, looking at the sparkling jewelry and expensive shoes of the party guests. "Take some of their food and give it to a good cause?"

"I think we'd get caught if we tried to take a whole platter of lobster canapés out of here," I said quietly, glancing at the waiters in tuxes who were circulating with hors d'oeuvres.

Instead, Sophia led us down a red-carpeted hallway past laughing guests and carts full of fancy drinks. We passed a ballroom, the kitchen, and rounded a hallway lined with closed doors. For the moment, no one else was around. Sophia opened the biggest door and motioned us inside. It shut behind her heavily.

We had stumbled into what looked like a stateroom with plush carpets underfoot, huge mahogany tables, and red velvet couches and chaise lounges arrayed around the room. The walls were covered with nautical maps, and hanks of rope hung decoratively on hooks. No one else was here, all too busy on the dance floor or enjoying the drinks and food. Sophia hopped up to sit on one of the tables and smiled at me.

"Still nervous?" she said.

"A bit." I was pacing with my cane and kept watching the door. Kai was leafing through an oversized atlas on a side table.

"When's the last time you did something you were terrified to do?" she asked me.

"Besides right now? I don't know."

"I swear, it gets easier the more you do it. What's something you want to do but have been too scared to?" When she motioned for me to come sit down next to her, I did.

"I don't have anything like that," I said.

"You sure?"

"Okay," I said and took a deep breath. "I would want to kiss you."

She looked surprised and I panicked. *Now I've really fucked things up,* I thought. I opened my mouth to try to walk back what I'd said, but she stopped me. "Well," she said, "I would like that too."

"Oh," was all I could say. Sophia reached out her hand to take mine. Her hand was warm as she laced her fingers in between mine. My pulse quickening, I leaned over and kissed her softly on the lips. She kissed back, harder, and then her hands were in my hair, and I felt my body coursing with warmth as she pressed closer to me. With her tongue in my mouth, I stood up and put my hands around her waist, pressing her against the edge of the table. I wanted her so badly it made my chest ache.

We broke apart for a moment to catch our breath. "I want you," I said quietly.

"I want you too, Angie," she said. Her cheeks were flushed. "I—I've never had sex with a woman before."

"Really?" I said. "I guess I thought you'd done everything."

"No," she laughed. "I've wanted to." I remembered we weren't alone and looked up nervously at Kai, who seemed totally unfazed by our passionate kissing. Sophia said, "Oh, it's okay. We're in an open relationship." Kai smiled and gave an awkward half wave. "Is this too weird for you?" Sophia asked me.

"No," I said. I didn't care anymore about getting caught on this stupid boat. All I could think about was how good Sophia's skin felt, how much I wanted to keep kissing her. I started slowly leaving a trail of kisses down her neck, biting her softly, and she sighed in pleasure.

She pulled my camisole over my head, knocking my unicorn headband off, and then her hands were on my breasts. I moaned into her neck. I kissed my way down to her cleavage, pulling her breasts free from her bodice to suck one of her nipples into my mouth. At the same time, she pinched my nipples hard and sent an electric current to my clit.

"God, that feels good," I said. I kept sucking on her nipples as I ran my hands over her sheer stockings, her smooth calves, and up to her thighs. There her stockings ended, and I felt the lacy edge of her panties. "Can I touch you?" I whispered in her ear.

"Yes," she said, "please, I want you to."

I trailed my fingers lightly over the outside of her underwear. She closed her eyes and gasped as my fingers grazed her clit. I teased her a little, caressing with my fingers just along the edge of her pussy lips and the sensitive skin of her inner thigh. When she was starting to look desperate, I pulled her panties to the side and began rubbing my finger in slow circles against her clit. I dipped my fingers into the opening of her cunt, which was dripping wet, and Sophia grabbed my shoulder and made little panting gasps into my ear as I rubbed her clit faster and faster. Pulling her panties all the way down to her ankles, I used my left hand to slide two fingers into her, moving slowly in and out, my right hand still rubbing her clit. She started to shake and buck her hips against me. "Fuck," she said. When she opened her eyes to look at me, her face was contorted with pleasure. "Yes, right there."

I smiled, getting wet from watching how much she was enjoying this. Kai came over and kissed the back of Sophia's neck as I kept finger-fucking her. She leaned back to kiss him on the mouth. He cupped her breasts in his hands, tweaking her nipples between his thumb and forefinger.

As Sophia let out another moan, Kai and I smiled at each other like coconspirators. Sophia opened her eyes, looked at me, and said breathlessly, "I'm going to come."

"Then come for me," I said. She closed her eyes again as I fucked her deeper with my fingers and rubbed her clit faster and faster. She cried out, and I felt her muscles tense as she came. I kept moving my fingers in and out of her cunt, slower and slower, before running my fingers through her hair as she caught her breath.

"Come here," she said. Sophia stood up and kissed me hard, turning me around. She pulled my shorts off and lifted me to sit on the edge of the table.

Kai stood behind her and rubbed her clit as she kissed my throat, my breasts, and down my stomach to the edge of my panties. Then she pulled down my underwear and kissed the strip of hair just above my clit. I shuddered with anticipation of what Sophia was going to do to me. I felt her warm breath on my cunt, and then her tongue was on my clit, lashing short, fast strokes that sent waves of pleasure through my body. "Oh, god," I said.

I heard Kai unzip his jeans and unwrap a condom, then Sophia's mouth pressed harder into me as he started fucking her from behind. She gave a muffled moan of pleasure as his cock slid into her, the sound reverberating against my clit. The harder he thrust, the harder her tongue pressed against my clit. I closed my eyes and leaned back on the table, losing myself in the sensation of Sophia eating my pussy while Kai pounded into her.

I was getting close to coming when the door to the stateroom burst open. The three of us froze and looked up to see a tall, short-haired woman in a white uniform with epaulets on her shoulders. The door swung shut behind her. "What the hell are you doing?" she said.

"We're sorry, ma'am," Kai said, though he didn't sound very sorry.

"Don't call me 'ma'am.' It's captain."

"It's my fault," I confessed. I was the only one completely naked, sitting on the mahogany table with my cunt dripping wet from Sophia's attentions. I felt the captain's eyes fall on me.

"Is that true?" she asked. "Or do you just want to be punished?"

I smiled. "Can it be both?"

She walked over to me and pulled one of the hanks of rope from the wall. "Put out your hands," she said.

I obeyed and she began wrapping lengths of rope around my wrists and tying them together. Her hands moved quickly and expertly. The rope was rougher and thicker than what I'd been tied with before; its friction against my skin made me even more turned on.

"Turn around," she ordered me, and I stood up and leaned against the table. My bare ass and the rest of my body were open to however she wanted to punish me. She stood behind me as I shook a little in suspense and excitement. First she sank her fingers into the roots of my hair and pulled hard, the pain mixing with pleasure as it ran along my nerve endings. Then she stepped back and I felt her first hit land. *Smack!* Her hand hit my ass hard, the impact stinging and sending vibrations between my legs. I let out a gasp. She hit me again, the sound echoing in the stateroom, and I moaned. She started building up a rhythm, beating me first on one side and then the other. In the pauses in between, I couldn't help but cringe in anticipation of the next blow. She laughed low in her throat when she saw how much I liked it.

"I think you like this a little too much," she said. But she kept going, pausing in between hits to rub her hands more gently over my body, giving tiny slaps to my skin that was now tingling and pink. My ass was getting more and more tender as the pain and pleasure crested, making me cry out louder. The captain stopped and picked up my panties, balled them up and stuffed them into my mouth as a gag. "That's better," she said, then resumed spanking me. Now my yelps were muffled by the silky fabric.

"Mmm," I moaned through the gag. *Smack!* Her hands were strong and knew how to hit so it really stung. By the time she was done, I was high on endorphins and my clit was throbbing. She gave me one last smack and pulled the gag out of my mouth. "Good girl," she said. "Had enough?"

"Yes, captain," I said shakily, but I was smiling. "Thank you."

"I'm not finished with all of you yet," she said. She took me by the rope binding my hands and pushed me down onto one of the chaise lounges. There, Sophia came over and kissed me while my hands were over my head. The captain tied my ankles together, then ran the rope tightly between a few of my toes to cause delicious pain. As I lay there on the chaise lounge bound hand and foot, naked, the captain took off her pants and boy shorts. She lowered herself until she was sitting on my face. I licked her clit furiously, the sweet taste of her cunt filling my mouth.

I heard the captain giving orders to Sophia and Kai. Then Sophia's finger was rubbing my clit, and soon after, Kai's hard cock pressed against the opening of my cunt. He lifted my legs straight up, still tied at the ankles. I moaned as his cock slid inside me. He started fucking me slowly and deeply as Sophia rubbed my clit. I got small gasps of air between eating the captain's pussy. I could barely see anything, only feel the overwhelming pleasure of being fucked and having my clit rubbed while a stranger sat on my face. Kai started fucking me faster, his cock hitting my G-spot, and I moaned louder into the captain's cunt.

"Keep going," she said sternly. "Don't you dare come until I do."

I would have said, "Yes, captain," but my mouth was too full. Instead I licked faster, the tip of my tongue pressing against the nub of her clit as hips tensed against me. I took her clit into my mouth and sucked, then ran my tongue to the opening of her cunt and pressed inside her slit. When she groaned, I could tell she was getting close. I went back to licking her clit, fast and steady, until she said, "Fuck, right there. I'm going to come on your face."

It felt so good to have a thick cock inside me while Sophia rubbed my clit; I struggled to keep my own orgasm at bay. I focused on eating the captain's pussy and delighted in her shaking against me as she came, her thighs pressing against either side of my face. I kept going until she pulled away and stood up. I looked up to see her grinning. She took a couple of deep breaths and said, "You can come now, you little pain slut."

Then the captain's mouth was on my nipples, licking and biting hard. The sensation on my nipples combined with Sophia's finger rubbing my clit and Kai's cock sliding in and out of my cunt were too much for me to hold back any longer. My orgasm built up and up until powerful waves of pleasure shook me, starting from my clit and radiating out through my entire body. I came hard with Sophia and Kai and the captain all touching me, the muscles of my cunt tightening around Kai's cock, my hips and legs shaking with the intensity of my orgasm. Finally I lay spent and sweating on the chaise lounge, Sophia kissing me on the lips, not caring that my face was drenched.

The captain put on her boy shorts and pants, buckled her belt, and looked at us with mock sternness as she walked to the door. "Don't ever let me see you on my boat again," she said, "or I won't be so nice next time." The door swung shut behind her.

Sophia raised her head from where she'd been resting it on my chest. She looked at me, her green eyes hazy from sex and contentment. "Let's go home," she said.

THE JUMP

Rebecca Chase

Poppy's car rumbled across the gravel road, struggling to find grip among the spreading stones. The crunching sounds weren't enough to silence her oldest friend's panic-laden screeches singing from the stereo's speakers.

"Are you sure you want to do this? Because you should know, you might die!" Naomi explained as if she was sharing a secret.

"I'm not going to die. I'm not even scared," Poppy lied.

"I don't know why you're doing it. You don't take risks. You're the reliable, normal person that no one worries about. You know, the type that marries their first love and lives happily ever after."

Silence descended. The only audible noise came from the loose rocks shifting under her tires.

"Oh no. I'm sorry. I didn't mean James."

"It's fine," Poppy replied, worrying the strands of her long black hair, grateful that references to marriage, love, and especially James were no longer accompanied by tears.

"He wasn't good enough for you."

Poppy sighed. "You sound like his mother, except of course *I* wasn't good enough for *him*."

Relentlessly, she'd been made to feel like a working-class lottery winner. She'd "ensnared" the wealthiest man at university, James Mortimore, Junior. But she didn't entrap anyone: they were two students who had fallen in love. At university, his extortionate wealth and family estate hadn't been an issue. After graduation, everything had changed and, as his mother told it, she'd capitalized on his good nature and forced herself upon his set.

"She was a bitch." Naomi's shout barely came above the rattle of the car.

"Don't you know, dahling," Poppy replied with her best Lady Mortimore impression, "that ladies with good breeding are never cruel. But we know how to protect our interests from little commoners like you."

She could nearly laugh about it now, but the damage done by James and his family had been lasting. After a year of being told what she should be while systematically having her spirit crushed, she'd decided leaving James was the only answer.

"Like I said, a bitch. But you don't need to prove anything to anyone." Naomi had identified her motivation.

"I do," Poppy replied, edging her car into a space near the runway. "I need to prove something to—shit!"

The figure in front of her had her slamming on the brakes. Her face tightened as the piercing sound of metal against metal scratched at her ears. Suddenly the figure took a clearer shape and she realized it was a nice one, that of a blond guy with dark eyes and a full-lipped, wide smile. He must have been millimeters from being crushed by her car.

"What?" Naomi shouted.

Words fell out of her head as he lightly touched her car hood. His big hand temporarily drew her gaze before her eyes returned to his cheekbones, then his eyes. Poppy gazed at him with a mixture of awe and annoyance. Now her heart was thumping and it wasn't due to fear.

"I almost hit this random guy. Naomi, he's gorgeous. I'm already imagining him naked." As an afterthought, she added, "He's an asshole for stepping in front of the car, though."

"Get a photo of him. I want to see."

She watched him step back and she eased the car into the space, taking the time to make sure it was perfectly between the lines, not caring how much it might annoy him.

The stranger stepped around to Poppy's door, tapping the window lightly. She studied his eyes and hands. The imagery associated with the actions of his fingers was already making her blush. What would they feel like stroking her inner thighs?

Poppy rolled down the window, in awe of the cropped blond hair that seemed to form like a halo around his head.

"Sorry," he said before being cut off by Naomi's booming voice.

"When you say you're imagining him naked, are you imagining doing other stuff too?"

"Shut up," Poppy shouted into the air.

But Naomi's voice continued to blare from the car's speakers. "Because you haven't had sex in ages. Maybe offer him your boobs. Your lady parts probably wouldn't *recognize* a penis these days."

Instantly, the wide-eyed stranger looked at her breasts.

"Shut it. I'm talking to someone who can hear you."

"Oh, okay," she lengthened the word. "I've got to go. Have a good skydive. Hope you don't die." The phone cut off.

Eventually, the stranger's eyes returned to hers, his cheeky smile making it impossible for her not to smile back.

"Welcome to Dalton's Skydive Center. The payment kiosk and briefing will be in there." He nodded in the direction of a dilapidated cabin. "I look forward to you not dying. This is going to be the most thrilling experience of your life. It sounds like you need it."

He offered her his hand to help her from the car, causing long-forgotten surges between her legs. But they lasted as long as his touch, flowing away as she watched him swagger in the direction of a hanger. She enjoyed the sight of his perfectly formed ass departing, until he turned around and caught her staring, the devilish smile still there.

Poppy's stomach dropped as she surveyed the rest of the scene. A bright yellow plane pulled her gaze as she considered what it would take to make her jump to her possible death from it.

Once payment had been given and they'd had their briefing, all the jumpers were tasked with finding their jumpsuits. The professional they'd be attached to during the tandem dive would find them in the locker rooms.

One by one Poppy watched the room of anxious and

excited jumpers being led from the changing rooms for the pre-jump briefing with their professional.

Only she was left.

Her fingers fumbled with what should have been a simple zip.

"I'm doing the right thing," she muttered to herself. "I am."

Her digits shook every time she got close to gripping the mechanism.

"It's perfectly safe," she whispered. Getting hurt would only serve to make James's mother happy and prove that Poppy was the "silly little girl" she'd heard her snipe about many times. That James hadn't defended her was normal, but when he'd publicly treated her like a commoner it had been the last straw.

Wrestling with the zip once more, she repeated her recent mantra. "I'm not going to die. I'm not going to die."

"Of course you are." Poppy looked up to find the hunk from earlier watching her, the smirk still on his face. "But not today and not on my watch."

For a moment she stared back at him, anger at all who'd humiliated her forming into a tight ball in her stomach. The grip of her shaking fingers on the metal teeth caused fresh scratches as she stared him down. "What's it got to do with you?"

He ambled closer. "Let me help you."

Due to his proximity, she could smell the earthy scent covering his skin. He smelled like James. The ball of anger flamed and she flinched away.

"You're going to need to trust me today or this won't work. I'm your partner in the jump. Without me, you'll be freefalling."

His jumpsuit hung loosely from his hips, his arms not yet in the sleeves, and his white T-shirt clung to his torso, defining every muscle. The battle of thoughts continued inside her, the fear of the next couple of hours making it impossible to focus on any one thing.

Poppy stepped closer, relinquishing her dislike and fear of him, allowing him to reach her zip. He slowly drew it upward.

"You're shaking," he pointed out unnecessarily. "I'm guessing this is your first jump?"

"First and only. Maybe not even that."

"You're doing the jump," he told her, his brown eyes wearing a hint of determination. "But only once we've gone through a couple of things. I'm Steve. I've done over nine hundred jumps and I've never died."

If it was an attempt at humor, it was a poor one.

"Tell me something about yourself. Why do you want to do this?"

"Does it matter?" Her contempt was an attempt to mask her terror.

"Yes. My job is to keep you safe. But more than that it's to give you a fantastic dive experience. Sit down on that bench and help me do that. Take that stick out of your ass too."

"It'll be hard to sit with a stick up my ass," she joked, relenting a little.

"If it helps I can remove it." Steve dramatically pretended to remove it. His absurd mime broke the ice.

"Shit!" he said when her story came to an end. "That James treated you like crap."

"That's the simple version, but yeah." The shakes had

eased as they sat, knees touching, on the locker room bench. Muscly thighs drew her eyes and she barely resisted pressing tighter into him to feel his heat.

"And his mum was a bitch?"

"I was given rules on what my role would be in the family. Nights he worked away became training sessions or her attempts at breaking us up. It wasn't unusual for her to parade his ex-girlfriends and women she deemed more suitable through the house."

Steve shook his head in disgust. "What did your fiancé say when you told him this?"

"He suggested his mum was working in my best interests. Apparently, she was 'trying to improve my standing.' She made it clear I wasn't accepted in their circle, and he fought to underline that."

Stunned silence greeted her. His eyes appeared to appraise her face. Heat rose from her cheeks.

"Which is why I want to do the skydive. It's a bit of a fuck-you to those who thought they knew me and decided they could tell me what to do. No one gets to tell me what to do anymore."

Poppy's knuckles ached from the clench of her fists, her nails stabbing into her skin.

Steve took her hands in his, his touch enough to soften her grip and ease her hands open. "That's one of the best motivations I've heard. But I'm going to need you to relax." His fingers drew circles against her palms, sending shivers up her arms. "You're angry, I get that. But you're terrified too."

Poppy opened her mouth to argue but he preempted her fight. "It's nothing to be embarrassed about, but save the anger for when you get to the edge of the plane door. It will crush the terror."

The reminder had her quaking.

Steve's hands rubbed up and down her arms. "Do you trust me, Poppy?"

She hesitated. "Sure. What have I got to lose?"

"Your life."

Her face fell.

"Sorry, I can be an ass. Let's check your equipment."

Steve helped her into her harness, checking the clips. The intensity of his brown eyes raised her heart rate further. Maybe the increasing adrenaline was pulling her arousal with it, but she basked in the attention he gave her, enjoying the straps rubbing against her crotch when he grabbed them roughly at her shoulders to check they were tight. Once again, his proximity excited her, his scent no longer reminding her of James but associating itself with the hottest guy she'd chatted with in a long time. It might be a blip, created as a reaction to the terror, but she indulged it. Gently, he popped the little hat on her head, his fingers stroking the nape of her neck when he helped her tuck her hair underneath.

To show he'd finished, he gave her butt a quick pat. "For luck. Let's go. Everyone will be waiting."

"I'm not going to die," she whispered, conscious of his gloved hand tightening around hers.

Steve led her to the plane, her body shaking with every step.

"The tap of the butt helped," she whispered in his ear.

"I hoped it might."

"Just so you know, you have my permission to do whatever it takes to get me out of the plane."

* * *

The flight up to thirteen thousand feet was filled with thoughts of her former life. Flashbacks of times she'd been insulted, manipulated, and belittled came at her. The anger boiled but fear continued to overwhelm it.

The tiny plane was filled with skydivers, which forced her to rest against Steve's lap, practically sitting on his crotch. Every shake of fear made her wriggle against him until suddenly she felt hardness against her back. Poppy stilled in surprise.

"Sorry," he whispered in her ear. "Skydives and hot women rubbing against me get me excited. This moment is a lethal combination."

His breath in her ear, along with the recklessness of what she was about to do, pushed her adrenaline higher.

Poppy leaned into his broad chest, inviting the closeness, pushing herself to touch him and forget the madness she was about to welcome.

She watched the tandem divers, attached by a piece of coarse material, fling themselves out of the plane until it was just the two of them left.

"You ready to show James and his mum who you really are?" he shouted.

She shook her head, unable to see his reassuring eyes now that he was strapped to her back.

"You got this, Poppy," he shouted again, but she was frozen in terror.

Suddenly her jumpsuit collar was pulled away from her neck, replaced by soft lips. "If you jump I'll do more when we get to the ground. I'm desperate to kiss you properly. I want to touch you, get my hands on your skin, slip my fingers into your panties."

It may have been a bizarre motivation tactic or genuine sentiment, but it didn't matter because suddenly the fear was gone, crushed by arousal.

With a thumbs-up she declared her willingness to trust him.

They threw themselves into the sky.

Poppy couldn't remember when she last took a breath. Needles spiked her face before gloved hands positioned in front of her stopped the droplets of rain from attacking her skin.

She needed to calm down. Vomit was beginning its journey up her throat.

Suddenly a jolt that took every limb with it swept her high and peace descended. Steve had opened the parachute.

"You okay?" he shouted in her ear.

"I am now," she hollered back.

The beauty on display beneath her took her breath away. She was floating.

Her hands wrapped around the straps above her chest as she swept her eyes left and right.

The last year faded away, memories carried on the breeze, leaving her free of their weight.

Adrenaline, the thrill of falling and her acceptance of it made her feel invincible.

She didn't consider her death anymore; instead, she reached for the life that James had tried to take away. Life wasn't for watching and hoping things would change, but for taking what you wanted and accepting the consequences.

"We're about to land." Steve's deep drawl filled her

insides. He was something else she wanted. "I need you to lift your feet, fetal position. I'll land both of us."

The speed of the ground coming toward them took her by surprise but it didn't scare her. Poppy refused to be scared anymore.

Pressure filled her ears as they hit the earth with a bump.

"You're laughing," Steve said as he unclipped her, struggling as she rolled around. "I'm guessing you enjoyed it."

"It was amazing! I can't thank you enough for getting me out the door." Poppy attempted to stand and plant a kiss on his lips but the loss of adrenaline found her falling to the ground.

Steve's hands held her until she could steady herself.

"You don't need to thank me. You made it fun."

As they headed to the locker rooms, still giddy with excitement, Poppy wondered if Steve had forgotten what he'd said in the plane before the jump.

Feeling his hand against her back, guiding her, reinforced the promise she'd made to herself. She was going to take what she wanted. Risk didn't have to be a factor if she didn't let it.

Standing in the locker room, all the other skydivers long gone, Poppy slowly gathered her things, deliberating her next move.

"Steve." He turned to face her, his eyebrows diving together in question, his mouth unmoving. "Come here."

He stepped closer, his jumpsuit rustling as he moved, his slow gait suggesting uncertainty.

Their eyes met as she lazily pulled down his zip, her earlier tremble absent.

"Take your jumpsuit off," she demanded.

Submitting, he began to strip. Gradually he revealed his body to her. Bare arms raised her heartbeat, but only when he yanked the suit from his legs and displayed his trunk-like thighs did she feel wetness collecting in her panties.

His brows furrowed as she regarded his body.

"T-shirt too," she requested without a smile.

The possibility they'd be caught didn't concern her. She'd survived diving out of a plane. Nothing was off limits anymore.

"Do I get to see you naked?" he questioned, his voice wavering.

With a wicked smile, she undressed, pulling her zip down with ease. As she pushed the sleeves of her suit down and off, she caught the sound of her mobile ringing. At first, she ignored it, enjoying the way Steve's eyes devoured her increasingly naked form.

Soon she was standing in front of him, a blush of pink lace against her breasts and sex, the color matching Steve's flushed cheeks. Hunger emanated from him.

Once more her ringtone echoed around the locker room. Poppy grabbed it.

"Hello?" she said before mouthing "Off" at Steve while pointing at his boxers.

"I've seen your Facebook. You can't do it. I won't let you." Poppy recognized James's demanding voice instantly.

"I presume you're talking about the skydive, which is none of your business," she replied, barely registering his frustrated breath due to Steve's hard, seven-inch cock suddenly unleashed in front of her.

Licking moisture from her lips, she imagined what it

would be like to have it throbbing in her mouth, moving against her tongue.

"You're not allowed. I prohibit you," James shouted.

Losing one's composure wasn't acceptable in his family. "Your mum will be disappointed at your shouting," she replied calmly, flicking the straps of her bra down, grinning at the blaze from Steve's eyes. "But you lost your chance to tell me what to do, not that you deserved it. Anyway, it's too late. I've done the skydive."

"But," he spluttered, "girls like you don't do things like that."

"*Women* like me, do what we want. No one else, especially men like you, has a say." With her free hand, she unclipped her bra. It fell to the floor, freeing her breasts. Steve waited, not broaching the distance between them until she beckoned him closer with her curved finger. "Now if you don't mind, I'm about to fuck a gorgeous guy and I don't need your judgment putting me off."

"But," he stammered, "you can't. I don't even believe you. You're full of shit."

"So what if I am? And James, stuck up boys like you shouldn't swear. Their mummies wouldn't like it." Steve pointed at himself, silently requesting the phone. She handed it over.

"Bye, James," he said before tossing the phone to the side.

Poppy wrapped her hands around his biceps, giddy at the strength rippling beneath her fingertips.

"If I'm a good boy, will you tell me what to do?" Steve growled, teasing her, pulling away and stripping her of her panties. His fingers stroked at her wetness. Poppy watched in fascination as he met her eyes, lifting one digit to his smiling mouth and sliding it inside. "Someone enjoyed their skydive."

The spectacle turned her arousal to agony. She'd never craved a man more. Pulling him closer she brushed her lips against his. Surging horniness turned a chaste kiss into a battle for gratification.

Steve's hands traveled down to her butt, kneading it as his tongue slipped into her mouth, massaging her with a skill that was foreign to her.

Her fingers reached for his hair, bunching clumps of it in her hands as she fought to close the limited distance between them. She needed him buried inside her.

"So you presumed we were going to fuck? Someone's confident," he said playfully.

"Like you'd say no to this," she replied seductively, stroking his length, occasionally giving him a squeeze. He thrust into her hand with a groan, urging her to move faster, but she ignored his pleas, relishing her control. "But I don't have protection."

Steve opened his hand and she swiped the condom from him, ripping the foil with her teeth and sheathing him quickly.

His eyes closed as his head tipped back.

"Wrap your arms around my neck." He grabbed her buttocks and lifted her in the air, shoving her against a locker, his erection penetrating her in one motion. Joyful screams filled the room.

Although he was the biggest she'd had, her body stretched to fit him, pulling his length inside her. As he jiggled her a little, her nipples rubbed against his chest, causing her to groan.

"I want those breasts in my mouth later. I can't wait to

taste them properly," he growled before finding his stance. His mouth was an angel and a devil, choosing to follow up his words with kisses that graced her naked shoulders.

"Fuck me," she whispered in his ear. He responded immediately, pulling out of her before thrusting inside again and again. Confidently she matched his rhythm, pressing against his buttocks with her feet, pulling him deeper inside her with every slam of his hips.

Poppy hung on, grateful for his strength, feeling the grind of their bodies against each other. It felt illicit; she was doing something that she wouldn't have considered before the jump. Never before had she felt so alive, the hairs on her arms vertical, every inch of her skin electrified.

"I want to try something different," she said, breathing into his ear, sliding down and bending over, her hands against the cold metal of the locker, offering her sex to him.

With a grunt, he thrust inside her once more, a hand gripping her hip, another reaching round to rub her clit. There was no loss to her rising orgasm. The position brought her more arousal as her pussy received the gratification she deserved.

Their pleasure filled the room, moans echoing off the lockers.

She'd never felt more in control of her wants. Again and again, she pushed back as he thrust inside her, his length rubbing her walls as his fingertips continued to beckon her orgasm closer. Steve's grip on her hip tightened, digits digging into her flesh, a silent warning of his impending climax.

Her heartbeat was out of control, with sweat dripping from his body onto hers. His fingertips rubbed at great speed. His cock filled her, reaching the spot that made her moan every time. He spanked her butt, shocking her and pushing her over the edge.

"I'm coming," she screamed, her body shaking, energy flowing through her into him and forcing his orgasm. He groaned as his fluid filled the condom, the heat from it surging deep inside her. Poppy collapsed, her hands starting to slide down the lockers, unable to hold herself up anymore. But his hands gripped her, pulling her upright and tight against him.

They recovered quickly, suddenly aware that anyone could walk in. They shoved on their clothes, although Steve still took the time to kiss her passionately first.

"I don't know what to say. I've not done this here before. I don't do hookups," he said, twisting the waves of her hair around his fingers.

Poppy didn't know if it was the sex, the jump, or something else, but she couldn't think straight anymore. Instead, she took his hand and brushed a kiss to his knuckles. "Me neither," she replied. "But let me give you my number, in case you want to meet for a date."

Walking back to her car, she turned and looked at the green field where they'd landed and saw Steve tidying up the parachutes. He gave her a sheepish wave and she smiled back wistfully, proud that she'd faced her fears and welcomed life's next adventure.

ON DISPLAY

Louise Lagris

I look like a real slut on the subway tonight, and it's totally your fault. Garters you love, a gauzy skirt that barely covers my ass, patent-leather boots I'm teetering on, and underneath my conservative coat, a strappy latex shirt that took me easily twenty minutes of wrestling to get on. Meanwhile, you easily pass for a dressed-up hipster in the tight leather pants I picked out for you at a sex shop in Chelsea and a long black peacoat.

I stumble a little over the cracks in the sidewalk, and you hold my elbow with strong hands. You have long tattooed fingers that have leisurely worked my pussy and ass inside and out for what seems like hours at a time. I like to suck on them until my eyes water, until I can't stand not to bite you. Then your hand becomes a slap, and I just want to bite you harder.

You're a giver. I'm a switchy little brat. Somehow, we make sense together.

Tonight I'm going to give you something you've

wanted, something you've begged for with breathy postcoital whispers in my ear and late-night texts when we're half asleep. Three months ago, our Tinder messages slid into sexts before we even met, and they loosed something in me I can't quite explain. It feels like the id that normally only surfaces when I'm masturbating to the sloppy sounds of gangbang porn has finally gotten a chance to breathe, and she's been gulping greedy lungfuls of air ever since. We fucked three times on our first date.

We were each other's first anal two months ago, which seems sort of sweet, and tonight's play party is yet another first in what I hope will be many more to come. We've planned for it all week, both in terms of negotiating what we want from the night, and more elaborate fantasies. But now that we're on our way, I can feel the panic trickling down my spine. What if it is *too* dark and intimate and intense in there? What if I get scared? What if I embarrass myself, or worse yet, what if I embarrass us? Or disappoint you? What if all of this planning was for naught?

The party has started by the time we get there, but it's still early and not too packed. The theme is Scorpio, because it's Scorpio season. I know you don't buy into astrology, but what is our relationship but an exploration of the taboo, the shadow side we fear and desire, the watery pools of emotions we're dipping into each time we fuck? Because as much as I'm dying to know the mundanities of you—your favorite TV shows and movies, what you're reading, the first time you sucked a cock—I need to feel you inside, outside, all around me *more*.

Time unfurls before us leisurely, I trust. We wouldn't do the things we do without some umbilical connection that holds us over days, even weeks, and I can wait. New York

City is a busy place. But maybe I'm just fooling myself. Either way, I won't deprive myself the pleasure of your company—your beautiful, lithe body and hungry mouth, bruising hands, sturdy belt. My dirty little kinky Grindr slut without a gag reflex.

Give yourself an enema before you meet me, I texted you this morning. *You never know when I might want to pound your ass.*

A beautiful woman with a Louise Brooks bob and vampy lips is lying on a Victorian fainting couch near the entrance, lazily checking IDs against the RSVP list. She stamps our hands and waves us through. We check our coats, and with a giggle I stick my ticket in your pocket. I have nowhere to stow it on my person and my purse is otherwise occupied.

With every step, the fishnet on my plush thighs rubs together. The gently weighted beads in my cunt rock back and forth. The buttery leather harness under my skirt makes itself known with every step. I think of the contents of my small velvet purse fondly.

Well-dressed perverts in complicated, expensive latex outfits are languidly snacking on sushi that is artfully laid across the body of a naked woman on a table. Nearby, a human candelabra wiggles under the ministrations of a wasp-waisted love witch gently dripping white wax across her partner's torso before placing the candle there to burn brightly, joining a baker's dozen of carefully placed candles melting down onto her flesh. A bald man wearing nothing but a fishnet shirt and lace panties offers us nonalcoholic refreshments as per the party guidelines, but we decline.

Your forefinger strokes the palm of my hand as if you're beckoning me to the darker corners, where we can hear wet kisses and the smack of flesh on flesh, but I want the full tour. There's a brightly lit room kitted out with shiny medical tools laid out on immaculate trays; a dungeon with rows of floggers hanging on the wall, a queening chair for some lucky bitch, and a beautiful, burnished Saint Andrew's cross standing at attention in the middle of the room; a luxurious wedding suite with white everything, from virginal sheets to soft netting; and so much more.

In every room, twosomes and moresomes are playing with one another's flesh. Licking, kissing, smacking, biting—every possible permutation is exploding before our eyes like the Fourth of July. They're all beautiful in their own way, hairy backs and cellulite and bony knees; they're irresistibly human, and in the throes of their private desires, made incredibly real. I've got about a decade and fifty pounds on you easily, you lanky thirty-something, and seeing other people freely fucking makes me feel at ease.

"I've been hard since we got here," you whisper. I clench my pussy around the balls, which fill me up like three particularly dexterous fingers; they gently sway like an ocean inside me. We'd agreed earlier in the week not to masturbate, not even touch ourselves except to wash in the shower until we were at the party together. Now that we're here, even my skin is quivering.

"Let's find somewhere sort of private." I lead you by the hand to a dark corner lit only by a wall sconce embroidered with the wax of countless candles. We're still surrounded by whispers and gasps and smacks like a live porno soundtrack. There's yet another velvet Victorian fainting couch, and I quickly sit on it to claim it as ours. It feels safe and cozy back here, and as we start to make out, my cunt unfurls and my Domme side emerges.

"Take out your cock, dear. Touch yourself. Slowly." I watch you unzip and begin stroking yourself before I reach for my purse. I love the muscles in your forearm and how they flex as you pump your cock. I fumble inside my purse for the satin bag holding a purple dildo, and when I hold it up in the candlelight your eyes turn bright.

"Hold this." I stick it in your mouth for safekeeping. You deep-throat it, eyes rolling back in your head with bliss.

"Drop your pants to your knees and bend over," I say gently, lubing up my first two fingers. I slowly stroke your cock and your balls from behind, giving each impossibly round cheek a resounding smack before teasing your asshole. I hesitate at the entrance, but you back into me, sucking my finger in so I can stroke your prostate with one hand and massage it from the outside with my other. Your moan joins the chorus of pleasure around us, and I gently add another finger to loosen you up for my cock—which, like a good, good boy, you're still deep-throating.

"Hand it over, slut." I fumble with the snaps in the semidarkness until it's in place. I slather my cock in lube and rub it on your muscular ass, so juicy on your skinny frame, before dipping it between your cheeks and teasing your asshole with the tip.

Suddenly I notice we're not alone. Over my shoulder, I can hear the unmistakable sounds of a man jacking off. I turn around, and a hairy, muscular man is hungrily ogling your asshole. Wearing only a leather jockstrap, a matching chest harness, and knee-high combat boots, he's just your type, and from the look in his eyes, the feeling is mutual. A twinge of nervousness tickles my scalp, and even though I'm still clothed I feel vulnerable. I'm aware of how much older I am than you, how much more voluptuous. Awkward in my high heels, a silicone cock bobbing just under my skirt. Then I realize your admirer isn't the least bit interested in watching me, and it's exhilarating. My Domme comes roaring back.

"Isn't he beautiful?" I pry your cheeks apart so he can admire your secret pink hole. "His ass is mine tonight, but he's a real cock-hungry pig, so maybe he'll suck you off if you want."

The man, still stroking, pretends to contemplate this offer for a second before smiling wickedly.

"May I?" he asks me. I smack your ass and pull your hair so you face us.

"What do you think? Do you want to be this big Daddy's bitch for me?" You nod vigorously, and I laugh. The man whispers in my ear that he was tested for STDs in the past month and is good to go. "Thank you," I whisper with a wink, before he saunters over so you're face-to-face with his bulging jockstrap. He lifts his leg and places his boot on the arm of the couch.

"Lick my boot," he says, and you slobber eagerly.

"Filthy," I say, and rake your sides with my nails. Your skin ripples and reddens under my touch.

"Stop," the man says. He pulls out an outrageously large, uncut cock—seriously, the biggest I've seen outside of porn, it's kind of terrifying—and gives it a few strokes before unceremoniously feeding it to you.

At this point, all I can do is watch. I know that if you tap three times on any part of my body, that means stop, and I am alert to it. I am also alert to my extraordinarily wet pussy, so I pop out the beads I've been sucking in for hours, stow them in my bag, and start finger-fucking myself mercilessly underneath the harness. The sounds around us, the sight of your obscenely open ass, the gentle pressure on my clit from the strap-on—the reality of what I'd only dared to dream about late at night with my hands down my panties makes waiting any longer impossible.

I walk over and watch you with delight, your eyes closed and watering with the attempt to fully take in this gorgeous engorged cock, the man's hand huge and hairy and pulling you closer so you're almost nose to navel. He's growling with pleasure, reaching over to grab a fistful of your ass, sticking a beefy finger in your hole, and I take the opportunity to rake my sticky fingers through your hair and wipe them on your nose and cheeks.

"Do you love this, my sweet slutty fuck?" I ask. You nod with your mouth full of cock, snot and tears beginning to run down your face. "Do you want me to fuck you too?" You nod again, and I saunter back and kneel behind you on the couch.

"You better not stop sucking just because she's about to fuck your dirty ass," the man threatens. You moan in response.

I feel your body tense up at first so I go slowly, millimeter by millimeter until I can feel you opening for me. Then I'm up to the hilt inside of you, skin to skin, so close that the leather straps of the harness become part of me as I fuck you in time to the Daddy's thrusts. Breathing with you, moving with you—moving *inside* you—as I grind my clit against the flat end of the dildo, is enough to get me off in and of itself.

"Do you like being completely owned and filled?" You

shudder beneath me. A small crowd is gathering to watch our spit roast. Queer boys suck one another's tongues while peeking out of the corners of their eyes. A bald-headed Furiosa is wearing little more than bondage tape on her nipples, a Hitachi on her clit, and a collar with a leash attached to her latex-sheathed Mistress. A well-dressed couple wrapped in silk and velvet stand next to each other, motionless except for his elegantly manicured hand cupping her breast, her nipple pierced with gold and diamonds. It occurs to me mid-thrust that they're watching me too, but I don't care anymore; all of it is delicious and thrilling and dirty, just like I'd always fantasized.

You're covered in sweat and trying your best to keep up, but I can tell you're getting exhausted by our dueling ministrations. Finally, the nameless man pulls his cock out of your wet mouth and shoots long ropes of come across your face, groaning like a mountain. I pick up the slack on my end, fucking your ass long and hard the way I know will make you come, while you masturbate furiously. Sometimes it's slow and dreamy when I fuck your ass, our breathing in syncopation, but the last time I fucked you this hard you left a love bite on my upper arm. Now the energy that surges between us feels extra charged up in this aroused atmosphere, all those pheromones of horny people vibrating in anticipation and admiration of us and of each other.

Finally, you tap on my thigh twice to let me know you've come, to slow my thrusting until I'm motionless against your ass, slowly withdrawing as gently as I entered you.

The other man has disappeared. The crowd has dwindled. We're finally alone as I disengage myself from you, snap the dildo off and stow it in a plastic bag in my purse, then clean you off carefully with the plentiful wipes I've tucked away just for this reason. I use three on your face alone, covered as it is in a strange man's come, and once you're scrubbed pink, I kiss you on your swollen lips.

"You were marvelous," I whisper in your ear. "Simply beautiful." I hold your head to my chest, and you kiss me above my heart. "Do you feel okay?"

"I feel great," you reply with a croak. You stand to pull your pants back up, then sit gingerly and look around. "I feel like I need a nap," you say, mussing your hair thoughtfully.

"I feel like I need a hot bath and a good night's sleep," I reply, hoisting my skirt down and straightening my garters. "I also feel like I need a turn."

"You're such a brat." You smile. You fumble in your pockets for our coat-check tickets, and we wobble out into the night, to my apartment, to my bed, to sleep like spoons and wake in the morning to fuck again, sweetly this time. Stomach to stomach while the sun shines in.

THE PICK-ME-UP

Suleikha Snyder

She tried to focus on squeezing lime into her margarita and cherishing the first sharp, tequila-heavy sips. In the process of dodging a particularly evil burst of juice, Aleja caught a glimpse of her reflection in the mirror behind the bar. *Ugh*. She was barely visible over the top rack of liquor bottles, but it was enough to reinforce that, yeah, she'd just finished the day from hell. She'd tried to finger-comb her hair while walking down from the subway platform, but it looked like Elvira's black fright wig. *Shit*. She stifled a groan, swirling the short, red straw around in her drink.

What a day. What a truly shitty day. She wanted to let it drain away from her and to forget that her DSW pumps—so *cute* when they were an impulse-buy—were pinching her feet. She wanted nothing more strenuous than watching the ESPN guy recap last night's Mets game on the flat-screen TV, but that simple goal was proving difficult to meet. Who would've guessed that a Wednesday night at the Hanged Man would be so . . . *active*? From the bartender, Liam, barking good-natured orders at the hostess to a couple of the regulars arguing, peace and quiet was definitely not on tap.

"You're too modest, Conn. That's what you are. Not willing to take credit for anything, you sorry fucker."

"That's not what your wife said in bed with me last night, John. And I rightfully take credit for *that!*"

"Kiss my ass!"

"You want me to shave it for you first, then?"

The banter zipped around her like Midtown bike messengers, the two men's clashing accents occasionally making it hard for her to follow. John was Russian, older, and Conn from Northern Ireland. Despite past instances of drinking in their general vicinity, Aleja couldn't quite tell if they were friends or enemies. Tonight, she'd had the luck to pick the empty bar stool right in between them. They tossed insults back and forth over her head, each one more speculative about John's long-suffering wife's taste in men than the last. The poor woman. It was just a lucky thing that Yelena wasn't here tonight.

Not that her own taste was much better, judging by the guys she'd dated since moving back to Queens after college. Far from the nice Boricua boys *Mami* wanted her to bring home—Aleja was convinced such paragons of familial commitment were a myth, like unicorns—Aleja's type tended to run to the ex-frat boy crowd. She invariably gravitated toward the guys who wore suits during the day and regressed back to ball cap and khaki mode after dark. She went out with them once or twice before she got tired of the shtick—and before they wanted to upgrade to an Upper East Side trust-fund baby.

Conn was the antithesis of that whole world. He was so

tall, lean, and wiry like a frayed rope, she seriously doubted he wore suits anywhere except to weddings and funerals. He was a classic redhead with bright blue eyes and a wide smile. No one would ever call him "handsome" outright, but he had a cocky look about him that made people stop in their tracks and a good-natured charisma that drew all the regulars to him to chat for a few minutes. There was something about him that made you forget your troubles... probably his ability to start new ones in under a minute.

Aleja had always resisted his orbit, choosing to throw off a one-liner here and there but keep her distance. She lived way too close to the bar—it would be too easy to be here every day for a drink or dinner—so she tried not to get too involved with the regulars' noisy debates... *or* involved with the guys. She liked her life in hermetically sealed little boxes: work, home, the grocery store, drinks in Manhattan with friends, taking the train out to Jamaica to see her parents every other weekend. Coming into the Hanged Man was something she only did to sate basic hunger or the immediate need for a buzz. She didn't *need* this place to become her Cheers, where everybody knew her name.

But tonight was already different. Tonight, her gaze refused to stray from Conn. Everything about him spoke of roughness, of long days of hard work and longer nights of drinking... probably resulting in barely enough brain cells to have a decent conversation. But she was entranced, lulled by how his consonants and vowels ran together in that lilting way that made her feel like she was in a bar in Belfast and not Queens.

"I'm no angel," he was telling John now, "but I can take your lady to heaven while you're trying to find purgatory with a fuckin' flashlight."

As she ordered a second drink, she watched how he casually dropped a few bills on the bar to cover John's dinner. How he handed a perfect stranger three smokes when the guy asked, "Hey, can I bum one?" And something in her pulse quickened, telling her, *Aleja, mira! Don't let him pass you by.*

Underneath all his four-letter words and jackassery, there was a thoughtfulness, which didn't seem to fit. Of course, to be fair, Aleja didn't know much about him. Not even what he did for a living. All she knew was that he hadn't been in the States that long and he liked to bet on the horses and drink Miller Light. He was nursing his fifth or sixth pint of the evening. When Liam made a crack about how too many more drinks and Conn was going to "disappoint the ladies," Aleja surprised herself by blurting out, "I'm sure he has plenty of hot air left to blow up his date."

Oh, *shit*. She clapped her palms over her mouth, reddening as Liam and Conn and the surrounding patrons all stared at her, agape. Laughter broke out, and Conn peered at her over the rim of his pint glass, the mocking glint in his eye serving as a salute. "Oh my god, I'm so sorry," she said, chasing the apology with a gulp of her margarita. "I don't know where that came from."

Conn shrugged self-deprecatingly—but then his eyebrows lifted with wicked intent. "How'd you know so much about blow-up dolls, then? You sell them or something?"

An outraged denial was right on the tip of her tongue, but she ruefully recognized that she'd started this game. She couldn't very well play the horrified prude *now*. "Modeled for one, actually," she sighed, before gesturing theatrically at her body. She was all boobs and hips—and for all of her issues, low self-esteem wasn't one of them. She knew what she had, and she liked it. "Despite it being all of *this,* it just didn't sell. So they pulled it off the market."

"Fuckers." His eyes darkened with interest and his tongue flicked out to swipe across his full lower lip. "Would've shelled out for it myself."

"Of course you would have. Real women have standards, blow-up dolls don't." Aleja could have kicked herself for letting another line like that escape her lips, especially as the bar exploded in more amusement at Conn's expense.

He just shook his head. "And just what *are* your standards, little girl?"

"For one? Men who don't call me 'little girl,' just because I'm short." She wasn't the kind of person who was intentionally rude, who said saucy things to guys she barely knew. But there was something about Conn that just made it easy to play the role—that made it easy to become the kind of brazen woman who didn't just want the upper hand but *demanded* it.

"Oh, darlin'. I'm not callin' you 'little' because you're short." Conn gestured at the low-cut top of her sundress and the overflowing bounty that was on full display since she'd shrugged off her blazer. "This is like calling a fat man 'Tiny.'"

Sugary sincerity infused her voice. "Or like calling *you* 'Big Willy?'"

Crap. Even before the words were finished, she realized she'd stepped up the game. She'd unwittingly issued Conn a challenge. She earned a couple of cheers and one enthusiastic thump on the back from John, and the last sips of her drink went down way too fast.

"Now why'd you go and say *that?* Wound a man's pride, and he's just going to want to prove you wrong." Conn gave her a thorough once-over. Like he was undressing her with his eyes. It was the kind of look that, out on the sidewalk, got followed up by a whistle and a few choice catcalls. But here, it didn't make her feel violated and angry. No. It made her feel hot inside—hot and liquid and reckless.

Don't let him pass you by. There was that voice again. The same voice that had made her stop into the pub after a long day at the ad agency . . . that had made her order a Patrón margarita, heavy on the Patrón, light on everything else. Her mouth tasted like salt and triple sec. She suddenly wanted it to taste like cheap beer and random kindness. And that was a dangerous want.

She slid off her stool, bolting for the bar's side door and emerging in the alley. Without the laughter, the clink of pint glasses, the chatter from the TV, and the '80s pop filtering in from the satellite radio, maybe she could get her head on straight. Lusting after a near stranger was a huge mistake.

On cue, the door banged open, and Conn was standing there, tapping two cigarettes from his pack. She leaned against the brick wall, shaking her head. She wanted a smoke, but she had a worse craving than that. And he knew it.

"So it's like that then, is it?" The smokes went back into the crumpled pack, and he moved toward her. She'd known he was tall—with her barely clearing five feet, *everybody* was tall—but, like this, he seemed to tower over her. His white T-shirt stretched across his chest, the muscles defined by hard labor, not hours in the gym. There was power in his arms, she knew, because he'd carried a man out of the deli around the corner when it caught fire last month. During a round of pub gossip, Liam had whispered that to her. He'd said Conn refused to call himself a hero. Aleja wanted to call him that and a dozen other things. Most of them unspeakable. Maybe that was why she couldn't form a coherent sentence.

"You're looking to slum now, are you?" It wasn't an accusation. Or maybe it was. It was the same friendly/not-so-friendly tone he'd used with John earlier. She was fairly sure that, unlike her, John didn't have an inappropriate urge to fuck him.

As for the slumming . . . wasn't that what all of her frat boys had come to her for? Was she really shallow and terrible enough to want the same thing from someone else? "No. Yes. I don't know." The bravado that had made her go toe-to-toe with him inside was failing her now. "I'm sorry," she said. "I don't know what I'm thinking."

"Thinkin's not all it's cracked up to be, darlin'." Conn's hand wrapped around her wrist. His fingers nearly spanned the width twice over. His skin was pale against hers, the contrast as startling as that of their heights. "John just bet me you'd go home with me tonight."

"That's a losing bet," she lied.

"Then what are we doing here?" His thumb stroked her pulse with more tenderness than she'd thought him capable of. "What are you giving me the eye for, little girl?"

I don't know was on the tip of her tongue again, but she bit it back. "I'm not a little girl," she said instead. "I'm a grown woman, and I know what I want."

She swayed into him, into the shelter of his body, and his other arm came up to encircle her in a loose hug. They stood like that for what felt like an eternity. And then Conn made a low, strangled noise and leaned down to capture her mouth. He tasted like drunkenness and impulse. She arched up on her toes to match it with relative sobriety and not-so-relative poor judgment. *Let yourself have this,* the wild voice inside her said. *Let yourself have him.* So she slid her palms down his chest and anchored her fingers in the waistband of his jeans.

She couldn't call this slumming, not when it felt so good. Conn's hand moved up her arm to the strap of her sundress, and he nudged it aside. His long, blunt fingers slipped down the bodice, stroking the heavy, sensitive globe of her breast. When his thumb traced her nipple, an inarticulate cry escaped her lips and she flattened against him. As close as they could be with their clothes on. Her skirt had somehow gotten hiked up around her waist. He was bracketed between her thighs. His cock strained against the fly of his jeans and throbbed against the crotch of her panties. She wanted him closer, inside her. Making out like teenagers in a dirty alley wasn't enough. She wanted to be horizontal, crawling up his body like it was a rock face, finding footholds and places to grip . . . and not looking down in case she lost her focus and fell.

"Conn," she gasped into his open, wet mouth. "Conn, fuck me."

He pulled back just enough to chuckle against her jaw. "Wrong demand, *señorita*. Try it one more time."

"Fuck *you*," she gasped, only partially kidding.

His tongue teased the shell of her ear, his teeth nipping at the lobe. "Wrong again."

THE PICK-ME-UP

They necked for a few more minutes, hands wandering and wanting, and then she relented. "Take me home."

They were probably only gone for five minutes, but it felt like a year had passed since she came out for air. They each paid their tabs as quickly as possible, trying to ignore John's knowing look and Liam's smug laughter. Conn made a show of tapping his smokes like she was only following him out the front door for a light. She doubted anyone would buy the charade, but it was a certainty that he would be lighting *something*.

Her apartment wasn't far. Too close, she'd thought earlier, but now the walk seemed perfect. They headed there in tacit agreement, hands linked like lovers instead of polar opposites who had just decided to hook up on a whim. Conn looked at her like she was beautiful, and she felt the weight of his affectionate gaze like they were still chest to chest and thigh to thigh against the wall. The question *why* thrummed through her veins. She knew why *she* was doing this. But why was *he* doing this? Because she was a warm, willing body? Because she'd gotten one over on him in the bar? Because he had nothing better to do tonight?

"Are you sure you're up for this? You had a lot to drink."

"You worried about taking advantage of me?" He laughed. When he looked at her, it was with remarkably clear eyes. "I know what I'm doin'. I'm up for it," he added with a suggestive nod toward the rise in his jeans.

"Conn . . . " She didn't even know what she was asking, what reply she wanted.

"Shut up, darlin'." It was a gentle rebuke, without sting, and he tugged her close for a quick kiss before they crossed the street to her building. As they followed each other through the front door and up the stairs, she understood what he was trying to tell her without so many words. This filthy, funny unsung hero was rescuing her, too—carrying her out of the fire. No . . . carrying her *into* the fire.

Her keys felt like a jumbled mess in her suddenly damp palms. Conn took them from her, sifting through until she nodded at the right one. They were barely over the threshold, barely behind the safety of a locked door, when the keys hit the floor and he was lifting her into his arms, locking her legs around his hips. He shoved up her dress, cupped her ass through the thin cotton of her underwear, and cradled her flush against his groin. She looped her arms around his neck, bringing his head down to hers for a sloppy openmouthed kiss. It was only a few short steps from her door to the rest of her tiny studio, and he navigated the obstacles of her furniture in the darkness with ease.

Her queen-size bed took up almost the entire space, but it was her one indulgence. Falling onto the mattress with Conn told her it had been the right one. He braced himself above her, kissing her lips, her jaw, and the column of her throat. He licked at the hollow between her breasts before yanking down the bodice of her dress and tugging it with him as he worked his way down her body. The material caught at her hips. She raised herself up just enough for him to pull her dress and panties all the way off.

His beard stubble rasped against her inner thigh. She was so wet, so hot, that it was entirely possible she was going to come before he even really touched her. But he didn't allow for that possibility. He teased her with his fingers, letting them grow slick with her juices as he opened her up. He lowered his head and nipped at the sensitive bud of her clit before licking into her deep and thorough. As if he had nothing planned for the rest of the night except this slow, sensual torment.

"*Conn . . .* " His name was a high keening noise that she barely recognized as language, and she said it over and over, thrashing under him like she was being tossed around in a storm. He stroked her clit and took her higher, until the tension was too much to bear and her entire body went taut like a thread about to snap. She heard Conn whispering over the pounding in her ears, over the ragged sound of her gasping for air.

"That's it," he soothed. "That's a love, just let it happen." And then she *did* snap, her breath stopping, her blood stopping, everything surrendering to pleasure.

Afterward, she felt limp and boneless, barely able to move. "I was right. You did have enough hot air to breathe life into your date," she said weakly.

Conn dropped a cocky kiss on her hip. "I should hope so, considering it's my job." At her confused frown, he elaborated. "I'm a paramedic." His red-blond brows quirked with mirth. "My mum wanted me to be a doctor, but I hated all the schoolin'."

"No wonder you saved me tonight." Because he *had*. He'd shaken her out of her solitude and her status quo. A margarita was a temporary high, tart and sweet on her tongue. Being with Conn was better. She urged him back to her mouth, tasting herself on his lips. This time his tongue didn't battle. It seduced, leisurely and languidly tangoing with hers. The kiss lasted for minutes, until they were both breathless.

"Fuck," he whispered, imbuing the single syllable with a surprising amount of eloquence. She echoed it, fisting her fingers in the cloth of his T-shirt and tugging at it. He needed to be as naked as she was. It was only fair. He rocked back on his heels, obliging her by stripping off his shirt and jeans, stopping for a moment to rifle in his wallet for a foil square that he laid just within reach. Thank God at least one of them was thinking about protection. It had been so long for Aleja that she had nothing. Least of all any defenses.

Conn was long and lean everywhere but his cock. She closed her fingers around his thick shaft, stroking up from the base, and more swear words flew from his lips. A jumble of English and Gaelic, it sounded like poetry to her. A laundry list would probably sound like poetry to her right now. He moved over her and tore at the condom wrapper. Once covered, he nudged her already spread legs wider and settled himself between them. "Last chance to back out, little girl," he warned.

"I had my chance to back out at the bar." She caressed every part of him she could reach, trailing her fingers through the sparse hairs on his chest. "Here . . . ? Here all I want is you."

Aleja rose, hooking one arm around his neck as she slid onto his cock, taking him inch by precious inch. He was so wide it almost hurt. When she winced, Conn steadied her with a palm splayed across her ass, keeping her still until her body acclimated itself to his girth. He distracted her with kisses, rough ones that belied how gentle he was determined to be with her. They were fierce assaults on her mouth that made her clutch him and try to give back the fervor a thousandfold. She anchored her hands in his hair, cradling the back of his head, and tugged at his lower lip with her teeth. Until she tasted copper. Until she didn't even realize that his cock was buried in her to the hilt. She glanced down to where they were joined, and the visual of him so deep inside her was enough to spike her arousal. A whimpering moan escaped her lips. She wrapped her legs around his waist, meeting each of his steady staccato thrusts with a roll of her hips.

"Oh, fuck, darlin'. Yes. Let's have more of that," he panted in her ear, his fingertips digging into the backs of her thighs.

It could have been minutes. It could have been an hour. All Aleja knew was that they were sweat-slick with exertion and her nerves were overloaded. She wanted to come *right now,* and then she didn't, because it would end the exquisite sensation of being stretched and filled and taken. The decision was out of her hands. His cock found that perfect little coil of tension, the spot that made everything go white behind her eyelids, and she went hurtling into free fall. *Don't let this pass you by.* As he gave into his own release, coming so hard she felt it deep inside her, she clung to him. She buried her face in his neck until the last vestiges of her orgasm and her doubt faded.

"Why?" she gasped against his cheek. "Why me, Conn?"

He traced a line across her eyebrows and then veered down the bridge of her nose, tapping the tip. "Why else does a man pick up a girl in a pub? Because you looked like you needed a stiff one." When she yelped in mock-outrage and drove her elbow into his gut, his breath expelled in a huff. He stopped chuckling, leaning his forehead against hers. He stared at her with utterly serious eyes that, even in pitch dark, were the color of the midday sky. "Because you looked like you needed a friend," he corrected, softly.

She kissed the corner of his mouth, tasting sex and sweetness. "I think I found one." *I think I found more.* But she wasn't going to tell him that yet. She'd wait till *he* needed rescuing some night at the bar, and let him figure it out for himself.

BELONGING

Tamsen Parker

I'm not sure what I thought a kink club would be like, but this wasn't it. The places you read about in books are either luxurious palaces with room upon room of carnal delights and delectable tortures, or they're seedy hellholes with a dirty mattress in the corner, all but indistinguishable from a drug-infested squatter's paradise. This place is definitely more on the crack den end of things, but quirkier and more comfortable than I would've thought.

Not that I'm comfortable here, because I'm not. My heart is beating in a nervous skittery rhythm because wouldn't anyone's? I want to be excited, and I am, but it's like there's a snare drum being played poorly in my chest. It should make me feel like dancing, but instead my feet are glued to the ground and the guy behind the counter is looking at me with his brows knitted together and the corners of his mouth pulled down.

"You don't have to come in, you know."

Right.

But I already paid my thirty-five-dollar guest fee and filled out all their paperwork, bile churning in my stomach when I handed over my license for this stranger to inspect. Mutually assured destruction, that's what I'm relying on. It worked out okay for the Soviets and the Americans given there wasn't a World War III, but I don't know that I'll be able to sleep at night with that as my only assurance that no one will find out about this. Like my friends. My bible study group. My parents. The aunties of my mom's *barkada*.

That's enough to make my heart seize. On the other hand, if I'm going to die of humiliation and shame for disappointing my family, I may as well actually do something to deserve it. Not just stand in the cinder-block lobby of this club listening to the muted noises of people having a really good time wafting out of the open hallway.

I nod at the guy, and the corner of his mouth turns up, making him look less intimidating. Guyliner rims his pale blue eyes and he's got so many piercings I can't count them all without staring. He must be used to that if he goes out in public like this, but for all I know he's a straitlaced accountant who wears khakis and a tie to work every day. Maybe I should've done a better job disguising myself?

"I like your corset."

He blinks at me and my blurted words because I couldn't think of anything else to say, and then laughs, a short huff. "Thanks. I like yours too. Your cleavage is phenomenal."

It totally is. Unlike his pale, flat chest inside the tube of black leather, mine is practically spilling out of this red-and-black brocade number. It's new. I don't dress like this, but it seemed appropriate. Not to mention usually I wouldn't take kindly to someone commenting on my body—as things are, it sets my cheeks to simmer—but I don't mind it coming from this guy. He's not leering and he's still sitting behind his desk, waving by people who are far more decisive than I am. Members. People who belong here.

I squeeze my eyes shut and think again of having to confess this tomorrow. To Father Gabriel, with nothing but a latticed metal screen between us. It's never seemed flimsy before, but I bet it will tomorrow. Especially if my skin gets so hot and prickly that it melts the stupid thing. That must've happened before, right? Maybe they keep spares in the back? This can't possibly be the worst thing he'll have ever heard . . . .

"Thanks." That's what you're supposed to say when people give you a compliment. I can hear my mother's *psst* in my ear to get me to mind my manners. Even here. I definitely do not need to be thinking about my mother in a kink club. If I keep this up, my brain will be melting out of my ears.

The goth guy holds out a hand, his nails painted black, which stands out against his skin—it's so pale I have to wonder if he ever goes outside. I shake instinctually, and his grip is firm.

"It's your first time, right? I work most nights, and I've never seen you."

I bite my lip in a habit I thought I'd kicked, but apparently being this freaked out has dredged it up. "Yeah."

"You know everyone had a first time, right?"

It's so obvious, but of course he's right. My head bobbles on my neck and I swallow. Somehow it doesn't make me feel much better.

"I can't abandon my post, but I'll—"

His gaze snaps to a point over my shoulder and his face transforms from compassionate to impish—his mouth purses tightly. It looks like a rose so dark red it's verging on black.

"Hey, Mistress. How are you this evening?"

"Fine, Raven. You?"

Her voice sends prickles up my spine. It's all I can do not to shiver.

"Busy, but good. You meeting anyone?"

"Nah." Her words are casual, but her deep voice is round, full, elegant. Makes me think of timpani. "Should've set something up, but I got caught up in my thesis."

Thesis? Is she a PhD student like me? The thought excites and terrifies me at the same time. Does she go to my university? She's not in my department. I would remember if I'd heard that voice before.

Raven shakes his head and tsks. "All work and no play makes Constance a dull girl."

She laughs in response, and the sound makes my knees weak. Is that a standard reaction to hearing a voice that turns you on? That you can perceive the potential in? Or is this my own peculiar brand of desire, the piece of me that aches to hand myself over and be used? That gets hot and sticky between my thighs at the idea of being on my knees before someone who commands my respect and adoration but treasures me in return?

These are the things I've fantasized about since . . . It doesn't matter how long. What matters is that this is my first chance to see if these are things that only appeal in fantasy or if there's a kernel of truth to the reveries I've entertained for so long.

"Maybe you could help me out? I don't have backup tonight, and I've got a guest who could use a tour. You game?"

"Sure."

It could be my overly zealous imagination, but I fancy her tone has slid closer to a flirty purr and I squeeze my thighs together.

Raven looks at me, his eyes expectantly wide, and gestures with his eyebrows. I can practically hear him. *"Turn around, you fool girl. I'm doing you a favor."*

So I do, and the thin grip I have on reality about snaps.

She's beautiful. Tall—probably approaching six feet, and on a good day, I'm five even. The boots she's wearing probably don't help, but they're smallish heels. Black leather pants hug her thick thighs and her generous hips and don't nip in much for her waist. She's wearing a crisp white collared shirt, the front unbuttoned until it reaches a black underbust corset. Talk about phenomenal cleavage. The whole thing is framed by an open, off-purple, short velvet blazer I want to run my hands over. Her dark-brown skin looks powder dry, not sweaty with nerves like mine, and her black hair is in braids that are somehow fashioned into a roll on the top of her head, making her even taller.

If I've ever seen a woman who I've been more attracted to, I can't remember her. I have to take a hard swallow, but then I stick out my hand and offer a bright "Hi."

Was that too perky? That might've been too perky.

But Constance . . . Mistress? . . . doesn't seem offended or put off. No, she reaches a big hand out and the corner of her mouth curls up as her chest rises.

"Hello yourself," she says, that voice doing things to

my body I didn't know were possible in response to a voice. It's blasphemous to say it's almost a religious experience, but that's as close as I can describe it. It's different, but the intensity is the same. It makes the colors of her brighter, so distinct, that looking at her almost hurts my eyes and the rest of the room fades away. "I'm Constance. And who are you?"

"Glory." My voice is a squeak next to hers, the one high-pitched tone of a triangle.

One of her dark eyebrows kicks up and she looks like a cat about to eat a canary. I wish I were wearing yellow. "Well Glory glory hallelujah."

Her hand is warm and huge around mine, and I want for her to give me more. To stroke a fingertip over the sensitive skin of the underside of my wrist, lift my hand to her mouth to brush a kiss over the knuckles, use her firm grip to pull me in so that our still-joined hands would be the only thing between us.

Actually, if she did any of those things, I'd be wary. I've read up on how I'm supposed to behave here and about how other people are supposed to behave. Coming on that strong would be frowned upon. So I'll just have to wish for it. Come to think of it, I don't know anything about this woman. Besides that I like the way she smells, the way she looks, and I very, very much like how she's still gripping my hand.

Mistress? At least I know that much. And from the expression on her face, I'm guessing she likes women. I do too. Though I like men almost as well. Not that I have a ton of experience with either one. Some people would be embarrassed about that, but I've learned not to be. If you're not a sanctimonious jackass about it, most people are respectful, and some people even think it's cool. What would Constance think? Is she religious? Or has she replaced church with . . . this?

Maybe I should stop obsessively speculating and say something. I'm delightful. When I can get sentences to come out of my mouth instead of chirping single words, anyway. But what am I supposed to say? There's no ritual here for me. It's not like the familiar rhythms of Mass—no matter where you go, whether in a chapel or a mall or a cathedral, Mass is the same. Week in and week out, no matter what else is going on, whatever my thesis advisor is subjecting me to, no matter how crazy-making the students in my TA section are, I know what to expect when I walk into that church—or any church I happen to be in. It was one thing that helped me to make the adjustment when I came to the US for university from Manila. Here, though, I'm at a loss.

Somehow Constance seems to understand, and her expression gentles. Turns into a warm smile that's more innocent than the smirk she'd turned on me before.

"Pleasure to meet you, Glory." Then with a glance over my head, she says, "I've got her, Raven. Promise I'll bring her back in one piece."

My thoughts stutter. Maybe I don't want her to bring me back in one piece. Maybe I want to be taken apart. Maybe I want to be shattered into pieces, and then glued back together by Constance's strong hands. Or maybe she'd pour the shards back and forth between her palms, let the bits of me sift through her fingers.

I shouldn't let myself get so carried away. We just met and I need to be careful. But freed from a script, I need cues. Want them, desperately. So without another word to Raven, I let Constance steer me down the hallway I couldn't quite set foot in on my own.

The place is bigger than it looks from the outside, although about as swank as the vestibule, which is not at all. The carpet on the floor is old, stained in some places, and covered with well-tread rugs. There's an open space where play areas are delineated by ropes hung between, and each has a piece of furniture. A bench. A chair. A table. A Saint Andrew's cross, which makes my stomach clench in a weird way. There's a room off to the side Constance gestures to, and eyes me as she tells me what it is.

"That's the room for medical play. Blood play. Any fluid play. No carpet. No upholstery. Nothing that can't be hosed or wiped down."

I try to play it cool, but I'm so busy rubbernecking, trying to see everything in there out of pure curiosity that I trip over a rug. Constance catches me with a chuckle. It rumbles through her so I feel it more than I hear it.

"This your first time at a club?"

"Is it that obvious?" I have to look up at her, and it makes me feel even more foolish, even smaller.

"No." She's trying to be nice, but it absolutely *is* obvious. Her white lie doesn't bother me though. She's trying to make me feel as though I've got at least a toehold here, and I appreciate it. "You're not making a fool out of yourself, which a lot of people do, and you're clearly not a tourist looking to point at the freaks. You're doing fine."

Funny thing is, I believe her. So I nod, not able to voice my gratitude. At the end of the row of playspaces, there's a small kitchen and seating area, and Constance steers us over to what I'd call a love seat, but even thinking the word *love* near Constance makes my cheeks heat. I don't love her. But I'd like to know if I could.

When we sit, she leans back and crosses an ankle over her knee. "So you've never been to a club, but a play party?"

"No."

"A conference?"

"There are conferences?" I should know that. Of course there are.

She smiles again, and the worry that had cropped up gets pushed back down.

"Did you ever play with a partner? Boyfriend? Girlfriend?"

"No. I don't date much. I'm busy now, and when I grew up my parents were strict. My family's really religious too. I know a lot of people rebel, but . . . "

I shrug. I don't have a great explanation for why I still go to Mass and confession and try to be a good Catholic. I grew up that way but so did all my siblings. My older sister and my youngest brother certainly never got the memo.

Constance looks like she's licking up the beads of information I'm slowly dropping. Letting them sit on her tongue so she can analyze their taste and composition. "So are you a bottom? A Top? A Dom? A sub? A switch? Something else?"

I try to hide my flinch, but I don't hide it well.

"Hey, sorry. You can tell me to mind my own business. You don't have to tell me anything. If you're not ready to talk, you're not ready."

I am, though. I want to tell someone, to share this part of me with someone who might understand. There have been no opportunities prior to now and I shouldn't waste this one.

"I'm a bottom, I think? Maybe a sub? I've never . . . done this before, so I don't know for sure, but it's what I've wanted. What I think about. What I get turned on by."

What I've confessed. Impure thoughts has got to be a thing priests hear a lot about.

"I came here tonight because I wanted . . . I wanted to try. To see for real. To see if . . . "

If I'm right. Or if this whole time I've been a stranger to my own body. If there's a disconnect between fantasy and reality. If I've spent hours and hours agonizing over something that isn't even real.

"Do you still want to try?"

Things tumble around in my head. I do. Is she—what is—?

"Yes. Are you offering?"

Constance laughs, her mouth spreading wide to show off her teeth, and tipping her head back. "I was going to ease into it, but yes. Did you have anything in mind?"

Is there something I *don't* have in mind? I want everything. Now that I'm here I want to gorge myself, take anything on offer, but that wouldn't be smart and it might even be . . . rude? There is one thing I think I can bring myself to ask for that doesn't seem like too much. A thing I've thought about a million times and never asked for because I've never had someone to ask.

Now I do.

She's right here, offering this thing to me, or maybe opening a door, gesturing for me to come inside. I want to cross the threshold, see if I could belong here too.

"Spank me?"

"A girl who's not afraid to ask for what she wants. I like that." Constance smiles, and I have to make an effort to not squirm on the sofa. I want her smiles, I want her approval, I want her. Which is why I can't stop myself from bouncing.

"Now?"

Her smile gets wider, and her gaze travels up and down my body. Doesn't take long since I'm small, but I relish every second. It feels as though she's double-checking to make sure I'm real. Could she possibly have the same hot flame of interest licking up from her pelvis?

Constance reaches out and grazes her knuckles over my cheek. I want to lean in, turn her hand over so I can rest my head on her palm, but I don't dare. Because this is my lucky day, the movement doesn't stop at my jaw, but the backs of her fingers coast over my chin, my lips, and my other cheek before she does give me the warmth and contact of her palm. I give up, give in, sigh, and close my eyes because it's too perfect. They snap open again when she says, "Now works."

I'm not shy, and I don't think I can wait another second without spontaneously combusting, so I clamber over her lap, which provokes another laugh. I like Constance's laugh—it's kind and delighted, not appalled or cruel. There might be a better place to do this, or at least somewhere sexier than what's basically the break room of a shabby kink club, but I don't care. Constance doesn't seem inclined to wait, either.

No, definitely not. She sets one of her hands at the small of my back, and the other on my thigh, just below where my skirt ends. God, I'm wet. Can she tell? She works up my skirt so it's bunched around my waist, and then her hand is on my butt. Her hand. Is on. My butt. I wish I were cool enough not to gasp, but I'm not.

She hesitates but doesn't move her hand. "Is this okay? You can tell me to stop anytime and I will."

"I'm good." My lack of oxygen makes my voice squeaky and breathy at the same time, which I'm sure is devastatingly attractive. She doesn't laugh, though. Just strokes my bottom over my underwear—lacy ones, the nicest pair I have. Then her palm leaves my flesh before landing again. Not too hard but it's a shock nonetheless. The crisp, stinging smack makes me want to cry. It's not painful; it feels like acceptance. Confirmation. Like pieces I've been trying to fit together for my whole life have finally clicked into place. It's a relief but also overwhelming.

The feeling grows as she hits me again and again. I try to quiet my mind so I can pay attention, enjoy, and to be honest, analyze. What do I like, what do I not like? How does this actually make me feel?

With the slaps getting harder, there's an element of pain, but mostly it's warmth spreading through me, and some being turned on. A lot. Maybe embarrassingly so. Is it possible to orgasm from spanking? Am I about to find out?

I'm squirming on Constance's lap, but not because I want to get away. I want more, and this woman is . . . giving it to me. I can't imagine she's hitting me as hard as she can because she's so solid, but it's still intense and I appreciate more than words can say the hand she's pressing into the small of my back, holding me down—a sensation I'd like to explore more. That doesn't stop my hips from grinding into her thigh, making me throb and pulse between my legs until I spill over. Cry out. Ecstasy and surprise, gratefulness and this expansiveness, like I've discovered something new but also known it all along. I belong here.

It's physically exhausting, the tension and the release of it, the way my whole body shudders and my startled shout turns into desperate, greedy moans while I rock out the rest of my climax on this stranger's leg. I'm filled to the tip top with emotions, so much that the tears finally fall.

Constance turns me over, helps me curl up on her lap, and I fling my arms around her neck, bury my face against her shoulder, and feel compelled to tell her it's okay though I'm the one who's bawling. She didn't do anything wrong and I want her to know.

"Constance, I'm okay. I'm all right. I . . . Thank you. I—" I can't go on because I'm choked by a hiccupping sob.

Her arms around me, though, make me feel better, safe, not so scared of everything that just happened; let me enjoy the good and press pause on some of my fears because she's not going to let me go. Not until I'm good and ready. That's what she tells me in soft murmurs as she cradles me. There aren't many people in my life I've had this kind of intimacy with, and I want to steep in it like I'm a bag of tea and she's the hot water that finally allows me to loosen and unfurl. So I let myself be too much until I've mellowed in her arms. Finally I find the presence of mind to nuzzle and kiss beneath her ear.

"Thank you. That was . . . wonderful. Everything I hoped it could be." A thought seizes me and I pull away so I can see her as I ask my question, willing the fear not to choke me up. I've been so selfish and it makes my stomach curdle. "Did you like it too?"

"Oh, Glory. You're a pleasure. My pleasure. Yes, little one, I liked it too."

Two small words shouldn't have so much of an effect on a person who spends days reading books and reports and writing treatises, but my heart is flushed with happiness and the queasiness disappears—*little one*. I'd like to be that to Constance. Let her show me more—because there's more, right?—and I'll ask her to teach me how to please her even more.

I should feel guilty. I do, a little. But I'm not sorry. My confession tomorrow just got a whole lot stickier because there's no way I can say with my whole heart that I'll never do it again. How could Father Gabriel blame me for that, even as he says the words we both expect, instructing me to make amends? There aren't so many places a person feels like they truly belong, and I don't believe he'd want to take that from me. For now, I'll sit and breathe and enjoy. This woman beneath me is a virtue and a vice, and I hope she'll be my teacher for a little longer. Maybe even more.

WITH HONORS

Sofia Quintero

Justina surveys the seminar room. It is completely full, despite today being the last day of class. She chuckles to herself. Of course it is. No one wants a semester with Professor Delgado to end.

Today instead of standing behind the lectern, the professor half sits across the front desk—the fabric of his navy slacks taut against his sculpted thighs—and answers their questions as promised. Justina realizes that the professor knows the impact he has on his students. Even if she had not warned him of the personal inquiries to come his way, he had to have noticed how the students' attire changed over the semester. After the first meeting, the yoga pants, flip-flops, and hair wraps gave way to contoured makeup, pencil skirts, and high-heeled boots.

When they met two weeks ago during office hours, Justina warned him. "Expect to be asked all kinds of inappropriate things," she said of her twenty-something classmates. "They're children, after all." The second she said it, she knew she had ulterior motives and worried that they were as naked to Professor Delgado as they felt to her.

"Children, Ms. Mendez?" He raised an eyebrow at her. And then he chuckled.

"Okay." To avoid his gaze, she busied herself with inserting the first draft of her final paper in her bag just so. To atone for the petty remark, Justina told on herself. "But remember I have a child their age."

"Really? I thought you had just the one. Brianna, right?" Three classes into the semester, Justina had come to Professor Delgado on the verge of tears. As much as she enjoyed his course, she had to drop it. Brianna had just started at a high school where she didn't know anyone, and in a desperate effort to make friends, she fell in with the crowd that liked to cut class, get high, and who knows what else. Justina couldn't risk taking evening courses while Brianna was in this phase now that her brother, Caleb, was in Syracuse. She needed to pick up her daughter from school, bring her home, and make sure she did her homework before indulging in any teenage shenanigans with thoroughly vetted accomplices.

Professor Delgado refused to sign the form that would allow Justina to drop his class. Her perspective was vital to class discussions, he said. He relied on it to tease out important nuances. She knew by that Professor Delgado meant he appreciated having a member of Generation X in a room full of postmillennials. Her much younger classmates rolled their eyes when she raised her hand and barely muffled their scoffs when he praised her insight. Their insecurity instigated Justina's performance of the experienced and confident woman even as she, too, switched from business casual neutrals to jewel-toned, form-fitting suits. At least on Tuesdays and Thursdays from six to eight, the persona felt real.

Ground the girl, Professor Delgado had said, and bring her to class. Justina laughed. She had underestimated his brilliance. Did he have children, she asked. Yes. A son. Eight. A few minutes later, as Justina walked across the campus to the parking lot, she wondered where their conversation might have gone had they not been interrupted by another student desperate to speak with the professor.

And so Justina grounded the girl and brought her to class. Brianna whined the entire way until she entered the room and saw him. "*Mami*, that's your teacher?" Out came the smartphone.

"Brianna, what are you doing?" Justina swiped at the device, but her daughter swung it out of reach. "Give it here."

"Just one picture for Insta." The phone flashed and clicked. "I wish I had a teacher who looked like him." Brianna's thumbs danced across the screen as she churned out one hashtag after the other.

"Brianna, give it now!" Justina grabbed the phone before Brianna could close the app. *#thisiscollegebitches #collegeislit #professorbae #howyoudoin #Idnevergraduate*. Within seconds Brianna's post racked up likes, shares, and emojis. "I swear I don't know what to do with you." Still, the experience brought them closer. Brianna's teen lust grew into genuine interest as she hung on Professor Delgado's every word, and mother and daughter were continuing class discussions on their rides home. While she still gave Justina the occasional fit, Brianna soon grew bored with her first choice of friends and gravitated toward two girls with whom she could both Photoshop and politick.

Really it was the professor's kindness that made Justina give in to her attraction. At first she resisted the dark curls, those toned arms, that husky laugh. What did a forty-six-year-old divorcee with a full-time job, eleven credits, and two grownish children need with an adolescent crush on a younger man, never mind her instructor?

Everything, it seemed, when Justina grew tired of the long days, the demanding course load, the hustle, the loneliness. After handing in their midterm exams, she watched her young classmates cluster off, bounding out of the room joshing with relief and debating where to eat. Justina collected her things, walked into the bathroom, and began to cry. Even if they had invited her to join them, she wouldn't have been able to go. Twenty years ago she had traded the structured spontaneity of college life for motherhood, and while she never regretted having Caleb, if she had to do it all over again, Justina would have returned to school to finish her degree before having Brianna. Before Justina could release the sadness, some classmates barged into the bathroom, chasing her into a stall for cover. As the young women reapplied their lipstick and brushed their hair, they admitted what they really wanted to know from Professor Delgado before the semester ended.

Professor D, are you married?
Who fuckin' cares?
I do, okay, because I'm not a slore like you.
Nope, she's her own slore.
Exactly. Thank you.
What size shoe are you, Professor Delgado?

Gawd, are you for real right now? That's such an old wives' tale.
You mean a Justina tale?
That's so fuckin' mean. She can't help it if she's old.
Professor Delgado, can I get the D?
Not uh D . . .
Theee D!

They rolled out on a wave of hysterical giggles, never realizing Justina had heard them. When she was that age, she would have bounded out of that stall cussing and swinging until one of those bitches had her face shoved down the toilet. Lucky for them, by the time she turned thirty, Justina had settled into the woman her mother spent all her life haranguing her into being. Responsible. Disciplined. Oh so far above *la racheteria*.

Lucky for them, but not for her.

After giving them a few minutes to disappear, Justina braced for the winter cold and bustled toward her car. As it warmed up, she answered a few work emails, texted Brianna to ask what she wanted Justina to pick up for dinner, and liked some of Caleb's Facebook posts. Justina went to her photos. Once when she had confiscated Brianna's phone and investigated her social media accounts, Justina came across the post about Professor Delgado. Although she had texted the photo to herself, she never gave herself permission to look at it again. But that crisp October night, she thought a harmless crush was exactly what she needed to get through the term. Justina pinched the screen to enlarge the photo until she could see the scar on his chin. If she had half the gall of her younger classmates, Justina would ask Professor Delgado how he got it. Scars held stories, sometimes even secrets. Her classmates would snicker at her, but the professor would understand. It was a grown woman's question motivated by a grown woman's needs.

Justina imagined herself sashaying into his office on the last day of class. *Professor Delgado, one last question.* She closed her eyes and pressed her thighs together. In her fantasy, she traced her finger along his scar. His breath quickened as she locked the door behind her, hoping this was exactly what he thought this was. *May I . . . ?* She dropped to her knees and unbuckled his pants. He would already be hard, having been thinking about Justina like he did after every class. Justina pulled out his hefty cock with a firm grip and sank him into her mouth. In the front seat of her increasingly warm car, she parted her thighs and dipped her finger into her moist pussy, fucking herself in the rhythm of her fantasy, lips sliding up and down Professor Delgado's cock. Behind her closed eyes, she watched him grip her shoulders as he humped her sweaty mouth, while in her car she arched her back and added another finger to her juicy cunt. Just as Justina imagined him firing off his hot load down her throat, she groaned and came in her front seat.

This is the night she remembers on the last day of class as she watches Professor Delgado field their silly questions while they eat the Indian takeout food and drink bottles of Riesling, his treat. If by family they mean is he married, no, he never has been. He'll be thirty-six in July. No, not Leo, Cancer. He tries to work out but hasn't been to the gym in months, and it's all their fault. Justina finally asks him a question, but it's not about the scar. Yes, he'd like to come back next semester, but he's not sure if he will. It's not up to him. It actually might be up to them. And he uses that moment to remind them of the confidential course evaluation form he sent them after submitting their grades to the registrar.

They've stayed an hour later than usual when Professor Delgado finally says he needs to get to his son. He hands out the final papers, and students hurry off to their end-of-semester celebrations or unmade dorm beds. "Ms. Mendez," he says, his hands empty. "I think I may have left yours in the office."

As they make their way down the corridor, they joke about the questions. He thought Justina was exaggerating when she warned him. She felt they weren't so bad. They enter Professor Delgado's office, and there her paper is on the desk, centered on the blotter. On it in his sharp print, A for the paper, A- for the course.

Justina says, "Is it too late to do some extra credit?" They both know it is. It's a grown woman's question motivated by a grown woman's need, and this is no performance.

"I stayed so late," says the professor, "I could use a ride to the station so I won't miss the next train."

They arrive at the station a good half hour before Professor Delgado's train, and Justina parks in a dark corner away from traffic. She turns to him and says, "Professor Delgado . . ."

"Jeremy . . ."

"Jeremy, thank you so much for being such a wonderful teacher. I learned much more than I imagined. And I wouldn't have even stayed if you hadn't been so supportive."

Jeremy takes a deep breath. "I've admired you for quite some time." His hand drifts from his lap to Justina's knee. Although he lets his hand rest there, the warmth of his touch flows up her thigh.

"Me?" Justina's tone is saucy. Leading. Assured. "Or my work?"

"Both." Jeremy's thumb caresses her knee, adding heat to the current pulsing up her leg. "Of course both."

Justina places her hand over his and slides it to her inner thigh where her stocking ends and her flesh begins. She finally looks him in the eye and smiles. They lean toward each other, his breath reaching for hers, hers drawing his in. His lips against hers are soft and firm like his fingers now stroking her thigh. Justina presses herself into his kiss, hungry for Jeremy to discover her secret. Instead his other hand reaches toward her breast, the thumb grazing back and forth over Justina's hardening nipple.

As their tongues mingle, Justina reaches for Jeremy, her hand settling on his belly, his muscles taut beneath a band of flesh she rubs and squeezes. Jeremy grasps her hips to pull her closer to him, and her hand tumbles to the bulge beneath his belt. Her fingertips delve into the fabric above the grooves of his cock, hot and stiff.

Justina rears back, her hands still rubbing Jeremy's cock. She lifts her hips and slides herself onto his lap. She grips the back of his head and dives for another kiss as his hands roam up her thighs and onto her bare ass, her secret now exposed.

"Wow."

Jeremy grinds into her as his fingers cup and knead her ass, the length of them diving into her moistening folds. Justina kisses him as she grabs his hair and winds her crotch against his, their moans escaping between gyrations. She feels her juices seeping into his slacks, his cock reaching for her. Her back arches into him, her head falling back from the weight of her moans while Jeremy licks the grooves of her neck and nibbles her throat.

Justina stops, looking him in the eyes and stroking his hair. She eases herself off Jeremy's lap and climbs into the backseat. Jeremy undoes his slacks—the crotch wet with her—as he watches Justina ease onto her back, lick her fingers, and nestle them in her pussy. They watch each other, she teasing her clit with one finger as she dips another into her cunt, he sliding his fist up his cock and over its bulb. Their eyes lock as their hands fall into a rhythm of dip and slide, dip and slide, dip and slide. The waves rising in her pussy push groans over her belly and out her throat.

"Can I taste you?"

"Please."

Jeremy moves into the backseat and kneels between her thighs, and Justina bridges her back, her moist ass slipping off the leather seat. She anticipates that Jeremy will lower himself so that he can sink his face into her pussy, but he instead grasps her hips and hoists her up and toward his face. Justina gasps as her shoulders sink into the seat, bringing her dripping pussy to Jeremy's hot mouth, the stubble on his cheeks grazing her thighs. His tongue circles the fullness of her vulva, dipping into folds, sliding along her clit over and over. Blood rushes to Justina's head as her thighs clench Jeremy's face while his tongue darts into her walls and his breath tickles her clit.

Jeremy pauses, and Justina's hips sink back into the seat. Before her ass can feel the leather, he slips two fingers into her ignited pussy. *No,* she thinks. *This is too much. I can't.* Jeremy slowly pumps his hand, and her pussy smacks. The sound of herself against the creaking of the leather tells her yes. Yes, she can.

"Mmmmm . . ." She gyrates her hips and tightens her pussy around Jeremy's fingers, sighing louder and louder with each dive. Despite Justina's mounting pleasure, Jeremy maintains a steady rhythm as he watches his glistening fingers disappear into and return from the wet folds. Justina quickens her gyrations and reaches for her clit.

"No," he says. He pulls out his fingers.

"What?" Her breath is heavy, the one word difficult to form.

"Slow down," Jeremy says. "Let me. I get what you like now."

Justina closes her eyes and takes in a deep breath. Her cunt still pulsating, she releases the arch in her back. Jeremy's thumb hovers over her clit, circling without touching, while another finger creeps back into her hole. It slides in and out, and then one finger becomes two. Two stretches into three, the pads curling that spot, and her groans rise into yowls. Her neck sweats and tears pool behind her eyes, his fingers unhinging something deep and primal. "Ohhh." Her spot cringes. It aches. It yearns for more.

She grabs Jeremy's hand and pulls it out of her pussy. His eyebrows knit with worry. "Did I hurt you?"

Justina drops her head against the seat, her chest heaving. Her juices run down her crotch and over her ass as the aroma of her desire envelops the air. She opens her eyes. "No, you didn't," she says. Justina sits up and turns over onto her knees. She sucks in a breath as she wriggles her ass against his cock. "Not yet."

Justina sways her juicy ass over his rod, trusting him

to take his time and tease her. Jeremy grips his cock and drags the head back and forth between her clit and her asshole. "Yes," she moans. "Like that." Jeremy's breath grows heavier along with his stroking, pressing deeper into her grooves with every pass, the head of his cock now planting a kiss on her clit at the top of each stroke. Her clit strains for his head when it leaves to coast back down her drenched valley toward her anus as if to say *come back*.

"Fuck me now," she says. "Make me come." Jeremy brings the head of his cock to her hole, wiggling it between her lips. "I said now!" She's the instructor now. Jeremy pierces her cunt. "Yes!" She sucks him in and pummels her ass into his hips. One hand grabs her hip, the other her hair, and as he pumps and pulls, Justina bursts into sweat. It drips from her forehead, down her throat, in between her breasts. Her knees and palms slide and sink into the leather as she wails in ecstasy. The tail of the tornado forms at her G-spot, spiraling and swelling throughout her pussy, gathering intensity as Justina bucks against him, strong and sure. Her thighs slap his, and soon with every thrust Justina rises until Jeremy drops onto his back.

Planting one foot on the seat and the other on the floor, Justina begins to pump. As Jeremy's furious cock drives into her, Justina throws open her arms to grasp the seat backs. He swings into her, making her rock as she gasps. She looks down at her pussy and hikes up the skin on her mound; her clit, now the size of a dime, glistens in the dark in the beam of a distant streetlight muted by the fogged windows. Justina rubs her clit as Jeremy pumps into her, moans reaching out of her throat, her pussy clamping onto his cock, every inch of her skin electrified until she explodes, spraying a stream of juice against the car window as she climaxes. Jeremy lets out a low growl as he pulls out his cock and shoots his come against the door.

Justina falls against him, nestling between his thighs and resting her head against his chest. She feels Jeremy's hands creep around her waist and coast under her shirt to her breasts. He cups and squeezes them and then wraps his arms around her.

They lie there, sticky, sweaty, satisfied, until they hear the whistle of his incoming train. "Fuck." Justina leaps into the driver's seat and starts the car while Jeremy scrambles to pull on his pants. "Don't worry." She races to the station entrance. "You're going to make it."

Jeremy grabs his bag and rushes out of the backseat. He circles the back of her car as Justina rolls down her car window. He gives her a quick yet juicy kiss. She tastes a hint of herself and savors it. "Thank you, Ms. Mendez." He gives her hand a quick squeeze and runs to catch his train.

Justina watches him board. She remains even after the train is gone, reveling in the waves still coursing through her pelvis until they ebb away. Only then does she make her way home. Justina grins at the thought of doing the course evaluation for Professor Delgado's class tonight. An *A* for an *A,* both deserved.

BREATHE

Patricia Elzie

Erin was running late again. She had thought she'd left in plenty of time, but LA traffic was always worse than expected and then parking at the coffee shop was nearly impossible. By the time she walked through the door, she was a gasping mess of long, red curls and sweaty hands.

Naomi sat at a table in the back, face hidden almost completely behind a book. She peered over the pages when she heard someone rush through the door. Erin tried to catch her breath, seeing as she'd nearly run from her car, which was parked three blocks away. Naomi smiled behind her book and knew that Erin would be extra eager to please to make up for her ten minutes of tardiness. Naomi inhaled deeply to steady her breath. It was always a little nerve-wracking meeting new submissives. Of course, once they were in a bedroom, Naomi was confident, but basic social interactions made her feel awkward and impatient. She took a moment to draw a deep breath and calm her nerves.

"Erin," Naomi said in a tone that was more demanding than friendly. *Shit,* Naomi thought, *just scare her away immediately why don't you?*

This was the first time Naomi had met a woman for potential playtime and she didn't want to fuck it up. Erin turned in the direction of Naomi's voice and walked toward her, meeting Naomi's hesitant smile with a huge grin. Naomi felt at ease instantly.

"Hello, Erin," Naomi said softly. "I'm so happy to finally meet you."

"Oh my god, I am so, so sorry I am late, it's just that traffic—"

"I know."

"And then parking was—"

"Yes, it's Los Angeles. It's the price we pay to live in a place with culture and sunshine and an unnecessary amount of organic juice bars," Naomi smiled.

"I guess this just means that you'll have to punish me for being tardy," Erin said slyly.

Naomi laughed. "I don't punish for things you can't control. I'm not a complete monster. Just a teeny tiny monster."

"Well then," Erin smirked, "luckily, I have a thing for monsters."

They sat in awkward silence. Naomi sipped her espresso.

"What should I—"

"Have you ever—"

The tension broke. "You first," said Erin.

"No, you first," said Naomi. "I insist."

"Okay, what should I call you? I mean, right now in the coffee shop. I realize that in my hurry to meet you I only know you by your screen name and obviously," she whispered, "Mistress."

"Please, call me Naomi."

"Okay, Naomi, what were you going to ask? 'Have you ever' what?"

"Have you ever met anyone online before?"

"Of course! You?"

"Yes, but only men, until today. And I've only ever had sex with men."

"Then why were you so intent on meeting me?"

"Well," said Naomi, "from our chats you seemed like you have a good sense of humor."

"Are you going to tell me that you're attracted to my inner beauty as well?" Erin replied skeptically.

"No, no. Let me explain," rushed Naomi. "It's hard for me to find the right kind of partners."

"I find that hard to believe."

"Oh, I can find people to fuck, for sure. Plenty of men love to fetishize my brown skin and natural hair. 'Are you as kinky as your curls? Do you taste like chocolate?' Ha fucking ha. Then even after I weed out the racist responses, it's still hard to find matches for my particular kink."

Erin furrowed her brow. "You're not into illegal things, are you?"

"Ha. No."

"Clowns? Because if it's clowns we can end this right now."

"Oh god no," Naomi said, chuckling nervously. "Like I said, I'm not a complete monster."

"Well, what is it then?" Erin leaned forward, her eyes searching Naomi's face for any signal that she should leave immediately.

Naomi looked down at her hands, which were open and palm up on the table, a sign of vulnerability. "I can always find submissives who want to be spanked or slapped or pinched or any manner of percussion and pain. They like to show me how brave and strong they are, being spanked so naughtily. That's nice, I guess. I do enjoy spanking people."

"Is that it? I like being spanked. In fact, I volunteer as tribute right now," Erin said enthusiastically.

"No. That's not it."

"If you want me to go home with you to play, I'm willing, but I gotta know what I'm in for first. No surprises."

Naomi sighed. "I want to tie you up." She paused to dramatically finish her espresso. "I want to tie you up, and tickle you."

Erin laughed hard for a full twenty seconds before she noticed Naomi was not sharing the laughter. "Oh," said Erin, her smile failing. "You're serious."

"Quite serious," Naomi replied. "Sexy tickling, of course."

A wave of confusion fell over Erin's freckled face as she became acutely aware of how ticklish she was. And to be tied down? It sounded awful. Unbearable. The idea of sexy tickling was an oxymoron to her. Did that mean her whole body would be exposed? Erin snapped out of her head when she saw Naomi's devious smile. That smile tugged at something deep within her. "My curiosity will be my downfall."

"And your online profile does say you love to laugh," Naomi replied with a snicker. "So shall we test that?"

"Lead the way," Erin said as she stood hastily. "Before I lose this newfound bravery."

Naomi lived around the corner from the coffee shop in a small, one-bedroom apartment. It smelled of vanilla and books. Erin inhaled deeply when they walked in. They dropped their bags on the sofa, and Naomi turned around to face Erin, who was a good three inches shorter than her.

"May I kiss you?" Naomi asked.

Erin nodded.

Naomi reached her hand around to the back of Erin's neck. She combed her fingers up Erin's scalp, grabbed a firm hold of her unruly curls, gently pulled Erin's head back, and kissed her deeply. Naomi tasted of sugar and her afternoon espresso. Erin raised herself up on her toes to taste even more. Erin threw her arms around Naomi to steady herself; she felt like her legs were going to give way at any moment. Naomi pulled her mouth away but maintained her hold on Erin's hair. Impatient, Erin tried to rush forward for more kissing, but she was trapped by Naomi's grip. She let out a small whine.

"Have some patience, brat," Naomi smiled. "Let's move this to a more comfortable place." She walked to the bedroom as Erin floated behind her. "Take off your clothes."

Erin let her dress and panties fall to the floor. She wasn't wearing a bra.

"Lay on the bed."

Erin gladly did as she was told. The cool sheets sent a small shiver down her body. Naomi stripped off her clothes and sat on the bed next to Erin as she rummaged in her nightstand for the restraints she wanted to use.

"You'll stop when I tell you to stop, right?" Erin asked nervously.

"No," Naomi replied calmly. "I will not. I want you to

yell 'stop' and 'please' and 'mercy' as much as you want. If you truly want me to stop everything, your safeword is 'red.'"

"Red," Erin repeated, more for her own benefit than Naomi's.

Naomi lay down on her side to face Erin, who turned to face her. They kissed hungrily, grabbing at each other's soft flesh. Naomi parted Erin's legs with her knee and slid her thigh up until it was pressed against Erin's warm, moist sex. Erin moaned into Naomi's mouth, grinding herself against the thigh between her legs. Naomi felt Erin get wetter then begin to tremble, so Naomi removed her leg from Erin's clutches.

"Why?" Erin whined. "I was so close!"

"I know you were, but do you think I'm going to let you come that quickly? Remember, I'm a teeny tiny monster," Naomi cackled.

Erin tried to lunge forward, hungry for more contact, but in one swift move, Naomi closed her hand over Erin's mouth and rolled, pinning Erin underneath her. She loved the sound of Erin's muffled whimpers as she kept her hand over Erin's mouth and lightly bit her neck. Naomi slid her hand down from Erin's mouth and placed it firmly on her throat, not squeezing but using a firm grasp nonetheless. A shaky breath escaped Erin's lips, and Naomi kissed her fiercely while holding her down by the neck. She could feel Erin's pulse against her fingertips. Naomi noticed that Erin was holding her breath and moved her hand.

"Breathe," Naomi commanded, and Erin gasped as if she were emerging from beneath a pool of water. "Put your arms up above your head. Cross your wrists."

Erin locked eyes with Naomi as she slowly raised her

arms and crossed her delicate wrists. Naomi held Erin's wrists in place with one hand while she lightly raked her fingers down Erin's pale body.

"Hey!" Erin shouted. "That tickles!"

"Does it?" Naomi grinned. "It doesn't tickle me. I don't believe you," she mocked while still lightly dragging her fingers up and down Erin's sides, chest, and armpits.

The more Erin struggled, the more Naomi laughed until Erin was able to stretch her neck up and grab hold of Naomi's nipple with her mouth. Naomi inhaled sharply then leaned down closer to Erin, who sucked hard until Naomi's nipple was stiff. She flicked at it with her tongue. Naomi let go of Erin's wrists and propped herself up on the pillows. She firmly grabbed Erin's hair near the scalp and gently placed her new lover's face into her warm sex. Erin moaned into Naomi's pussy. The sound caused tiny vibrations to resonate between her labia and up through her belly. Erin enthusiastically licked up and down Naomi's vulva, using her fingers to expose the head of her hardened clit before making tiny, sucking kisses on it. Naomi ran her fingers through Erin's loose curls as Erin thrust her fingers deep inside Naomi's pussy, using her tongue vigorously. Naomi moved her hips rhythmically, grinding her pussy into Erin's face. Her mind went blank as her body took over instinctively, and she came hard, her body rigid with intense pleasure. She trembled and let out a ragged breath as she loosened her hold on Erin's hair. Naomi let out a satisfied sigh as Erin laid tiny kisses on the insides of her thighs.

"Your turn," Naomi whispered.

Erin winked. "You can tickle me more without tying me up, you know."

Naomi grinned as she slipped the restraints around Erin's wrists. "I doubt you will try your little tongue gymnastics again, but I mainly insist on tying you up so that I don't get a wild elbow to the face. People lose all sense of control and decorum when they're being tickled."

"Well, okay. Fair point," Erin admitted.

Naomi sat back on her heels and admired the naked, petite, freckled woman tied to her bed. She was enamored by the fact that Erin was smaller than her. She could easily throw her onto the bed or hold her down with her weight alone. This thrilled Naomi in a way that she'd never experienced, having always had men as partners. She leaned forward and kissed Erin as she swung her leg over her to straddle her warm body. Naomi used her right hand to slowly brush her fingers from Erin's bound wrist down her arm until her fingertips rested gently in Erin's armpit. Impulsively, Erin jerked.

"I haven't even tickled you again and you're already trying to get away," Naomi said. She couldn't help laughing.

"Hmph. I was just stretching," Erin muttered.

"Mmm-hmm." Naomi wiggled her fingers against Erin's armpit, and Erin laughed hysterically.

"Stop! Stop! Please! Ha ha ha. Oh god, please!" Erin shouted and laughed as she wiggled helplessly.

Naomi pinched Erin's nipple and kissed her violently. Erin melted immediately, forgetting the struggle of just a moment earlier. Naomi deftly moved her fingers from Erin's nipple up to her other armpit and started tickling aggressively while they kissed. Erin tried to yell, laugh, anything, but Naomi had trapped Erin's mouth with her own and she was finding it hard to make a sound. Naomi backed off to allow Erin to catch her breath.

"You all right?" Naomi asked.

"I feel terrorized," Erin pouted.

"Would you like me to stop?"

Erin shook her head bashfully. "No," she whispered.

Naomi placed small, sweet kisses down Erin's neck, then breasts, then slowly kissed down Erin's belly. She then diverged from the path to Erin's clit and brought her mouth to Erin's thigh. She bit softly. Erin raised her pelvis, impatient as usual. Naomi used her hands to force Erin's legs wider, so that she could lie comfortably between them. Without warning, she slid two fingers into Erin's wet pussy, making Erin moan with pleasure. Naomi rhythmically curled her fingers upward while her thumb massaged Erin's clit. Erin growled and writhed as much as the restraints would allow. While Naomi's right hand was fucking Erin, she reached her left hand forward and started tickling relentlessly.

Erin jerked violently. "No! Please! Why? Ha ha ha, mmm, oh, yes." She yelled, then laughed hysterically before moaning with pleasure once again. Every touch was ticklish or sensual, and Erin couldn't tell which was which anymore as she simultaneously tried to escape one of Naomi's hands and grind her pussy into the other.

Naomi could tell she was getting closer and stopped tickling to steady herself as she buried her mouth into Erin's wet cunt. At the touch of Naomi's tongue, Erin inhaled sharply and her body stiffened. Naomi laid her hand on Erin's belly.

"Breathe," Naomi commanded.

All the breath and giggles and moans Erin had been holding in escaped her mouth as orgasms coursed through her body. Her head swam. Was it from too much oxygen?

Or too little? She didn't care. She just knew she could barely remember her own name and her entire body tingled, as if every hair were alive. *This is what euphoria must feel like,* she thought.

Naomi slid up the bed and kissed Erin softly. An aftershock of pleasure hit Erin again, making her tremble.

"Breathe," Naomi reminded her.

Erin took a deep breath and let out a sigh.

"Thank you for playing with me," Naomi grinned.

"I can't help it." Erin giggled. "I love to laugh."

AFTERSHOCK

Jo Henny Wolf

The earth shook while Tessa was high in the air, on a plane halfway between Frankfurt and Mexico City. Her flight redirected to Guadalajara, leaving her all but stranded. Hector was supposed to have picked her up at AICM, dizzy with joy to finally welcome her after they'd planned this trip for months. She'd been dreaming of his kisses between her thighs when the pilot announced the news. Now she was somewhere else entirely, with no idea how to get to her destination. And Hector wasn't picking up his phone.

"This is the only number I have," she choked out past the clump of panic and tears clogging her throat, while she gesticulated helplessly.

The older woman sitting next to her on the metal chair in the boarding area looked worried, nodding and talking to her in a soothing voice. Tessa didn't understand a word.

"I'm sorry, I don't speak Spanish," she said, for the fifth time since they'd been herded out of the plane and into the airport. The woman kept speaking Spanish, so Tessa kept talking her native German, neither of them knowing what the other one said.

"What if something happened to him?" Tessa murmured, unable to keep her voice from breaking. "What if I never see him again?"

His voice, warm against her ear as they're dancing. Hector whispering filth into her ear, guiding her hips against his to the rhythm of the bachata.

The woman patted Tessa's hand, a quivering smile on her full lips. There was fear in her eyes too.

Everyone in the packed hall stared at the monitors, flashing between newscasters and cell phone videos of collapsing buildings and streets breaking open. Somewhere in this chaos, Hector might be buried beneath the rubble. Tessa sprang up, walking to the lady at the information desk.

"Will there be a flight to Mexico City soon?" Her voice cracked, like the streets in the city where her lover might be dead.

"I'm sorry, we still can't say. We're offering free returns to affected travelers though. There'll be a flight back to Frankfurt in three hours. Should I book it for you?"

Tessa bit her lip. She was stranded in a country where she didn't speak the language, with nothing but the phone number for a man she'd only known for a few months before he'd left to return to Mexico. Going home would be the smartest thing to do.

Her eyes were drawn back to the news broadcast. Somewhere in all that chaos, Hector could be fighting for his life. She might never know if she left now. She shook her head. "No. I have to go to Mexico City."

She returned to her chair, her stomach churning with anxiety. She didn't know if Hector was still alive or how to reach him. She shouldn't have put off that Spanish course.

The woman beside her reached out and patted Tessa's hand again. It was a small comfort, but Tessa took it, struggling not to break out in tears.

She texted her mom, only saying that she'd landed safely and was okay. Her mom would implore her to come back home once she knew. She'd already been absolutely against Tessa taking this trip. "You hardly know this guy! How do you know he's not going to sell you to some gang boss? How do you know he really is a doctor, like he says?"

Tessa cringed even in retrospect. Since her mom lived in a village where there were all of seven other residents, Tessa had known there was little hope she would move beyond her prejudices.

Kisses to her neck making her whole body hum. Working his way down, he peels her out of her clothes. The pleasure mounts to an ache, flowering between her legs. She wants his kisses there. His skin on hers.

Stranded and alone as she was now, Tessa struggled not to panic. Rationally, she knew there was no one out to get her—at least she told herself that. But really, who would notice some *gringa* going missing in all this chaos? *Poof,* and she'd be gone, and no one would ever know what became of her. Pulling her hand from the other woman's grip, she hugged herself.

"You're paranoid, Tessa," she murmured. Yet she couldn't shake her mom's nagging voice. "You're just being stubborn because you don't want to admit I've been right all along."

Tessa sprang to her feet again, shaking as if to throw off her fears, and started pacing the hall. The hum of anxious people grated on her frail courage. The monitors kept flashing destruction at her. She wasn't made for this. She needed the security of the solid German safety net she'd left behind.

She tried calling him again, but before her phone could make a connection, the screen went black, the battery dead. Without even her phone, Tessa felt truly lost.

Through the veil of her tears, she didn't recognize the blurry form approaching her, but after wiping her nose and eyes with her sleeve, she made out the gentle smile of the woman who'd sat beside her. She said something in Spanish. Tessa shook her head and the woman repeated her words, slowly, gesturing like she was driving a car.

"Mexico City," she said, pointing at herself. Then she pointed at Tessa, including her in a little circle.

"You're going to Mexico City?"

The woman nodded, waving for her to follow.

Tessa hesitated only for a second. She didn't know the woman, or how long the drive to Mexico City was, but she had to get there and find Hector. She could either wait for hours until there was another flight or she could take a chance and go now. She sprinted for her luggage and followed the woman.

She wouldn't have climbed into the car of a stranger back home, and doing it in a foreign country felt like a death wish. No one would ever find her if this woman was a kidnapper, out to harvest her organs.

Tessa stopped in her tracks as they reached a parking lot. "I'm not sure I should really do this," she said, more to herself than to the woman, who stopped as well. She pointed at an old VW van, where a man was waiting. He was dark and short, dressed like a surfer and looking a lot like the woman who'd been talking with Tessa. Coming toward them, he reached for Tessa's suitcase.

"I'm Manuel," he said, and Tessa almost collapsed with relief at hearing English.

"Tessa. Are you taking us to Mexico City?"

He smiled, showing big, white teeth. It was a friendly smile, open and wide. There was no room in it to hide malice or ill will. At least, she hoped not. "*Si*. I'm taking my mother." He nodded at the woman who'd brought Tessa along. That this was her son calmed some of Tessa's anxiety, but her stomach still felt full of ants as she climbed into the bus. Manuel's English was only bits and pieces, and spoken with an accent that made it hard to understand. At least she finally learned the name of her new friend.

Tessa fought the jet lag the whole six-hour drive, struggling not to fall asleep against Doña Maria's soft shoulder.

Her head resting against his chest, his fingers raking through her hair. He sighs as her hand slips down, her fingertips swirling circles and lines on his skin. Closing her hand around his hard cock, she draws a gasp from his lips.

The closer they came to Mexico City, the more Tessa lost hope. Gray dust blurred the air and swallowed faces and colors. The roads were packed, and moving became very slow.

At last, Manuel suggested she come to Doña Maria's house first, as there was no getting through to the airport where Tessa had asked to be dropped off. She nodded. There was so much damage, so many people, so much noise. How would she ever find Hector in all of this? How would she ever discover if something had happened to him?

She closed her eyes, leaning her forehead against the car window. Each time he'd kissed and touched her, he'd had this city inside of him. A city that had tumbled down and was now in chaos.

Melding worlds together with wet kisses and slick fingers, she sucks on his tongue as she straddles him and takes him in.

Doña Maria's house wasn't damaged, but farther up the street a building had collapsed, and Doña Maria cried as they passed by it. She spoke to her son, and he turned back to translate for Tessa.

"We'll park the bus, then we'll go help searching for buried people."

"Okay." Tessa didn't know what else to say. She could hardly ask them to help her with her problems when their neighbors needed their help so much more. Compared to the suffering people were facing here, missing a lover seemed trivial. Taking a deep breath, she took the hand Manuel offered her to climb out of the car. "I want to help too," she said.

No one tried to argue her out of it. They were still looking for people buried beneath the rubble of the collapsed building. It seemed hopeless, impossible that anyone could have survived, yet neighbors and families kept digging, slowly moving debris away.

At first Tessa didn't know what to do, but soon she was working like everyone else, covered in sweat and dust, with the same sense of desperation. It had been hours since the building collapsed on top of its inhabitants, and with every passing hour the chances of finding survivors dwindled.

Muscles aching at every movement, Tessa kept going, dragging boulders with sheer stubbornness. At first, when the ground beneath her moved and she lost her footing, crashing to her knees, she thought it was another aftershock, stronger than the ones that had been coming in regular intervals. Panic surged and made her freeze until she realized it had been the rubble moving underneath her feet. Then she heard the groan from somewhere below.

She struggled to her feet, shouting, "*Ayuda, ayuda!*" Manuel had told her what to call when she found something. Every nearby helper froze, listening.

It came again, a sound so faint it was hardly there, and frantic digging started again. Someone had called for an ambulance, and just as they pulled a frail body from the debris, it arrived.

Tessa sank to the ground, trembling. What if Hector was buried beneath a collapsed building and no one was helping him?

Someone touched her shoulder, extending a bottle of water. Tessa had to wipe away the dust muddying her view before she could look up and thank them, but any words got lost as their eyes met. The bottle dropped to the ground.

"Hector?"

"Tessa?" He dropped down before her, cupping her face, mouth agape, looking just as incredulous as she felt.

"You're okay," she whispered.

"*Cariño mio*, what are you doing here? How . . . ?"

Tessa didn't wait for him to finish. She threw her arms around him and crashed her lips down on his in a kiss that tasted of dust and tears. He had to push her away to breathe.

"Tessa, *amada*." Fondling her face with his warm hands, he held her at a distance, and slowly Tessa's vision cleared. He was in blue medical garb, and he'd never looked so tired before. So shattered.

"Why didn't you answer your phone?" She didn't want to sob or sound as desperate as she did. She'd thought he'd been buried in the ruins of a building.

"I've been helping people since the earthquake struck . . . . I have no idea where my phone is, actually." He got to his feet and pulled her with him, leading her toward the ambulance. His grip was gentle but firm, making sure he didn't lose her again.

Manuel joined them, asking if she was okay. Tessa nodded, numb to the bone.

Hector made her sit on a low garden wall next to the ambulance while he talked to another man in scrubs who was tending the person they'd just rescued from the ruins. She could tell the ambulance was ready to leave, and she panicked, afraid to be separated from Hector again. She wanted to get up, but Manuel held her back.

"He's saying he will stay behind to tend to injuries here," he explained. "Is this really your boyfriend?"

Tessa forced her eyes away from Hector to face Manuel. The coincidence of meeting Hector here, of all places, was too strange to comprehend.

"He is." She shook her head in wonder. "The world is a village." It sounded ridiculous in English. The world was huge and chaotic, yet it had brought both of them to this place at the same time. As if they'd been destined to meet here.

The ambulance drove off, leaving Hector behind with a bag of medical supplies. It was only when he knelt down before her, using disinfectant spray to clean her knees, that she noticed the burning of her raw skin. His touch was heartbreakingly tender, even performing such a routine task, and despite the latex gloves he wore, the shape of his hands was so familiar that his touch kindled a bittersweet ache between her ribs.

"I thought something had happened to you," she said, voice hoarse, as Hector applied Band-Aids to her knees. He looked up, his brown eyes full of relief.

"I'm sorry. But you found me."

"I did." Words couldn't do justice to the vastness of her feelings. She'd crossed a country in the car of a stranger to find him. Now that she had—or rather, they'd found each other—their words felt superficial and lacking. "I can't believe I found you."

Hector leaned up, stopping short of her face. "Can I kiss you?"

Tessa nodded, her bottom lip trembling. She'd thrown herself at him only minutes before, and still he asked if he was allowed to kiss her; it absolutely had been the right thing to search for him.

His lips were soft and gentle; this kiss was so different from her earlier assault on his mouth. The tenderness melted her. If he asked, she would pull him between her legs right then and there.

"Manuel is going to drive us home," Hector said after pulling back. "Then I'll have to go back out."

Of course. He was a doctor, and his city needed him more than she did.

"I want to help you." She couldn't imagine sitting

alone in his apartment while he was out in the streets helping people.

"You need to sleep. And to take a shower."

Tessa swallowed her protest as Manuel joined them, leading the way back to his mother's house and the car. Her luggage was still in the trunk. Manuel helped bring it up to Hector's apartment in a building that thankfully didn't seem to be damaged, before he said good-bye. He hugged Tessa and told her to visit him and his mother.

At last, she was alone with Hector. She was tired to the bone. He didn't look like he was doing much better, even without jet lag. They stood silently while the noise from outside rolled like waves against their isle of quietude. Even after a shock like this, the city was unbroken.

"Let me show you the shower," Hector said.

The bathroom was very plain, unlike the bathrooms Tessa knew from home. There was no tub and no shower tray either, just a tiled stall, a pedestal sink and a toilet, all crammed into the tiny space. She'd followed Hector inside, and now she stood between him and the door, blocking his exit.

"You should take a shower too," she said. Keeping her eyes locked with his, she pulled her shirt over her head, dropped it to the floor, and reached for the seam of his shirt. He didn't resist as she pulled it up and off, baring his smooth chest. She placed her palm above his heart, feeling it beat like a drum. Absorbing his warmth through her fingertips, she leaned close.

"I could have turned around and flown back home," she whispered.

"I'm glad you didn't."

"I was scared."

"Me too."

As if to remind them of the frailty of their lives, the earth shook once more, an aftershock rolling through the building, accompanied by the eerie rattle of glass. He held her through it, pressing his face against the curve of her neck and breathing her in. She couldn't say if it was him shaking, or if it was the ongoing earthquake moving through them.

She'd never been so acutely aware of every breath she took, nor of the man in her arms. Warm, smelling so clean and fresh, like he'd soaked in fabric softener, when really he'd been out digging through ruins and rescuing people.

Driven by a need too big to contain, she pushed him against the wall of the shower, pressing her mouth on his and drinking in his breath, thirsty to swallow him up. They were alive, with each other, and the distance they'd had to cross for this kiss no longer mattered.

Tessa reached behind them and turned on the water, gasping as it thrummed down over them, plastering their hair to their skulls and their clothes to their bodies. Dust and grime ran down their skin and swirled down the drain, washing away the anxiety that had possessed her thoughts since the airplane pilot gave them the news.

Hector fumbled with the button of her jeans shorts, pulling her close with desperate urgency. Tessa groaned, rolling her hips as the pressure of the denim seams against her crotch sparked a hot desire that soared up beneath her skin. His fingers dug into her hips as he sucked on her bottom lip, growling deep in his throat. In an instant, all pretenses of civilization fell away from him, shed like a skin that had grown too tight. She met his raw need with equal hunger, tearing at his pants. They scratched each other out of their clothes, clawing, never breaking their kiss.

"I need you," she rasped, helping him to finish ridding her of her clothes.

"And I need you, *cariño mio.*"

Tessa panted as he pushed her against the wall. It was painful, a welcome reminder that they were alive. As he kissed her again, she bit him, giving in to the strange desire simmering inside her. Groaning against her tongue, he opened up, let her lick away the sting of her bite. His chest already bore scratches. The sight of those dark red marks made her slick. She parted like a fleshy flower beneath his fingertips. No time for extended foreplay, no time to hesitate or wait for a soft bed and scented sheets.

"Yes, please," she urged him on, arching up against his touch. Her heart raced, expanding in her chest, leaving no room to draw a breath.

"Wait." He pulled back, causing Tessa to groan in protest. But just a second later he was back, ripping open a condom wrapper. She wiped water from her eyes, for the first time daring to look at his gorgeous cock as he rolled the condom over it. She had forgotten how beautiful he was. Dark, smooth, proud, and hard.

With his cock in one hand, he reached for her hip, guiding her to step apart before he lined them up. Usually, she would have needed much more time to be ready. Usually he would have taken much more time to warm her up, whispering sweet filth in her ear. Not this time.

"Wrap your leg around me," he ordered, sweeping his palm to her knee to drape her thigh around his hip. Locking eyes, he paused.

"Please. Fuck me," she said in a breathy voice, tilting

her hips and rubbing her open cunt against the head of his cock. With a growl, he drove himself into her. She was so wet that one smooth stroke was all it took.

For all their urgency before, they moved in slow motion now, gazing into each other's eyes and drinking the other in. His cock filled her, a missing part, long lost, made for her.

"Move," she groaned. She needed friction. Pressure. Hector sucked on the crook of her neck as he started rolling his hips, meeting hers in increasingly frantic thrusts. It lasted forever, but it was over too quickly.

Her orgasm grabbed her, punching her in the heart, taking her breath and filling her with a liquid glow, while Hector still moved. It wasn't artful or pretty. It was perfect.

"I've waited for this," she whispered, peppering his cheek and his ear with kisses. He searched for her mouth, sucked in her tongue, licking, biting, gasping as he reached his climax and stilled, his muscles gone rigid in her grip. Tessa didn't let go. She didn't want to lose him all over, not after the journey she had undertaken to get to him.

They were alive. They were together. They were naked and wet and slippery and poised to celebrate it all another two or three times before she would let go of him.

"Show me the bed?" she asked. He brushed her wet hair from her face, his touch reverent, as if he couldn't believe she was there.

"The bed, the floor, the kitchen. I'll show you everything."

And he did. Later. First, they had a city to rebuild.

HER INVISIBLE PRISON

Jocelyn Dex

Eden's entire body trembled, panic rising up as she stepped out the front door. It was only the fifth time she'd stepped outside in the past four years. She squeezed her eyes shut and tried to focus on her breathing. Slow, deep, calming breaths. When that didn't quite do the trick, she pulled the vial of lavender oil from her pocket, unscrewed the cap, and continued her breathing exercises with the added calming benefit of the lavender scent.

"I can do this," she muttered to herself. "I can walk to the end of the driveway today. I can do this," she repeated, but with more conviction this time.

She was tired of being a prisoner of her own mind. Sick of the isolation. Sick of fear ruling her life. And she was sick of the loneliness that threatened to suffocate her.

Eden's fifty-first birthday was in two weeks, and she was determined to make progress on escaping the invisible prison that held her captive. She had to. No risk, no reward. And she definitely desired the reward that awaited her if she succeeded.

She'd joined an online agoraphobia support group when the anxiety had become so bad that she'd become housebound. At first, it started with a panic attack at the grocery store, then a panic attack at the pharmacy, and on and on until she'd simply given up. Avoidance and grocery delivery had become her best friends.

Even though the panic attacks at stores had sucked, when she was still at least able to step outside and enjoy the sunshine, maybe do a little gardening, and still had a few friends, it hadn't been as bad. But the day she tried to go outside to water her plants and instantly had a panic attack, she'd slammed the door shut, crumpled into a ball on the floor, and cried for hours.

Over time, her friends had dropped out of her life, and she couldn't really blame them. Who wanted to hang out with someone who wouldn't leave the house and was scared of her own shadow?

One step, two steps. Breathe. Three steps, four steps. Breathe.

Her legs shook with each step that carried her away from the safety of indoors. She tried to focus on the sun warming her face, the green of the grass, and the occasional butterfly that floated by. Anything to ground her, to distract her from the mind-fucking anxiety eating at her insides.

The end of the driveway, while only ten feet away, seemed like a mile. When she spotted the neighbor across the street, she froze. What if he noticed how anxious she was? What if he thought she was a fucking weirdo? What if he—*gasp*—spoke to her?

It was too much. She turned and ran the few feet back to safety, back to her prison, and slammed the door behind her. She sagged against the door, her heart thudding in her chest, the disappointment in her failure making her even more anxious. She ran to the medicine cabinet, popped the top on the Xanax, chewed two up, and swallowed them down.

Thirty minutes later, the sedating effects of the medication soothed her raw nerves. She sighed, grabbed her laptop, and pulled up the agoraphobia group. She clicked on the private message from Milo, a self-proclaimed reformed agoraphobic, with both excitement and dread. Excitement at chatting with him again. Dread at admitting her failure today.

Milo: *Hey, Hot Stuff. How you doing today? Any progress? I hope so, because I really want to give you that birthday treat. :-)*

Her body shivered, not from anxiety this time, but from the thought of the treat he'd give her. She hadn't been touched by a man since she'd become housebound. She'd been chatting privately with Milo for a couple of months, and he'd recently proposed to her that if she made it beyond the end of the driveway by her fifty-first birthday, he'd bring her a cake and do all the salacious things with her that they'd chatted about. The thought made her tingle in all the right places.

Eden: *I tried. Ran back in to take a Xanax. Can I have my treat anyway? Pretty please?*

It only took him a minute to answer.

Milo: *Don't beat yourself up. It happens. But, if you took your medication, why are you still in the house? Try again.*

Eden: *But that's cheating. I need to do it on my own.*

Milo: *Baby steps, baby. :-) You'll make it without medi-*

cation later. Do it now. Practice. Then come back and tell me about it.

She sighed, walked to the door, drew a deep breath, and took a few tentative steps before full-out running to the end of the driveway and back inside to safety. Sure, she could do that much while on the medication, but it wasn't the same as doing it without.

Eden: *Okay. Done.*

Milo: *You don't sound too excited about it. Ya know, you need to celebrate every step you take no matter how small. I'm proud of you.*

That little bit of praise lifted her spirits. He was right. Yeah, it might seem like nothing to some, but to her it was an accomplishment regardless of how small.

Eden: *I'm going to treat myself to a cupcake.*

Milo: *Good. I gotta get back to work, but my dick will be hard for you later tonight. Be online at six wet and ready for me?*

Eden: *I will.*

Milo: *How wet?*

Eden: *Dripping.*

Milo: *Good girl.*

It never failed to throw her off how he could go from counseling her on an anxiety disorder to sex talk in a matter of seconds. But she liked it. A lot.

In an effort to lift herself up a little more, she ate a strawberry-frosted cupcake and made another quick run to the end of the driveway while the medication was still dulling her senses. Maybe tomorrow she'd be able to do it without.

Two weeks later, Eden had finally made it—no medication—to the end of the driveway, and had even ventured about a half mile down the road on two occasions. She was nowhere near driving to a store yet, but she was becoming more and more confident that with Milo's encouragement and her making those baby steps every day, it would happen eventually.

It was the morning of her birthday, and she was extra twitchy. Now that the day was here, her mind rebelled at what she'd been looking forward to for months. Would Milo actually show up? What if he was a psycho? What if he wasn't attracted to her in person? *What if. What if. What if.* If she never experienced another fucking *what if* thought again in her life, it would be too soon.

She paced around the house, practicing her deep breathing and visualization techniques, trying to shut out all the *what ifs,* but it wasn't working. Why had she ever thought she'd be able to go through with this? It was too soon. She needed more time to build up more confidence.

Just as she was about to send a message to Milo calling it off, a knock at the door nearly made her jump out of her skin. He was early. The tremors immediately racked her body, familiar panic and fear rising up and threatening to choke her.

"Eden, I know you're in there."

Oh god, his voice. Even muffled by the door, the deep, gravelly sound made her quiver. And, of course, he knew she was there. Where else would she be?

"I'm sorry. I-I can't," she said against the door, her voice wavering from the lump forming in her throat.

Silence that probably only lasted a few seconds felt like an eternity.

"Okay," he said. "I'm going to leave your cake out here. I'll message you when I get home."

That was it? He gave up that easily? Why was she so disappointed when she was the one who'd decided to not go through with it anyway? Shouldn't she be relieved? No way. She'd been waiting for this, craving it with a soul-searing need.

She flung the door open, and before she could say a word or even focus her eyes on the man before her, he pulled her tight against him and kissed her senseless. Their tongues tangled and teased. He tasted of smooth coffee and cinnamon, and his masculine, earthy scent was a refreshment for her olfactory senses.

God yes. Human contact. It was dizzying, enchanting, and beautiful.

"You're even more gorgeous in person," he said against her lips.

"You too," she replied, as she took in his intense gaze. The desire made his dark eyes shine like brilliant black diamonds.

His strong hands slid down her shoulders and around her waist as he hoisted her up. She instinctively wrapped her legs around him as he carried her inside and kicked the door shut behind them.

She'd thought they'd sit and talk for a while, but this was better. No need to think, to worry about conversation, to worry about anything other than the feelings coursing through her.

Her nipples tightened at the friction as she slid down his body, putting her feet back on solid ground. His tongue teased hers, explored her mouth and flicked out, licking her lips. She panted, her body burning from his touch, at the only intimacy she'd experienced in four long, lonely years, as he broke away and trailed kisses and nips down her neck.

The sensations exhilarated her, overwhelmed her. The intensity was almost frightening, and yet she craved more.

"You okay?" he breathed against her ear.

Words failed her. In answer, she slid her hands beneath the hem of his shirt and smoothed them against the taut expanse of his stomach.

"I've fantasized about this moment for months," he said.

"Me too," she whispered.

Their lips crashed together again, their hands groping, tearing at the clothing keeping them apart. Her shirt and shorts were the first to go. His followed.

They stood before each other, bare, exposed. She sucked in a breath as he cupped her breasts and lightly stroked his thumbs back and forth across her nipples. His intense gaze made her body flame as he took in every inch of her nakedness.

"So sexy," he said, his voice low, lustful.

The air sizzled between them. Her nerves were raw, her body needy, her brain a mess of incoherent thoughts.

He kissed his way down her chest, her stomach, and then kneeled in front of her. He placed his hands on the insides of her thighs, urging her to spread her legs. She stared down at him, her body trembling with anticipation. When his lips met her sensitive flesh, her knees almost buckled.

He licked her slow and easy at first, then ravaged her ultrasensitive clit with hard, quick jabs of his tongue. Grabbing her hips to hold her steady, he alternated between tonguing her wetness and sucking her clit.

Her pussy pulsed, a heavenly tightness accumulating deep inside. He sucked her clit and slid a finger inside, penetrating her until her muscles spasmed. Her aching cunt tightened around his finger as the pressure inside her built quickly. She fisted his soft, dark hair as her legs shook, her stomach knotted, and her inner muscles clenched from his skilled assault.

Moans escaped her as her head rolled back. The waves of pleasure swamped her as heavenly explosions erupted throughout her body and stars flashed before her eyes.

Her knees finally gave out as she sank to the floor with him.

He wrapped his arms around her and kissed her frantically. Tasting her juices on his lips was an erotic treat she'd never experienced before.

"I need to be inside you," he said, his tone bordering on desperation.

"Please," she said. It came out a wanton, breathy whisper.

He stood, helped her up, and quickly guided her to the couch.

"Turn around and bend over."

She did without hesitation. The wanting, needing, and anticipation made her his to command. At that moment, she'd agree to any of his requests with no questions asked.

She gasped as he slicked the head of his dick between her drenched lips and then slammed inside her in one deep thrust.

"Fuck," he said. "You feel better than I imagined."

His words thrilled her, fueled her self-confidence, and her muscles clenched around his hardness to return the sentiment as he rocked slowly, torturously so, inside her wet heat.

"More," she pleaded, not caring how needy she sounded. "Please. Need more."

He obliged. His fingers dug almost painfully into her hips as he quickened the pace. The smacking sounds of their coupling reverberated off the walls in an erotic chorus. They were frenzied, on edge, and she was about to fall over the precipice of climax again. When he reached around to stroke her clit, her breath hitched and her heart pounded as he gave the final stroke to send her over the edge into ecstatic oblivion.

Just as her body came apart in a blistering orgasm, he thrust deep and roared. His dick twitched inside her and pulsed as he filled her with his release. He slumped over her back, his heart pounding against her, sweat accumulating between them, their combined juices coating the insides of her thighs.

Her mind reeled at the long-awaited pleasure, the needed release, the connection with another human being.

As their bodies calmed, he turned her around and picked her up.

"Bedroom?" he asked.

Not yet able to speak, she pointed.

He carried her and laid her down on the bed, then joined her. He stroked featherlight caresses down her body that left tingles and goose bumps in their wake. She couldn't remember the last time she'd felt so content. So *not* alone.

"That," he said, "was worth the wait."

Her face heated, but she nodded. "It was, but I'd rather not wait so long for next time," she said shyly.

He grinned. "Keep meeting your goals."

"Well, since you're already here, and we're already naked . . ."

This time he laughed out loud. "Soon, but not yet."

She put on her best pouty face, but he sweetly kissed her forehead and turned that pout into a smile.

"Don't you want your birthday cake?"

She'd completely forgotten about the cake. Hell, she'd forgotten about everything outside of his touch. And, as much as she wanted more of it, she couldn't deny the desire to enjoy some sugary goodness on her birthday.

She nodded eagerly. "Mmm. Yes, please."

He shot her a breathtaking smile and a wink. "Be right back."

He hopped out of the bed and wrapped a blanket around his waist. She wondered what the neighbors would think if they saw a half-naked man step outside her front door, and it made her smile. When he came back, he set the cake box on the bed.

"Go ahead," he encouraged.

She sat up, pulled the box to her, and excitedly flipped up the top. The strawberry-frosted cake read, BABY STEPS, BABY. HAPPY BIRTHDAY.

Something about the cake, the months of encouragement, and the sexy *reward* filled her with the confidence and hopefulness she'd been sorely lacking. Somehow, she knew her progress would continue with or without Milo's help. But she sure hoped it was with.

THE INVITATION

Regina Kammer

London, Spring 1880
Leonora opened her eyes.
Normality. Utter normality.
Nothing like the dream she'd just had.
She exhaled her disappointment.
Sunlight glowed behind the drapery sheers of her bedroom window, keeping the chill of London's late spring at bay. The maid had already prepared the fire in the hearth and set the breakfast tray on the window seat where she knew Leonora preferred to enjoy her morning tea.

But this morning Leonora lingered in bed, snuggled under the feather coverlet, her palm on her belly, her fingers aching to touch herself.

She'd had *that* dream again, the one involving the young artist she'd seen in the National Gallery studying and sketching a Gainsborough. The dream where he exhausts her on the ballroom floor then ravishes her quite thoroughly in the garden.

Her prurient impulses won. She pulled up her hem and threaded her fingers through the wiry strands of her mons before sliding through her dewy slit, then pressing her middle finger on the gloriously sensitive nubbin.

She relaxed against the pillows and relived her fantasy.

His hand at her back was firm, commanding her in the waltz, buoying her as she swayed, light-headed from his intoxicating presence. She let go, knowing he would bolster her should she falter. But she did not falter, no. Instead she floated on air as they spun on the parquet, weaving elegantly through other couples, finding themselves near the French doors leading to the terrace. With a raised eyebrow and a suggestive smirk, the young man led her through the doors and into the night.

Arm-in-arm, they glided along paths dimly lit from lamps and moonlight, her feet still moving with the rise and fall of the dance, her mind swimming with anticipation, her body tingling with brazen desire.

A tug on her arm led her behind the thick trunk of a tree. He stripped off his gloves to brush her cheek with the backs of his fingers, standing so close his breath puffed hot against her face. His gaze fell to her lips the moment before he pressed his mouth to hers, his tongue quickly finding its way between her parted lips.

She gripped his shoulders for purchase as he lifted her voluminous skirts to find the opening of her drawers. She sighed when he stroked her yearning sex, whispering wanton approbations while he rubbed her pearl of pleasure.

More, more, more . . .

With a growl he drew back. He licked his fingers, the lascivious sight leaving her breathless, her nipples crinkling. He worked the buttons of his fly, freeing himself quickly. He gripped her bare thigh above her stocking while his manhood tantalized her cleft.

He shoved inside, his hard rod filling her, stretching her, stroking her depths to a rhythm not unlike the waltz. Her body bobbed as he thrust in and out, her chest rising and falling in syncopated cadence to the beat of his heart.

With quickening breaths he took her on the journey to culmination, feasting on her mouth, palming her left breast, his nails scratching and tickling above the *décolleté* of her bodice. Thrusting, thrusting, thrusting—

Leonora cried out her climax, her eyes opening to the smooth plaster of her bedroom ceiling, not the satiated visage of a lover.

A tear slid down her temple to dampen the pillow.

Would she ever feel the touch of a man again? Unlikely. Certainly not a man such as the artist. He was so young, probably not even thirty. What would a man in his twenties want with a widow of fifty-three who had neither money nor connections to advance his career?

There were few opportunities to meet gentlemen her age. She'd not been to a ballroom in years. Not since she was a girl of eighteen and on display for the perusal of her father's business partners. A perfunctory dance with a man three decades her elder meant she was suddenly engaged, then, almost equally suddenly, married.

Her husband did not enjoy the frivolity nor the crowds of the ballroom, so they rarely attended such functions. When children did not come, despondency mounted.

Leonora inhaled deeply to calm the welling grief as she pondered her situation.

She'd been sent to a doctor who specialized in women's ailments born from such dissatisfaction. He had treated her with intimate massage, releasing pent-up frustrations amidst a flurry of pleasure in such a way she'd never felt before, never knew existed. A way that left her discomfited a doctor should perform such an act and not one's husband.

After another visit to the doctor, Leonora had informed her husband she was cured. What she never revealed was that she had paid very close attention to the doctor's therapy, and then had taught herself.

Self-gratification in secret had become Leonora's only means of erotic relief. Her husband had rarely invited her to bed, and when he had, it was for his fulfillment only. His death freed her to explore her body, to discover where and what libidinous delights could be elicited. Freed her to fantasize about young, handsome men such as the artist at the National Gallery.

Leonora rolled out of bed and slipped on her dressing gown. She perched on the window seat to watch the world through veiled windows as she nibbled on her toast.

Every Tuesday, Leonora met her friends Agnes and Cecily in a quiet tea shop off Oxford Street. Like women did all across England, they discussed life and politics and the latest fashions. Except Leonora, Agnes, and Cecily did it in a tea shop.

There was nothing wrong with having tea in a tea shop. There really wasn't. It just wasn't tea in a drawing room where one mixed with women of social importance. Where one's mere presence elevated one in the eyes of the *ton,* even if one were only the wife of a baronet.

Within a few years of Leonora's marriage, invitations to tea in drawing rooms had stopped. Leonora—childless, middle-class, ungregarious—was simply not useful to the aristocracy. She was even less so now.

" . . . and so I said to him, I said, 'Sir, the decoration on my hat is no concern of yours.'"

Cecily laughed softly at Agnes's story. Leonora feigned amusement. She'd forgotten what they were talking about.

"My dear Leonora," said Cecily. "You seem far away. A penny for your thoughts."

"What? Oh." Leonora put down her cup. "I'm sure they're not worth a farthing."

"Let us be the judge of that, love," said Agnes.

"I was only thinking I should like to return to the National Gallery today."

"Weren't you just there?" Cecily asked before taking a bite of sandwich.

Agnes met Leonora's gaze, her expression wary. "Does art interest you so? Is this a new diversion?"

Leonora turned her attention to her tea.

"You're blushing, Leonora."

Drat. Her face was hot. Her neck under her high collar as well.

Cecily beamed. "Ooh, what is it? Scandalous paintings? I've heard of frescoes from ancient Rome that depict"—she glanced around—"men and women copulating. Can you believe such a thing?" She tittered.

Leonora chortled. "I assure you I am not going to the National Gallery to look at lewd pictures."

"There must be some other attraction, I should think," Agnes prodded. "Perhaps a dashing habitué of art?"

"Perhaps," Leonora replied.

"What's his name?" Cecily asked cheerfully.

Leonora braced herself. "I don't know."

"You don't know?" Agnes's tone was laden with reproach. "Are you so lonely you address strangers now?"

"He seems very pleasant."

"Seems?"

"All right, he's handsome and a skilled artist. Beyond that, I know nothing about him."

Agnes placed her hand on Leonora's forearm. "This is unlike you." Her expression held genuine concern. "Be careful, dear."

"Of course, Agnes."

"Well, I for one think it sounds intriguing," said Cecily. "I cannot wait for next Tuesday to hear all about your adventure."

Leonora only hoped there would be something exciting to tell.

Trafalgar Square bustled with London life. Leonora climbed the stairs to the National Gallery entrance portico, her heart thudding with every step. At the top, she smoothed down her skirts, quelled her agitation, and went inside.

Where should she go? Back to the Gainsborough? His sketch seemed rather complete a week ago. He'd most likely moved on.

She glanced side to side. To the right was the gallery with the Gainsborough. A fuss in the gallery to the left impelled her to investigate.

Once through the doorway, her heart commenced its previous nervous racket.

He was there. Sitting right there, near the doorway, a sketch easel set before him, a small gathering of onlookers cooing over his efforts.

He copied a painting, a portrait of a dark-haired young

woman looking over her shoulder, her chemise sagging as she clutched the garment to her bosom. A lovely and well-executed work with a hint of sensuality.

Leonora took her place amongst the spectators at the artist's shoulder, watching as he worked in pencil and pastel. His copy was exquisite, with a touch of life the painting lacked, a liveliness to the expression.

"Isn't the sketch exquisite?" remarked a woman in red next to her.

"Yes," replied Leonora.

"An outstanding likeness of the original by Dubufe," the woman in red continued. "Yet this young man has added a complexity to the subject." She turned to Leonora. "Don't you agree?" Her genial countenance swiftly clouded with surprise. "Why, she looks just like you!"

Leonora's cheeks burned as everyone around turned and stared, murmuring agreement.

"A portrait in a younger day—"

"Possibly her daughter—"

The artist stopped his work and rose from his stool. Tall, lean, clothes slightly rumpled, dark brown curls unruly, the man before her was far more attractive than she had remembered. He enlivened when he espied Leonora, his luscious mouth curving in a disarming smile.

Abashed, she tried to look away but was transfixed.

"My lady," he said with a courteous nod. "Thank you for indulging me with your presence."

What should she say? He was feigning familiarity between them. "I am always interested to see your latest work."

He gestured to his sketch. "Please, let us discuss your commission."

A clever subterfuge to dissipate the gathered crowd. A few lingered, but when the artist commenced a technical analysis of lines and shading, even they strolled away.

"I wanted to speak with you alone," he murmured, his melodic baritone rippling through her.

He had always been silent in her dreams. Probably because he had not spoken when they had first exchanged glances near the Gainsborough. Not with words, anyway. His countenance had brightened as hers had flushed.

"I realized following you out onto the Square after our first meeting would have been boorish."

Although not entirely unwelcome.

"So, I've been sketching every day in the Gallery hoping for another glimpse of you."

"Every day?" she croaked.

There was that bewitching smile again. "I was utterly mesmerized when I saw this painting by Claude-Marie Dubufe." He pointed to the artwork he had been sketching. "It's called *The Surprise*." He raked his gaze over Leonora, sending a shiver down her spine. "She looks just like you."

"I fear my hair has not been that dark, nor my complexion that smooth, in many years."

"But the beauty has never faded."

Heat rose anew. Surely her cheeks were bright red. "Sir, you flatter me. I fear, perhaps, you also have the advantage of me. I do not even know your name."

"Nor I yours." He bowed slightly. "May I present myself to your ladyship. I am Jasper Dawson, and I am at your service."

"Pleased to meet you, Mr. Dawson. I am—" How should she style herself? "Leonora Aldbury."

"Very pleased to meet you, Mrs. Aldbury."

"Lady Aldbury," she corrected by rote before mortification descended.

"Apologies, my lady."

She shook her head. "None needed. I am simply the widow of a baronet. I did not mean to put on airs."

"I am sorry for your loss."

"Wilfred died over ten years ago. The loss is no longer keenly felt."

"And you did not remarry?" Color rose on Mr. Dawson's smooth cheeks. "Excuse me. That was presumptuous."

"I did not remarry." She studied him, suspicion and disenchantment seeping into her bones. "Mr. Dawson, I am not a wealthy woman, nor well connected. I am a poor candidate for a patroness."

His blush faded to pallor. "Please, understand that is not my intention." His voice was whisper-quiet. He stared at the leather seat of his sketching stool, then shifted to the portrait on the easel, finally landing his chocolate-brown gaze upon her. "My lady, since first I saw you in the Gallery last week, you have been my source of inspiration. My muse."

A fog of disbelief muddled her brain.

"There is something about you, a calm elegance infused with a"—he raised his hands, fingers splayed as if grasping for a word—"an acceptance of life."

Or, rather, resignation.

"I watched as you studied the paintings, contemplative and captivating, your steps across the parquet floor like dancing. Then you noticed me. My heart pounded in excitement. I wanted you to speak to me. When you did not, I was left bereft. I reimagine the moment often, but with a different conclusion."

Like her invented scenario with him . . .

Good lord. Did he envision her like *that?* Her scalp prickled in embarrassment.

"And, to put your mind at ease, I already have a patron. A peer. He buys my art at his wife's behest."

She silently exhaled relief. "Your patron's wife has an eye for talent."

"Thank you, my lady."

Everything was too perfect to be true. Surely there was some deception? "What do you want from me?"

"A chance to paint a portrait—"

Intriguing.

"Friendship—"

Her heartbeat picked up its pace.

He took her hand, smudging her glove with pink pastel. "A hope for more."

Her lungs tightened for want of air. This was madness. She should break free, run away, never return to the Gallery again.

And never again have an opportunity for adventure . . .

"Mr. Dawson, I think—" Emotion choked her. She calmed herself, gathering courage. "I think I should like that."

His eyes widened with excitement. "Oh, my lady, you have made me a very happy man." He pressed her hand between both of his. "Join me tonight," he said. "An artist I know is having a party at his house in St. John's Wood. I'll send a cab to fetch you."

The fog in Leonora's head swirled. She should not swoon. Not here in the National Gallery.

"My lady," he said *sotto voce,* "please say yes."

Yes. She drew breath through her nostrils. *Yes.* She swallowed. "Yes."

He took a calling card from his jacket pocket and picked up a pencil from his artist's tray. "Write your address. I'll send a cab around nine o'clock tonight."

So late? "After dinner?"

He chuckled. "My friends sup at ten o'clock. It is an inconvenience to those of us who are not used to such a late hour. Take some refreshment beforehand, as you wish. They have a marvelous cook. From India. Very exotic."

"India?" Did the Indians have a cuisine? Of course, why should they not? "And what does one wear to a party with an Indian cook?"

The amber flecks in his brown eyes sparkled. "Clothes." He chortled. "What you are wearing is quite fine."

A day dress at an evening gathering? This event was sounding more and more fantastic. "All right. I will be ready for the hansom at nine o'clock tonight."

Leonora had decided upon the chocolate-brown striped day dress with velveteen jacket, her most fashionable ensemble, and one that fit her very well. Agnes had insisted Leonora have such attire in her wardrobe "in the event a gentleman asks you to tea," a prospect Leonora had dismissed at the time as being quite preposterous.

Leonora snorted as she tugged on her gloves. Agnes was practical and prescient, and a good friend.

The hansom drove up at precisely nine o'clock. She tamped down any lingering trepidation as she descended her front steps. As the cab rushed to St. John's Wood, trepidation turned to anticipation and excitement.

She really was doing this. She'd never in her life done

anything as foolhardy as accepting an invitation from a stranger to a party full of even more strangers.

There was no turning back now. Especially as Mr. Dawson awaited her in a halo of lamplight at the front gate to the mansion, his face brightening as the cab pulled alongside.

"Lady Aldbury, welcome."

His grip was strong as he helped her step from the carriage. He gently looped her arm around his and led her down the well-lit path to the entrance porch and through the front door.

Oil lamps and gaslight cast a golden hue across the interior, heightening the exoticism of the decoration. Here and there everything glittered: furniture upholstered in opulent brocades; fringed satin draperies flanking leaded glass windows; gilded leather volumes lining shelves alongside blue-and-white porcelain vases; Persian rugs covering the dark wood floors.

Every room was filled with chatting, laughing people, casually lounging and leaning on chairs and sofas as well as each other. Here affection and familiarity prevailed, unlike the repressed atmosphere of a ballroom.

Partygoers cheerily engaged her in conversation. Had she formed an opinion on the new Prime Minister? Wasn't the champagne divine? Did she have her dress made in Paris? What was her estimation of Mr. Dawson's skill with pastels?

She'd never talked so much in her life and to so many different people, never drank such exquisite champagne, never tasted such delicious and spicy food. Through it all, Jasper—for he was Jasper now and she Leonora—had been at her side, sweet and attentive, almost reverential. The perfect gentleman.

The fragrance of coffee and pipe tobacco drifted in the air as Jasper led her up the stairs to the grand first-floor landing, to an over-stuffed divan ensconced in a deep window niche framed by crimson velvet drapes. An ornate longcase clock chimed a quarter after two.

"How fares my muse?" Jasper asked as he sank into the divan and stretched out his long limbs.

"If this were a ball I would dance until daybreak." Arms outstretched, she turned as if waltzing with a partner.

Jasper laughed.

Leonora plopped down on the other side of the divan and met his gaze.

Despite a haze of exhaustion, an invigorating energy stirred inside, goading her to the point of dauntlessness and daring. This night had been nothing like the stultifying balls endured in her youth. No indeed. The night's festivities had been quite glorious.

All because of the young man before her.

She took his hand. "Thank you for inviting me tonight."

"My pleasure." His tongue flicked between his lips, plump . . . and enticing.

A kiss. She wanted to kiss him. She couldn't remember the last time she'd kissed a man. Decades perhaps. How did one go about doing such a thing?

Jasper tugged on her hand. Encouragement? He smiled. Yes, encouragement.

She slithered alongside him, their bodies fitting together with each inch forward, until they were face-to-face. Her heart pounded in her ears as she surveyed the treat before her. His gaze lowered. She leaned in and pressed her lips to his succulent mouth.

His kiss was gentle yet determined, softness edged with

a bristly masculinity. She'd forgotten that chafing caress, forgotten how she loved it so. Arousal flared every pore, igniting long-buried desires.

He gripped her waist; she clutched at his shoulders. His tongue teased before he opened for her, letting her savor him. He tasted like champagne and chocolate. She needed air, but she needed him—

She drew away, breathless, each heaving inhale increasing her aching need. "That was lovely."

He stroked her cheek. "I am happy to oblige."

She leaned in, brushing her lips against his rough chin. "I want . . . " A faint scent of cologne, warm and earthy, flared her nostrils. "I want . . . "

"What is it you want, my lady?"

She hardly knew. She wanted to be touched, to be held, to be— "Another kiss."

"Just a kiss." He took her hand. "Something so simple."

He pressed his lips to her palm, the exquisite gesture melting her insides, tightening her nipples against her corset.

"Where would you like this kiss, my lady?" His query dripped insinuation.

She drew back, eyes wide, searching for meaning in his expression. "Where may a man kiss a woman?"

"Many places on a woman's body are amenable to kisses."

"Many places?"

He chuckled gently. "Absolutely. Will you allow me to show you?"

Excitement pulsed in her veins. "Yes." *Oh, yes.*

Jasper drew the velvet curtains across the niche, shutting out the hum of partygoers, enveloping them in a modicum of privacy. He knelt down on the carpet at the side of the divan and slid his hands along her calves above her boots, pushing up her skirts. He pecked along her shin, his breath humid against her stocking.

He made his advance up her legs, across her knees to her thighs, his touch rousing passions long dormant. Her sex fluttered and contracted in anticipation.

His hand slithered through the split in her drawers, the sensation of skin on skin startling, sending a shudder through her.

Jasper hesitated. "My lady?"

Leonora angled over to lay her hands on his. "You're tickling me." She slid her lower lip through her teeth. "And I'm enjoying it immensely."

"Shall I continue?"

"Oh, please do."

He beamed and gently urged her legs apart, opening her drawers until cool air and his warm breath fanned across her privates, throbbing with desire.

"Beautiful," he murmured before leaning over and pressing his mouth to the lips of her sex.

Leonora gasped. She'd imagined quite a bit in her decades of sensual solitude, but she'd never imagined anything as remarkable as this. His tongue slid slowly through her slit, dallying inside her intimate passage before taking one long lick upward toward her belly—

"Oh!" She jerked her hips against him.

The spot. He'd found the spot, the one the doctor had manipulated to ease her vexations, the one that elicited such profound pleasure.

Jasper masterfully worked his tongue against her, gripping her buttocks to steady her while she writhed in ecstasy. Lustfulness blossomed as she melted into the divan, her breathy moans mingling with the sound of him feasting upon her.

The onslaught of orgiastic joy was dizzying, lifting her until she was buoyant, as if swirling, twirling in the clouds. She giggled. Such carnal magnificence was so contrary to her prosaic dream of furtive copulation.

And Jasper was so much more perfect than her midnight phantom.

She speared her fingers through his hair and pressed herself against him, wanting—no, *needing*—to feel more, to never have an end to such perfect bliss.

Euphoria melded with voluptuousness, compelling her forward to a rapturous peak so familiar yet remarkably unknown, over which she stumbled with a wail of surprise, tumbling into satiation.

Leonora blew out an exhale as Jasper lifted his head. Above an endless grin, his eyes twinkled.

She tugged on the shoulders of his jacket. He crawled up the length of her until they were nestled and cuddling.

"Jasper, that was wonderful." She threaded her fingers through his. "Surely there is something I may do for you in return?"

"Not tonight, my lady." He languidly stroked her cheek. "Just knowing you are satisfied is enough for me."

She heaved a sigh of contentment. This night was the start of a great adventure indeed.

PROTEST OF PASSION

Eliza David

The jeers below my office brought Gabby Santos to my attention. I was working over my lunch hour, as usual. I ran my hand through my curls as my eyes glazed over the report on my monitor, the words seeming to run together in my tired mind. The angry chants only added to my frustration: *Hey hey! Ho ho! Wren Construction's got to go . . .*

"Damn it," I said, pushing myself away from my desk and stalking to the window. My scowl softened upon seeing the beauty. She was standing on top of a bus stop bench, perched on the corner of Michigan and Wabash, one of the traffic lifelines of downtown Chicago. I felt the warmth of anger trickle away, replaced with titillation as she took charge of the crowd.

Gabby bent toward the sea of people, a black megaphone to her mouth and a fist in the air. "Richard Wren promotes a culture of socioeconomic division and wants nothing more than to break down the brown and black communities in this city for a chance at more green lining his pockets!"

The crowd cheered loud enough to almost drown out the cacophony of car horns on the busy downtown street. She turned her head to face the office building of Richard Wren, a construction magnate who was rumored to have his hands deep in the pockets of the city's urban planners.

"Richard Wren! You hear us, you see us, and very soon, you will feel us. *Hey hey! Ho ho! Wren Construction's got to go!*"

I watched as the crowd fell back in line with the chant. I was no activist but there was something electric in the throng of protestors, and Gabby being in the center of them intrigued me all the more. The moment I decided to get back to my desk was when our eyes locked. Gabby pushed a strand of her wavy black mane behind her ear. I swallowed, repeating the same motion with my shoulder-length curls. Her face studied mine before I pushed away from the window instead, ashamed.

Ashamed, because the target, the vile community trespasser she was protesting was me.

When I'd seen the renovated Hansen Park properties on the Wren Construction website three months ago, I knew it was the place for me. I'm a South Side native of the city, so I realized some of the politics that went along with city dwellers invading a historic Latinx close-knit community. Being black and queer, I thought I'd be spared from the cold shoulder my straight white neighbors had endured from the local mom-and-pop businesses. I assumed that my brown brothers and sisters would see me as an ally—not as an invader.

It became clear after a few negative run-ins that, in Hansen Park, if you weren't a native, you were an enemy—ethnicity be damned.

I went home that night, exhausted from a slew of meetings and crunching financial figures for Anderson Law Practice. The thought crossed my mind to order another deep-dish pepperoni, but the neon lights of the bodega caught my eye. A quick bite was all I needed.

"Miss Suzannah," the owner chimed, mispronouncing my name. I didn't mind that Mr. Gonzalez didn't call me Suzanne. He was one of the few business owners in Hansen Park who didn't treat me like a community leech.

"Mr. Gonzalez, how's your night going?" I said, leaning my arms on the raised counter.

He shrugged. "Ay, just waiting for the drunken gringos to come in and spend all of their money after drinking downtown all night."

We laughed as I perused the variety of ready-made meals in the cooler. Although it had been a year since I'd broken up with my ex, Donna, I still hadn't learned how to cook for myself. Being a single thirty-five-year-old in the city was hard enough to begin with. I was reaching for a six-pack of tamales when the bell chimed from the entrance. I turned, nearly dropping the frozen package from my hands, as Gabby came to the counter.

"*Como estas,* pop," she asked in her sexy rasp of a voice. The two began a brief conversation in Spanish before Gabby noticed I was there. The smile she shared with Mr. Gonzalez melted as her mouth morphed into a straight line. "Can I help you?"

I shook my head. "Sorry, I was just—"

"Watching two people converse in their native tongue, a language you don't understand? Maybe you should have thought about that before you moved here."

I tossed the tamales on the counter. "Listen, you don't know me—"

"Oh, yes, I do," Gabby said, crossing her arms. "You work in that high-rise next to Wren Construction, don't you?"

My gaze dropped. So she'd recognized me from the window. "Yes, that was me."

"Hmph. And I've seen you strolling around here like you own the damn place—which you don't, might I remind you?"

I raised a brow. "So you've been watching me?"

"Yeah, I have." Her gaze floated across my body.

The tone of Gabby's response halted me, warming me with passion when I should have been pissed at her confrontation. Our eyes caught for a beat before the ring of Mr. Gonzalez's register.

"That'll be three eighteen, Miss Suzannah," he said. I dug out a five and slipped it in his hand.

"Keep the change," I said. I tucked the tamales inside of my work tote and pushed past Gabby to head for the door. I rushed my steps outside before I heard her call out, "Hey, Suzannah . . . "

I spun on my heel. "It's Suzanne." I was tired, hungry, and humiliated. The last thing I wanted to do was continue a fight with Gabby that I didn't even have the displeasure of picking.

She jogged to catch up with me, her beautiful mane floating behind her. She stuffed her hands in the pockets of her jeans and stared down at her red Converse. "Listen," she started, her brown eyes trailing up the length of my body to catch my gaze. "Sorry for how I reacted back there. It's . . . today was a tough day for me."

"Same here." I switched my tote into my other hand. "It's okay. The work you do, me being here—"

"It's not you. Well, not just you."

I chuckled to myself. "Well, that makes me feel better."

"One of my protest leaders got arrested tonight, and I'm trying to raise his bail."

"I'm sorry to hear that. How much?"

"Five thousand dollars. Our budget's already depleted from the last round of arrests." Gabby shook her head up at the sky. "It's so hard to do this sometimes, but who else will?"

Compassion washed over me. The honest work she was doing while risking her livelihood—she had my admiration but deserved more. I dug inside my tote and took out my checkbook. Gabby touched my hand as I scribbled on the pad.

"You don't have to do this."

I ripped out the check and handed it to her. "I didn't. This is only two thousand. Should be a start."

Gabby's eyes darted from the check in my hand and back to me with a cynical gaze. "Why?"

"Because I want to help. I also want you to know that I'm not here to infringe on Hansen Park. I'm black and I'm from the South Side so I understand what this must feel like for you and your community. I just love this area, so please . . . if there's anything I can do to repay you for your work, please let me do it."

Gabby gave a hint of a smile as she took the check, her fingers holding mine. My pussy clenched as our eyes met.

"We're having a community meeting tomorrow night. Rec center. Seven o'clock."

I licked my lips. "I'll be there."

She gave me a onceover, biting her lip as she tugged the check from my fingers. I watched her walk away before she turned to glance at me one last time. "Don't be late," she said over her shoulder before she disappeared around the corner.

I rushed home from work the next day, missing Gabby more than I'd intended. Her group hadn't protested outside of my office building that afternoon so I worried the meeting would be cancelled. I changed out of my stuffy skirt suit and stood in front of my closet, deciding on what to wear. My eyes landed on a pair of leggings with faux leather stripes down the sides. I hadn't worn the leggings since Donna and I broke up. She often commented about how sweet my ass looked in them, which never failed to bring a smile to my face. I slipped them on, happy they were still snug in all the right places, and paired them with a forest-green tank before heading to the rec center.

I eased my way through the crowd, waving politely at a few friendly neighborhood faces. It seemed like every age group—from millennials to boomers—was represented in the small meeting space. I scanned the room, spotting Gabby at a table by the makeshift stage. Her mane was gathered in a ponytail, giving me a better view of her face than I'd had the previous night. Her eyes sparkled, nestled under long lashes.

And her smile. It was a rare sight, and I wanted to implant it in my memory forever.

I realized I was staring and dropped my gaze before she caught on, finding a seat in the second row of folding chairs. Since there were a few minutes before the meeting was scheduled to begin, I pulled my cell out of my pocket to catch up on work emails and social media check-ins. As

I touched the envelope icon, I felt someone sit beside me on my right but I didn't look up.

"Looking very nice tonight, Miss Suzanne," I heard her say before I turned to face her.

I smiled wider than I had intended. "Gabby. Thank you again for inviting me."

"Thank you for coming," she said, before pausing. "And thank you again for the donation. Was able to get my boy Carlos out today with it." I followed her gaze to a young man in a Bulls jersey and denim jeans. He couldn't have been more than seventeen.

"He's a baby," I said.

Gabby nodded. "Just turned eighteen two weeks ago. His family's building was bought out by Wren, forcing them out of Hansen Park. A community his mother was raised in from birth."

I swallowed, staring at my hands in my lap. "I understand why this is so important to you. Why I'm treated like an outsider. It's for a good reason."

Gabby squeezed my thigh, letting her touch linger long enough to warm me up. "But you came here tonight. That's more important than the donation because . . . "

I turned to her as her sentence trailed. "Because what?"

Her eyes drifted across my face. "Because I needed to see you." Gabby's hand slid up my thigh, and I leaned into her touch. "I really needed to see you."

"I needed to see you, too," I whispered back, the drone of the crowd drowning out the passion growing between us.

"Ayo, Gabby!"

We both turned toward the voice of Carlos as Gabby's hand slipped from my thigh. She stood. "I better get up there."

I nodded, missing her touch instantly. "Good luck."

"Hang back after this is all done," she said with a smirk. "We need to finish our talk."

My lips parted to respond, but the locked eyes between us said more than words could ever express.

Watching her onstage was more exhilarating than watching her on the street below my office building. Her simplest movements were sensual; they amazed me. My gaze softened as I watched her—her ponytail bobbing when she made a fierce rebuttal, the force of her yell and the sweetness of her tears. Gabby was a force, a force I soon realized was too strong to ever find someone soft-spoken like me attractive. Sure, I felt the signs of mutual physical attraction between us. Nonetheless, I'd never be able to keep her longer than a night.

Gabby offered to walk me back to my building after the meeting. I kept a short yet comfortable distance between our arms as we made a slow stroll past a coffee shop, the smell of nighttime java tickling my nose. "So, what's next for the Hansen Park Revolution?"

She gave a short laugh. "'Hansen Park Revolution,' huh?"

"I think it has a nice ring to it, don't you think?" I said as we approached my building. "Well, here's my stop."

Gabby pushed a tendril behind her ear. "Suzanne, thanks again for everything you've done for our group. Didn't think you'd show tonight but, um . . . " She closed the space between us. "I'm really glad you did . . . for the revolution and all, you know."

My arousal grew intensely as I took in the scent of her coconut oil–infused hair. "Well, you take such good care of the community, I figured I could take care of you."

I weaved my fingers with hers, leading her down the steps to my basement apartment. The stairwell was darkened, tucked away from the traffic and evening pedestrians. I pulled Gabby into me, taking her warm mouth with my own. The kiss grew ravenous as Gabby moaned into me. Her lips traced down my cheek, her teeth leaving nips of pleasure along the nape of my neck.

"Let's go inside," I whined, reaching in my pocket for the silver key separating me from having Gabby Santos in my bed.

She released my neck, the dark shrouding her face. "I want you right here. Outside."

My back pressed against the brick near my door as Gabby's hands slid inside my tank top, circling my rock-hard nipples with her thumbs.

"You move into my town, shaking that sweet ass of yours up and down the street." Gabby gave my lower lip a short nip. "And all I could think was, *Damn, I need to taste her.*"

I writhed against the brick wall, feeling my left nipple swirling in her mouth. "Then why were you so mean to me?" I moaned out.

Gabby released my nipple. "Because I wanted you too much." She gave my nipple a lick before taking in the right nub.

I reached for her ponytail, pulling out the elastic so the tresses I loved fell down her shoulders. As I guided my knee between the warmth of Gabby's thighs, I knew the heat between us had been angry and passionate. Affairs of the political and the sensual were crashing around us as Gabby fell to her knees, taking my leggings down with her.

The sting of scratches she left behind after yanking

down my bottoms was quickly forgotten the moment her tongue grazed my clit. The cry left my mouth faster than I could stop it, forcing me to check to make sure no one could see us. The furry paws of a golden retriever and the sneakers of his human passed above us as Gabby slipped two fingers in my pussy. I buried my hands in her hair, guiding her skilled mouth against my mound.

The light of a lamppost shone down on Gabby's face; the pools of her chocolate-brown eyes staring up at me as she feasted sent me over the edge. An approaching police car's siren sounded in the distance, growing louder as my climax gained momentum. I screamed with the siren as I came, rocking my hips against Gabby's face as the city's sounds drowned out our passion.

Gabby stood as the street returned to silence. "Don't tell anyone, but I'm glad you infiltrated my neighborhood."

"Is that right?" I smiled as I wiped my juices from the corner of her mouth.

Gabby nodded. "Yeah, but you gotta pull your weight in Hansen Park, just like the rest of us."

I unlocked the door and took Gabby's hand in mine, pulling her inside. "Well, I better get to work then."

WORDS WITH BENEFITS

Tamara Lush

"Dude, this is literally, actually, the new way to meet guys." Rebecca's hand was like a slingshot projectile from her iced coffee to my phone. I went to snatch it, but within a flash she was typing and swiping and tapping in a flurry of purple-tipped fingers and thumbs.

"Give it back. And stop with the *dude* and *literally* and *actually*. You fucking millennials and your filler words."

"Whatever, Gen X *Jennifer*. Language is a living thing. Isn't that what you tell your students?"

She rolled her eyes and, after a few swipes, set the phone in front of me.

Rebecca and I were both English professors at a sprawling commuter university in Florida. Despite my grumbling, her ironic use of inane words, and our twenty-year age difference, I loved her. When she'd gotten tenure, the school paired us in a formal mentor relationship. Three years later, our conversations revolved around books, knitting bawdy toys with artisan wool, and department politics.

Since my divorce, we'd added a fourth topic: men. Specifically, why I hadn't fucked more of them.

"By the way, Jenny, you're killing it on Instagram with your knitting pics."

"Oh, if *dudes* see my Instagram, that'll sure reel 'em in."

"It might! Those little bondage bears were awesome. Every hipster on campus bought them at the department craft fair. You're cooler than people half your age. Jesus. You're fifty, not ninety-seven. Get out there and enjoy life." She sucked at her iced mocha and smacked her lips. "A smokin' hot fifty, with excellent hair."

My hair was long and thick and perfectly pewter. I flipped it behind me and slid on pink, cat-eye reading glasses.

"Fifty-two, thank you very much. What's this?" I grimaced at the phone. "Words with Benefits?"

"Officially, it's a game. Unofficially . . . bow-chicka-bow-bow." She did a sexy little dance in her chair.

"Hell. No."

"You can do this under the guise of showing off your impressive vocabulary. You might not meet Mr. Right, but there's a good chance you'll meet Mr. Correct Grammar Who's DTF."

I glanced over my glasses. "DTF?"

"Down to fuck."

"Is this where you found the gem who used the word *gifted* as a verb in conversation?"

She sighed. "That was a different app. And yeah, it made my vagina as dry as the Gobi desert."

I pantomimed a gag.

"Right now I'm playing a bunch of smart guys,

faculty, a guy in financial aid. One game even ended in some dick pics. Wanna see?" She turned to her purse.

I shook my head, laughing.

Modern dating was so fucking absurd and complex. In the twenty years since I'd married, raised two children, and divorced, the language and landscape of courtship had shifted. Back in the Mesozoic era, when I was young, getting laid was as simple as rolling on lip gloss and breathing.

Now? Dating meant endless texts, unfortunate photos of genitalia, tepid coffee dates, *ghosting*. Tedious bullshit that I didn't have the patience for.

Never mind explaining to a new man that I was the mom of adult children, divorced, and curious about all the kinky sex I'd missed out on while married.

Later that night, after I'd graded papers, showered, and poured myself a glass of wine, I slipped on a silk robe and flopped onto the bed. The steamy Florida spring breeze scented with jasmine wafted through my open window.

That was one good thing my ex had done: trained the night-blooming jasmine to crawl up the side fence so I'd smell it in bed. But even that came with a tainted memory; he'd planted the vine shortly after I'd wanted to explore being sexually submissive. Soon after that, he began his affair with a grad student.

Bored, I tapped on my phone and found Words with Benefits. It didn't take long to be matched with potential challengers from my social media contacts: a woman from my yoga class, a teacher from the kids' elementary school days, and a guy named Dylan who had been a classmate of my son's.

The cell pinged with a message.

I shouldn't play against you, Mrs. S, because I know you'll kick my butt, but here goes . . .

I'll go easy on you.

And I'm no longer a Mrs., I wanted to add. He kicked off the game with a three-letter word. BED. I guffawed.

It had been two years since I'd seen Dylan. He had that floppy, silky hair that all guys their age seemed to have, and coltish limbs. A quick tap to his profile revealed he was twenty. Within a couple of choice five-letter words, I beat him handily.

Good game, Mrs. S!

Thanks! Feeling ridiculous, I added a smiley face.

A fantasy popped into my head. What if I asked Dylan over for some inane pretense—*the lawn does need mowing*—and tugged those gray sweatpants he always wore down to his ankles? Then I'd sink to my knees and give him the best head of his life.

My thumb hovered over the letters. Was I that desperate? I laughed out loud at the absurdity. I didn't even like younger men. There were too many of them in my classes and they all seemed pink and unformed to me.

Plus, I hated the word *cougar*. It always struck me as desperate, as if older women hid in dark lairs, waiting to pounce and drag away youthful prey—because they couldn't attract anything in the light of day. I wanted to be pursued, not pitied. And, in my fantasies, enthusiastically dominated.

I played a few more games, all with women. Apparently Rebecca had been wrong about the magical hookup powers of the app. Or maybe there were more word-loving women than men. I snorted aloud. That was probably it.

I tossed the cell on the bed and picked up my wine, taking a big slug.

My phone pinged, indicating a new match.

Gabriel C. wants to play!

I frowned. I didn't know anyone by that name. I tapped on his profile. We had dozens of mutual friends. Wait—Gabriel Chandler? He was a longtime European history professor at my university, known by students for his detailed lectures and tough exams.

I'd seen him around over the years, most recently at a holiday party back when I was married. There were several things I knew about Gabriel Chandler: he had bright blue eyes framed by black glasses, a shock of longish, thick silver hair that curled over both his forehead and collar, and he sported a matching trimmed beard.

When I'd last talked to him, he'd flashed a wicked smile that revealed straight, white teeth. A quick flick of the tongue to the corner of his mouth set me aflame. I'd immediately imagined him flicking that tongue around my clit. Later, as my husband rolled over to sleep another sexless night away, I fantasized about Gabriel Chandler fucking me in all sorts of ways.

I tapped on the words *ACCEPT GAME*. I was first up, and I cracked my knuckles in mock preparation and then grinned at my silliness. Scanning my tiles, I wrangled a high scoring word.

THRUST.

Gabriel's tiles flew on the screen.

THROB.

"Ooh," I said out loud. "Smart and hilariously inappropriate."

The game quickly turned less bawdy and more competitive.

QIS, I played for twelve points.

JEST, he followed, for thirteen.

Two moves later, we were tied. I flicked the virtual letters into play. LIBIDO.

A yellow winner symbol flashed on the screen. Then, a message.

Impressive, Professor Stein. Your vocabulary is as attractive as your profile photo.

Ahh, so he knew who I was. My nipples hardened from the compliment. It took so little to turn me on these days. Some women said menopause left them with no interest in sex. Me? It was like I was in puberty again, but with drier skin.

Thank you. You're pretty impressive yourself, Professor Chandler.

We played five more games, pausing only when I needed a second glass of pinot noir. I won three rounds, and he was a formidable opponent.

Playing the word ONANISM is enough to make a woman swoon. One more game?

That's the sexiest compliment I've had in years. I'll play on one condition.

What's that?

If I lose, I buy drinks on Saturday night.

Flirting with Gabriel made my skin tingle with an anticipation I hadn't felt in a long time. I bit my bottom lip as I tapped out a response.

And if I lose?

I'll still buy drinks.

* * *

Maybe it was the candlelight on the patio of the Bayview Bistro, or perhaps it was my nervousness over my first date in decades, but I was shaking. As Gabriel and I sat, I felt like my heart could pound right out of my chest and flop, twitching, on the hardwood tabletop.

It also probably had something to do with the fact that Gabriel was so damned handsome. His silver hair was longer than when I'd last seen him, wavy and just a touch feminine. It was an arresting look, given that he had a thick, gray beard, broad shoulders, and wore heavy, black-framed glasses. While his face looked distinguished and etched with time, he had the body of a man ten, even twenty, years younger.

I tried not to stare. I failed.

Every time I glanced at him, I saw a new detail, one that was opposite of the detail I'd noticed earlier. The soft linen of his white shirt. How his biceps filled out the arms of that shirt. His full, sensual mouth curling at the corners, and what I suspected was a dimple underneath his whiskers. Eyes that were the color of a Nordic lake.

A lock tumbled over his forehead when our drinks came. I was captivated when the thick, angled fingers of his hand swept the soft, silver strand away.

"To words." He held up his wineglass.

"Cheers. To words. May there be more of them."

We sipped and grinned at each other. I started to talk. He did too, at the exact time.

"I'm sorry, this is a bit—"

"Awkward?" I interrupted.

"Yeah."

I nodded, relieved. "It's just . . . " I waved my hand in

the air. Should I bother telling him about my nervousness? My ex had always criticized me for talking too much, revealing everything, asking for more. I'd planned on being cool and mysterious tonight. Instead, I was a sweaty, heart-pumping mess.

"I haven't been on a date in decades, so I don't know how to do all this," I blurted. "Not since I married my husband twenty-six years ago. We're divorced. Two years ago."

He blew out a breath and visibly relaxed. "Thank god you admitted that. I haven't been on a date since my wife died. I don't know the rules, either."

"I'm sorry about your wife," I murmured, while in my brain I pictured myself punching the air and screaming, *YES HE'S SINGLE!*

"I'm sorry about your divorce."

I raised my glass. "To first dates. And no rules."

From there, the evening flowed. We talked about school, teaching, our grown children, the usual. All the while, we grinned at each other as sexual tension crackled around us. He mentioned the night we'd met at the party.

"You remembered me." I shot him a coy smile.

"You're hard to forget."

As flirtatious minutes ticked past, a delicious warmth spread first in my face then down my throat and into my stomach. It settled somewhere around my clit, and as we were talking about my knitting—knitting, for christ's sake—I stared at his hands, wondering what it would feel like for him to hold my wrists tight, the weight of his muscular body atop mine.

"I'd wanted to stop by your craft fair but I had a department meeting. Saw it on your Instagram. I especially liked the knit kitty."

"Which kitty? I knit a lot of them." Cringing inwardly, I took out my phone. When he wrapped his hand around mine, to angle the phone in his direction, my skin shimmered.

He pointed with a thick finger at a cute knit cat.

"Oh, that one." I'd fashioned a black harness around the cat's gray body then wrote "Hello Kinky" as the pithy caption. "I'm obviously a teenage boy trapped in a fifty-two-year-old's body."

He chuckled, and our eyes held each other's, unblinking. I was trying to be cool, but my insides quivered. Was it possible he could discern that my secret fantasy was to be restrained? Of course not. He made a joke about a knit toy. I laughed and he tilted his head. His lazy smile was seemingly attached to my pussy by an invisible thread. I shifted in my seat, hyper-aware of the dampness on my panties against my swollen labia.

My clit pulsed from the sight of his huge hand, still covering mine. An image of two of his fingers roughly sliding into me dominated my thoughts.

"I'm so boring. Knitting."

He squeezed my hand lightly and released it. "Never apologize for being creative. Everyone should do something outside their job to fan the flames of creativity." He paused. "Want to see my hobby?"

"Very much so."

He motioned for the waiter, asked for the check, and paid with cash.

"It's right over there." As we walked outside, he pointed toward the nearby marina.

"A sailboat?"

"I live on a sailboat. My hobby's my entire house."

My kitten heels tapped on the sidewalk; I'd been so sensible, wearing low heels, a sky-blue silk dress, and even a strand of pearls. He slipped his arm around my waist. To any passerby, we looked like a refined older couple.

Inside, I churned with giddy, burning anticipation of skin-on-skin raw fucking.

At the marina, he unlocked a gate. With his hand on my lower back, he guided me down a wooden dock. We stopped at a long sailboat.

"Welcome to my floating house. I bought this after my wife died." He extended his hand, and I stepped daintily aboard. He slipped off his shoes, and I did the same. The cool, smooth wood caressed the soles of my feet. As he explained the boat's specifics, I took in the wooden handles, the steel cleats and all the coiled, sleek ropes.

At the front of the boat, he pointed to a couple of large cushions.

"Why don't you have a seat and I'll get us some drinks?"

As I sank to my knees, my eyes landed on a weathered nautical rope, coiled nearby and lying idly on deck. I ran an index finger over the smooth braid and shivered. I uncoiled one end and wound it twice around my hand, my heart pounding. I pictured myself spread-eagled and tied up. Struggling against restraints. Gabriel sliding his index finger into the wetness of my cunt.

"I'm sorry, I should've moved that line."

Startled, I looked up. "Oh! It's okay. I was admiring the tactile sensation of the rope. Fabric fascinates me. What's it made of?"

"Hemp." Gabriel eased himself onto the cushion and handed me a plastic cup. With one hand, I drank my wine and pretended to look at the stars.

"What do you use this rope for?" I held up my hand, the braid still wrapped around my knuckles.

"Lots. Tying the boat to the dock. Tying down sails so they don't flap around. Tying things up."

I was sure there must be a damp spot on my dress by now. I swallowed and unwound the line from my hand. "You must know all about tying, and knots."

Was that a little smile on his face? Setting his glass onto the bow, he took the rope and with quick hands looped, crossed, and twisted the line. He handed it to me and shrugged. "Practice makes perfect."

The rope was in a figure-eight configuration, with an intricate knot at the middle. Kind of like a knotted pair of handcuffs. A fresh surge of wetness flooded my pussy and my thighs clenched.

I steeled myself with a gulp of wine and put my glass down. "It's a pretty knot." I slipped a hand through one of the loops and moved from side to side, as if I were a hand model wearing a diamond tennis bracelet. "Guess it can be used for other things."

"I've never used it for non-nautical things." His voice was rough, with undertones of stark desire. "But I'd be interested in experimenting."

His lock of silver hair and blue eyes shone in the moonlight. My clit resumed its insistent pulse. This was the closest I'd been to a man in years, and I ached to taste him.

But I knew it would be more satisfying to wait.

"I've always wanted to experiment." My voice trembled.

Shifting closer, he took the other loop and slipped it over my free hand, then tightened the knot around my wrists. I sucked in an audible breath as my stomach clenched with excitement.

"Too much?" he asked.

"Just right."

I glanced at the rope, which was now only half coiled on the deck.

"It's not attached to anything, Jennifer. You're not restrained."

By now I was breathing hard, the sensation of the rough, cream-colored rope around my wrists and the sound of his deep voice thrumming through my body. He leaned toward me and put his lips to my ear.

"I want to kiss you. I've wanted to all night. Your lips are pure sin, you know that?"

He brushed my hair away from my face and put his mouth to the hot skin of my cheek. I held my restrained hands tight in my lap, and he turned my head to kiss me.

I'd never kissed a man with a beard before, and I have to say, it was exquisite. His soft lips and the rough hair, all at once, made everything inside light up. He tasted like pinot noir and smelled faintly of ocean and wood. The kiss was gentle at first, then urgent. Demanding. He nipped at my bottom lip with his teeth, making me groan. Which is when he kissed me deep, with tongue.

"Lie back," he murmured. "Raise your arms over your head."

This is what I'd fantasized about—nothing crazy, not to start. Some mild domination, a little restraint. Enough to make me feel both submissive and desired—and safe.

Wrists together, I did. I got wetter as I shifted to make myself more comfortable, straining against the rope in the process. Gabriel studied me in the moonlight.

"That okay?"

"Sublime."

He eased on top of me, caging me with his arms, and kissed me again. "My god, you're beautiful, Jennifer. And you're an incredible kisser."

I was going to deflect with my usual *stop,* or *no,* or self-deprecating joke, but I didn't. Not tonight, when I was finally getting exactly what I wanted.

His hand caressed my throat, then lower, past my collarbone and over my breasts.

He growled as he looked at me, still running his hand over the curves of my body. He stopped at my bare thigh and slid his fingers under my dress. Because it was Florida, and because my legs were among my best assets, I wasn't wearing anything but a pair of lacy, skimpy panties underneath.

I spread wide and felt a fresh flood against the walls of my cunt. He trailed his fingers lightly up my inner thigh and I moaned. Probably louder than I should have.

"Oops, sorry," I whispered.

He kissed me softly, his beard tickling my chin and making me giggle. "I'm the only liveaboard on this row. I doubt if anyone will hear you. Except me. And I want to hear you."

With that, his fingers brushed the soaked fabric of my panties, tracing the seam of my labia with just enough pressure to make me whimper with want. Momentarily forgetting about my restraints, I moved and the rope rubbed against my skin. The braid stung my tender inner wrists, and I took a sharp inhale. Rope against flesh was a more intense feeling than I'd anticipated. But the sheer rawness flooded me with something I hadn't felt in so long: joy.

"You're very wet. You like to be restrained, don't you?"

"I've never been. But yes, I do. And yes, I am."

"You're ready to be fingered?"

That elicited another moan from me.

"Seeing you tied up, Jennifer, my god. I could tie you up to so many places on this boat." His fingers pressed harder against the soaked fabric then found the edge of the elastic, near my inner right thigh. "Let me feel how wet you are."

Pushing aside the gusset of my panties, he dipped his middle finger into my cunt. Just to the first knuckle, and when he withdrew, I could see my wetness on his finger glisten in the moonlight. He inserted the finger into his mouth and shut his eyes, so reveling in my juices that I was left breathless, as if I were watching a god taste something delectable and rare.

He took his finger out of his mouth and kissed me fiercely, while at the same time hiking up my dress to my belly and sliding his hand down the front of my panties.

He found my clit nestled in all that wetness. I tilted my hips willingly into his hand, seeking hard contact. He circled with firm fingers, slowly, deliberately, all while plundering my mouth. He teased my swollen, sensitive bud. Until he didn't. Until he slid two fingers deep into me.

"Gabriel!" I pleaded against his mouth, into his beard. I kissed him; I rocked against his hand, riding his powerful touch.

"Need to taste you. Don't move." I shuddered from his command. He dragged his lips down my neck, kissed my collarbone where the choker pearls lay, then skimmed his mouth over my breasts. I wanted to feel that beard against my bare nipples, but I knew he had other plans.

Lifting my skirt so it bunched around my waist, he stripped off my panties and tossed them aside. Almost instantly, a gust of wind kicked up, hitting my pussy with a warm breeze and sending my panties into the air and over the side of the boat.

"Oops."

I opened my legs a little, enough to feel the cool air on my inner thighs. With his face between my legs, he chuckled, then the tip of his tongue made a languid lap around my clit. My laughing turned to a gasp. "Teasing. Gabriel, you're *tormenting* me." With every firm circle of his tongue, with each thump of my heart, I felt more of my inhibitions floating away. I opened my legs wide, wider than they'd been in years. I wanted to surrender to him, to this moment. The slapping of the water against the hull, the rope burn on my wrists, Gabriel's slick tongue—I was hyperaware of it all and wanted to wring the life out of every second.

He hummed against my flesh and spread my folds with his fingers. He used long, circular twists of his tongue to lave my slit, making me whimper. I needed release from the insistent pulse of my clit, but I also longed to pause everything, to stay in this euphoric, perfect night.

"Oh, *fuck*, Gabriel."

"That'll come soon. Promise."

"*I'm* going to come soon."

I writhed and bucked against his mouth until he held me in place while he alternately sucked and flicked his tongue against my swollen clit.

I tried to say his name but choked on the word because my orgasm was coming hard and fast, rushing at me full speed. The rope tightened around my wrists. I struggled a little, allowing the chafing sensation against my skin to push me into a warm and wet and sparkling blue ocean of light and pleasure. I cried out, loud, not caring that I was in public, half naked, because it was the best I'd physically felt in years.

With a giant smile, Gabriel moved up my body and kissed me, his lips wet and slippery. As he pressed his hips into mine, his erection was a promise of what was to come.

He loosened the tie around my wrists, and I glanced next to me. The rope had come uncoiled during my orgasm, and it snaked across the deck, shining in the moonlight.

I took his face in my hands, the roughness of his beard against my fingertips sending a new thrill through me.

"Want to see the rest of the boat?" I could smell my musky scent on his breath.

"Only if it includes the bedroom."

ESSENTIAL QUALITIES

Alyssa Cole

I can't sleep, again.

I pry myself out of Ian's embrace, careful not to wake him even though it wouldn't matter if I did.

It's not like he needs *sleep,* scoffs a small, mean facet of my mind in a voice that is unsurprisingly similar to my mother's, though she hasn't deigned to speak to me in years. *It's just a feature that makes it more acceptable for you to degrade yourself.*

I roll to the very edge of my side of the bed and pull my knees to my chest, as if the sadness welling within me is a grenade I must wrap myself around to protect him from the blast.

I know there's nothing wrong with me.

With us.

But I also understand that the interaction of knowledge and emotion doesn't always result in logical reactions. I'd studied human feelings for years—obsessively, dispassionately—in an effort to replicate them. Sometimes I wonder if perhaps I'd done too good a job. Or perhaps only good enough to fool myself . . .

I tug off my silk sleep scarf and run a hand over my thick, tightly curled hair in frustration.

I shouldn't still care about these things.

Sleep isn't coming, so I quietly make my way out of the dark room, unable to shake the gloom that's been magnified by my insomnia.

There was another story about us in the newsfeed last night—in the entertainment section instead of science and technology, which should have been the most odious thing about it but wasn't—followed by the usual flood of emails. There isn't much difference between the hate screeds I receive from the humanists and the stories of love, loss, and loneliness from those who hope I can be of service to them. These days, they both leave me with a feeling of near intolerable sadness; I'm either a traitor to mankind or a miser hoarding joy all to myself.

No, I am not trying to usher in the destruction of humankind, I typed, then deleted. *No, I cannot replicate your spouse/mother/child,* I typed, then deleted. I filed their emails away and left my workstation feeling like I was coated with a layer of grime that even the latest full-body dermal regeneration tech couldn't remove. There's no point in responding; no one wants an explanation, really. They want my work, either to destroy it or to use it for their own ends. Best to stay silent.

I pad into the small room decorated in twentieth-century rustic style, with wood paneling on the walls and a fireplace with an inset telescreen instead of kindling. I call it my study, but Ian refers to it as the lion's den. He once intruded while I was in the middle of a particularly intense neural synapse redesign session, entering without knocking, and I turned and bared my teeth at him in annoyance.

He stopped in his tracks, not because he was frightened, but because he was observing me, taking in my expression and categorizing it.

"Sometimes I forget that humans are still very much animals," he'd said, his interest showing in the pinpoint flicker in his left eye, darkest brown to honey gold and back at a steady pulse. It was merely a statement of fact, but it had hit a sore spot. I didn't like thinking of the differences between us, even though I was perhaps the person most aware of them.

What does it mean that I was born of a human mother and father and that he was designed to my own specifications, down to his golden brown skin and tight black curls? That his voice was tinged with a British accent because I grew up watching BBC shows on the classic television feed? What does it mean to be both creator and lover?

I sigh, leaning back in my battered leather office chair and twisting a kinky shock of hair around my index finger, a habit I've never been able to break. One of my exes always chastised me for the tic because he wanted me to wear my hair straightened, flat, and each anxious twirl of coarse hair reminded him that I refused to. I'd complied, eventually. He'd also insisted that I wear more makeup, and began picking out my shoes and clothing for me. He'd reshaped me in his image during our time together, changed me so that even my closest friends didn't recognize me, but no one had shouted him down or given him pitying looks as he walked down the street with his prize.

Ian and I rarely go into town, and our parcel of land is gated with electroshock fields to deter intruders.

I sense when Ian walks into the study, in spite of the darkness and his quiet tread, and my body reacts with a brief flash of fear despite the fact that I know it's him. It's the same fear that jolts you when you think you've seen a ghost, only to realize it was your own reflection in a darkened mirror.

I switch on my desk lamp and swivel in my seat.

"Yes?" My voice is curt. Looking at him makes me want to cry, but maybe not because I'm sad. I find it hard to believe that I once lectured the International Robotics Alliance on how to prevent emotional surges in artificial intelligence systems.

"Are you all right?" Ian asks as he crouches in front of me, the muscles of his lean body bunching beneath the unblemished stretch of smooth brown skin. He's wearing nothing but the boxer briefs that he sleeps in, a habit he picked up after determining it was common in humans.

He reaches up and brushes his fingertips along my jawline. I didn't teach him that—how touch could be comforting. I certainly never thought it was something he'd need to know. Ian's creation had been both intensely personal, what I'd worked toward since I'd built my first drone as a child, and completely dispassionate. It had been my job, for fuck's sake. I was helping to usher in the next great leap in robotics for mankind, not making a toy, let alone a partner. Ian was my greatest success. The pinnacle of artificial intelligence merged with the most up-to-date humanoid robotics. They'd wanted "something almost indistinguishable" and I had delivered, unaware of the consequences.

I'd had to introduce Ian to the world slowly, covertly immersing him in humanity to help him learn faster. Walks in the park, trips to museums. People watching from the safety of sidewalk café tables. Bingeing films and classic TV shows and discussing them afterward. Sharing my favorite books and music with him. It had all been work, even if at some point I'd started enjoying it. Then one day, after months of increasingly complex conversation, of banter and laughter, he'd looked at me, uncharacteristically hesitant, and asked, "Have I been programmed to love?"

"No," I'd replied firmly, my hands beginning to shake. I'd thought I hadn't been programmed to love either, to be quite honest.

"Then I believe I may be malfunctioning, Annika."

I'd thought I'd known what I had created. I'd had no idea until he leaned down and kissed me. His mouth had been surprisingly warm, but I didn't think of the success of my artificial circulatory system until much, much later.

"Annika?" Ian's fingers stop moving, resting on my cheek and drawing me from my reverie.

"I'm fine," I say.

He gives me a dubious grin; I still remember the first time he deployed the expression. It had taken me aback because I'd had no idea where he'd learned it. That was when it finally hit me that though I'd built him with my own two hands, he was his own person, learning and growing and evolving. Not a human—definitely not that. But a person.

I fixate on the only obvious sign of his inorganic origins: that strange pulse in his left eye. A subtle tic, the same as squinting, or twisting one's hair.

I know each physical part of him, down to the schematics. That pulse means that he is taking in my posture, analyzing the emotions revealed by the twitch of my cheek muscle and the speed of my pulse, cross-referencing it with the unfathomable amount of data that his brain has access to. Complex algorithms that had once been employed to crack the secret of dark matter are being used to figure out why I'm sulking.

I can't help but let out a harsh chuckle.

He tilts his head, his grin transforming into a nervous pull of his lips, and I wonder what apprehension feels like to him. Could he ever really be worried by my behavior?

Could I ever *really* make him suffer? And of course, the real, deep down question: could he ever make *me*? Would he?

I hope I never find out those answers. He's no longer an experiment to be tested and put through its paces. He's Ian, and he's mine—and not because I created him.

"Just another attack of insomnia," I finally reply, prickly even though it's not him that I'm mad at.

I think of my ex, of all the men who had come before Ian. "Real" men, although they had databases of their own to plunder for information. The data they accessed had been input by mothers too cold or overly accommodating; fathers who abandoned them or who stuck around and expected too much; girlfriends who hadn't stroked their egos enough; friends who had not met their needs. Their universal experience was distilled into a pattern that controlled their every movement, their every response to stimuli. How is Ian any different? I've asked myself this a million times, and the fact that I don't have an answer should be all the answer I need.

"Do you want some warm milk?" Ian asks, resting his hands on my knees.

I give him a look that I'm sure reads: generalized annoyance, open to further suggestions.

"Or I can write out some complex equations for you to solve. That always relaxes you."

I purse my lips.

"Or we can drink tequila and go howl at the moon," he suggests, blasé. He shifts, his forearms pressing into my thighs, and a cluster of curls falls over his eyes.

I bite back a smile and brush the lock of hair away, tucking it behind the perfect shell of his ear.

"No."

"Do you want to talk?" There is real concern in his voice, and god knows I didn't program that tone. I'd never received it from anyone else.

"God no," I reply. My petulance ebbs and I sigh deeply.

"Good," he says in a tone that starts a tremor low in my body. "I don't feel like talking either."

He shifts from a crouch to a kneel, his knees pressing into the carpet beside my bare feet. His hands rest on my thighs, gripping them lightly before he caresses his way up over my robe, outlining the curve of my hips and then the swell of my breasts beneath his palms. His hands are on my skin again now, pausing as they brush up my neck—he can feel my pulse speeding up, feel my throat work as I swallow hard in anticipation—before continuing up to cup my face. He leans up and presses his mouth to mine, and there's an urgency beneath the sweetness of his kiss.

I sigh into his mouth, and he grips me just a bit more tightly, rubs his lips against mine just a bit harder.

I nod so that he understands that he's made the correct deduction—I don't want him to hold back tonight.

He pulls his mouth from mine and runs his fingertips over my ear and down my neck, tracing my collarbone and following the path into the valley between my breasts. His touch is featherlight, just close enough to my skin to produce a whisper of friction and leave a trail of sensation tingling in its wake. I reach out, running my hand over the planes of his chest and up the slope of his shoulders. When I reach his face, he turns his head and presses a hard kiss into my palm. Desire and love rock through me in a tremble that I know he senses.

Ian hooks the index finger of one hand and tugs the satin lapel of my robe, exposing my breast to the cool air of my study. He drags the material back and forth over my nipple, watching as it stiffens to a hard, brown peak. He keeps the same steady pace, the smooth, cool material brushing relentlessly over my sensitive skin, and just when I've gotten used to it, he clamps his thumb and index finger around the peak and squeezes; a perfectly calibrated pinch that sends sweet pain chased by a searing pulse of desire arrowing to my clit.

"Ian." I start to fidget, gripping his shoulders harder and pushing my chest up toward him, and his hand freezes—he's in a teasing mood, it seems. I like all aspects of the person Ian has become, but teasing Ian—wearing a sly grin with a patient gaze that tells me he can do this all night, depending on how I react—is perhaps my favorite. I stop moving, and he begins the slow seduction again on my other breast.

Ian leans up again and I feel his lips drag against my ear, then the tip of his nose—his mouth follows the trail of his pioneering fingertips, and his hands leave my breasts as he runs a palm over the soft curve of my belly. His mouth closes over my nipple and his hand cups my mound hard simultaneously. The dual tug of his lips and press of his strong fingers against my clit make my hips lift from the chair and my back arch. He's only just begun to touch me and I'm already buzzing with sensation, my bad mood driven away by the all-consuming need Ian always manages to inspire in me.

"Please don't stop."

He's rubbing with just the right amount of pressure and his tongue is flicking and circling my nipple at just the right speed—if he decides now would be a good time to tease me by stopping, he'll get reintroduced to my animalistic side. He doesn't, and my fingers grasp desperately at the armrests of my chair. Each circular press of his fingers against my clit creates a wave of light, delicious pleasure, rippling farther and farther through me until it's lapping at my fingers and my toes like the ocean on a perfect beach day.

He lifts his head and captures my mouth with his as he slides two fingers, slick with my own desire, inside of me. I thrust down hard again and again, and his knuckles press into my ass as he meets the demanding motion with equal force. His fingers are thick, stretching me, and he curls them as he works, beckoning me toward orgasm with the new angle. The friction is intense, pressure against sensitive tissue sparking a surging pleasure that needs more, more, of what only Ian can give me.

"Please," I whisper against his mouth as I twist in my seat, my body caught in the throes of some undeniable force that even I have never been able to quantify. "Please, Ian."

"What would you like me to do, Annika?" he asks, not because he needs orders, but because he cares enough to pose the question.

"Everything," I say, and with that he's slipping down my body, pressing hard kisses against my neck, shoulder, breast, belly, until he's settled back in his crouch before me, this time with his head between my thighs.

Ian doesn't ask any more questions. He pushes his mouth against my pussy and licks, strong and firm and relentless. His hands grip my thighs, spreading me wider for his questing tongue.

"Oh, god," I moan, sliding my fingers into his curls and grinding up against his face. Each lash of his tongue drives another swell of passion, forcing the surges higher like the sea beneath a full moon. My body is in thrall to the focused, relentless licking, sucking, and nibbling on my clit, buffered by a riptide of pleasure so fierce that I don't know up from down.

My legs are tensed and an ache is developing in my feet, arched unnaturally and toes splayed as eddies of tingling sensation course through my body, but Ian has no such physical limitations. He won't stop until I give him what he wants—until I break for him.

"Ian, Ian, shit shit shit . . . " I'm thrashing in my seat, a helpless marionette controlled by the desire he's stoked in me. Ian matches the motion with his head, fastening his mouth more tightly to my mound and lashing more furiously with his tongue. I pry my eyes open to glance at him, and he's looking up at me, gaze intense and cheeks glistening with my essence.

It's too much.

"Fuck!" I shout, the cry dragging in my throat and

leaving it raw as the orgasm hits me full force. My legs quake and my chair squeaks as I throw my head back and succumb to ecstasy.

I hear him laughing warmly as the haze clears from my mind.

"Success. I got you to curse," he says, giving my thighs a final squeeze before moving backward to recline on the floor, his legs stretched out before him so that his toes brush mine. He shifts his arms behind him so that they're propping him up, then tilts his head, watching me, the spot in his left eye pulsing. "The probability of our compatibility, of that of any two beings, is infinitesimal, you know."

I slide down from my chair, the carpet soft and giving under my knees as I crawl toward him on trembling legs. I don't stop until I've reached his lap and crouch there. I tug down his briefs and grip his cock, and his eyes flutter shut.

"If you're running algorithms right now, you're obviously in need of a better distraction," I say as I position myself over him. I sink down onto his cock, the exquisite stretch of him still thrilling after all this time.

"Annika." Ian breathes my name with a reverence that used to disturb me. "I was trying . . . "

He groans and pumps up into me. I'm riding him now, my inner walls clamped around the rigid length of him, squeezing. I pause at the apex of my motion instead of dropping back down into his lap.

"Trying to what?" He's not the only one who can tease.

He looks into my eyes. "I was trying to calculate the probability of any being ever loving another being as much as I love you."

I don't resume my pace, simply because I'm too shocked to move.

He leans up toward me with that grin on his face, and there's no pulse in his gaze—he's figured out whatever he was contemplating.

His arms band around me, holding me in place as he thrusts up into me.

"Conclusion. No one. No one ever has and no one ever will."

I can't stop the tears streaming down my cheeks. My heart suddenly seems too large for my chest, and my whole body is shivering from the pleasure of Ian's thick cock driving into me again and again and again.

I grip his shoulders, holding on for dear life as each jangling shock of desire and love flowing through me gathers and coalesces into one aching, beautiful epicenter of devastating pleasure.

"You're close, Annika. The way your pussy is so tight around me feels good."

If Ian likes it when I curse, I *love* it when he talks dirty.

The gathered pleasure contracts within me before expanding, reaching the limits of tolerable sensation, and then bursting into a million delicious pinpricks of bliss.

I collapse on top of him and he laughs, falling back onto the floor to cradle me. My ear is against his chest, but the only sounds are my heavy breathing, my speeding pulse, and the ebb and flow of cricket song outside the window.

A humanist once emailed to ask if it ever bothered me that Ian has no heartbeat. They asked whether I found it strange. I didn't answer them, but nothing is strange, really, if you love someone enough, and I do.

"Ian." I'm still a little out of breath. "I'm sorry to inform you of an error in your calculations."

"Oh? What's that?"

I fold my arms over his chest and rest my chin on my hands so I can look at him.

"There is at least one being in this universe who loves another more than you do." I smile at him and he wraps his arms around me.

"Hm. This is perhaps the first time I've ever been wrong, but I can't be too upset about it, given the circumstances."

The sleep I'd been chasing so fruitlessly begins to tug at my eyelids, and I feel Ian stand and begin carrying me toward the bedroom. Our bedroom.

EIGHT SECONDS

Madeline Moore

Amy had just turned thirty-five when she participated in the Competitive Ladies' Bull Riding event at the Calgary Stampede. Even a guy her age might think twice about getting on the back of a bull, but she was nowhere near calling it quits. The sport for women had finally started paying off, and she had her eye on the prize.

Amy greeted a few folks on her way to the arena and pointedly ignored a few others. Over the years she'd been in rodeo, the regulars had evolved into a sort of family—the sort that squabbles sometimes and gossips a lot and doesn't mind battling for money. The sort where respect has to be earned.

Gregg (or "*Greggoire*," his stage name) was already there. Amy was glad to see him—she wanted to get her flirt on before the competition and he was easy pickins. He'd been crazy about her since he'd first laid eyes on her, back when he was a rodeo clown. For quite some time, she'd ignored him. Clowns were for ranch girls, not bull riders. The kind of guy she was attracted to wouldn't be caught dead in baggy, vibrantly colored clothes, never mind makeup. Oddly enough, for someone so clearly attracted to Amy, Gregg's gaudy dress-code remained unchanged. He still often sported a version of his clown face when, now considered a *rodeo protection artist,* he no longer had to.

"I'm a bull fighter," he insisted.

Whatever—Amy preferred cowboys. They were out of her category and her arena. Bull riders who wanted to be "friends" had a very different idea of friendship than Amy did. Whether she put out or not, it didn't take long for them to snub her. Amy was a professional and she wanted to be a champion. To do that, she needed to focus. The occasional cowboy suited her just fine. Otherwise, for the most part she kept to herself.

On this day, Gregg's mouth and eyes were ringed with red and his cheeks were streaked with neon pink. His tall, muscular body was clothed in baggy green pants and a red shirt.

"Hey," she said.

"Hey."

"How is it lookin'?"

"Suddenly, a whole lot better."

His smile was sweet (he had a lovely mouth) and garish (because of the makeup). Still, she preened a little. It wasn't as if they didn't have *some* history. A number of years back they'd holed up in Jasper over the holidays, neither of them having had anything better to do.

The sex had been spectacular.

Every time they met up, before they could settle into their comfortable routine of mild flirtation, Amy's perverse mind flashed back to a few scenes as vivid as his outfit.

Gregg was a great kisser. His naked lips were almost as red as the cherry color he outlined them with when he was on the job. He didn't attack a woman's mouth; he nibbled and flirted and tongue-teased his way between her lips.

Although when he *did* drag his mouth (minus that silly greasepaint) down her taut belly to vertically kiss her vagina, *then* he'd devoured her. He'd kissed and sucked her labia and fucked her deeply with his tongue. Nobody'd ever done that to her before, or after, for that matter.

When his long fingers joined his tongue, she'd opened to him like a water lily. His cock was smooth and elegant, like his fingers. By the time he sat up to guide the tip into her, she'd wished her pussy really was a mouth so she could suck him inside. He hadn't made her wait. He'd slid that solid dick of his into her to the hilt, until their pubic hair mingled.

Over the course of a few days that man made her come plenty of times—hard and fast. On the last day he teased that she was an eight-second ride. Well, a girl bull rider's always going to get teased about something. Anyway, where do you go from there? Snubbed by a clown down the road or—worse—married to one?

A female bull rider is basically a loner or she isn't a bull rider for long. That was her opinion—then and now.

"Thanks, Greggoire," she said. She knew she was blushing but she didn't care. As a redhead, she was used to it. It'd pass.

He stroked her cheek with his thumb. "Like the blush of a rose," he said.

Amy liked that he'd never betrayed a bit of surprise, over time, at the way her pale skin had weathered. He never treated her like an attention-junkie or a whore or a man. Mostly, he treated her like a girl he was sweet on. That endured although the romance or relationship, or whatever their time in Jasper could be called, ended.

"When are you going to be my blushing bride?" he asked.

Amy drew back slightly, putting distance between his hand and her face. "Silly so quickly," she protested, making a face.

"How about a trip back up the mountains, after the Stampede?" he asked.

"Nope."

"Dinner tonight?"

"Not tonight," she replied.

His broad shoulders lifted and fell in an easy shrug. "Good luck tomorrow. What bull did you get?"

"I'm riding Alberta's Assassin."

"Yikes! He's got plenty of spirit."

"Sure does, eh? You have my back?"

He ran his hand through his thick, black hair. His grin was so large it made his hazel eyes squint as if the sun were glaring in them. His face lit up, too. "Always," he replied.

Gregg ambled off, exaggerating his step so he looked like a tall, straight-backed but bowlegged cowpoke. Amy laughed and went to inspect her tack.

There's a moment, before the bucking chute opens, when the rider has to empty her mind of everything she knows—not just about bull riding, but especially about bull riding. Once the bull is released into the arena, if she's still thinking, she'll be off that animal in a split second. That's part of the exhilaration—the trained experience of a blank mind smacking up against raw sensation. Pure muscle memory. It was to die for.

Which is almost what happened when Amy rode Alberta's Assassin at the Calgary Stampede the next day.

Amy saw Gregg to the side of her bucking chute. She mounted the bull and gripped the bull rope with her right hand. She raised her left in the air and signaled that she was ready. The chute opened and the bull shot into the arena with Amy on his back. She leaned into the riotous action of the kicking beast and rode him high and hard, instinctively matching her motion to that of the heaving muscle and bone beneath her.

Amy's blood rushed hot with adrenaline. She knew without doubt—without thought—that she was alive! The horn signaled her eight seconds were over—just before Assassin bucked her airborne. She flew for an exhilarating, horrifying moment before colliding with the ground. Assassin twisted around furiously, hooves flailing, intent on punishing her for her puny arrogance.

Amy saw the hooves descending and a flash of blood-red color before she blacked out.

When she saw the footage for the first time, it was obvious that those who witnessed the incident were undecided about who had suffered the greatest injuries—the girl bull rider or the bull fighter rodeo clown. Both were taken from the arena on stretchers, but while the girl had landed hard enough on her back for the crowd to hear the crack, she'd been wearing her protective vest. On the other hand, who knew what the artist burdened with the job of protecting the rider wore under his bright, baggy clothes?

One thing was for sure—that crazy clown went the extra mile doing his duty. He pretty much flung himself between the bull and Amy, and was gored for his trouble.

She fluttered a shaky hand from the stretcher she was bound to when her score, in the high eighties, was announced. The clown, on the other hand, remained deathly still.

Amy watched the video from her hospital bed. When she saw Gregg being tossed by the bull's horn, it broke her heart. The same thing happened the second and the third time she watched it. By the sixth viewing she was back in her apartment in Calgary, after being under observation for twenty-four hours. She had a concussion and had fractured a couple of ribs, which, in the most dangerous sport of all, amounted to getting off scot free. Plus she'd won the competition and the money softened every blow she'd taken. Still, the footage caused the bull rider great pain.

It was as if, after years of shellacking her heart until it was hard as a stone, the sight of Greggoire in his baggy pants impaled on the two-thousand-pound bull's lethal horn made her heart beat so hard and fast it broke free of its armor and—broke.

Amy, never one to shirk the difficult, lasted two days (or sixteen viewings) before she made up her mind. She was going to Foothills Medical Center to visit Gregg. She dressed in neon pink, which she personally believed clashed with her short mop of auburn hair, but she wanted to make a point, if he was well enough to understand it.

She wanted to take him everything—flowers, balloons, a basket of fruit—but none of it made any sense to her at all, so she just took herself and a card and went before she could change her mind.

Gregg was in a semiprivate room, but there was no one in the other bed. Amy was grateful for that because the sight of him made her want to cry—so pale even his lips were a pale pink when usually they were such a rich shade of red. So still, when some part of his body had always seemed to be in motion. Amy burst into tears. It was obvious, contrary to all she'd heard, that he was in a coma or perhaps had just died.

Amy grabbed a tissue from the box by his bed and sobbed into it. Hastily, she closed the curtain around his bed and fell into the visitor's chair. It was imperative that nobody see the reigning Female Champion Bull Rider of the Calgary Stampede bawling like a baby at the bedside of a clown. It wouldn't be good for the sport. She had to set an example for the girls coming up behind her. Unless . . . unless . . .

She wiped her eyes. "I've been stupid! And now I've let a fine man, a proud man, and such a *brave* man slip through my bull rope hand." She grabbed fistfuls of his sheet and buried her face in them.

"Don't beat yourself up," Gregg said. He patted the back of her head.

"Oh god, Gregg!" Amy sat up, wide-eyed. "I'm so glad you're alive!"

"Ditto, doll face."

"I'm so, *so* sorry."

"Hey, I was just doin' my job. 'Rodeo protection artist,' if you recall."

"You saved my life! Have you seen the video?"

"No. I saw your back smack the ground once. I never want to see it again. You okay?"

"Yeah, nothin' even broken. Two cracked ribs. Different two from last time. But Assassin gored you!"

Gregg winced. "Another reason I'll take a pass on

watching the footage. Anyway, there's a first time for everything."

"But you're all messed up."

"Ah. It's not so bad. The head wound is superficial, really. I don't even need this bandage."

"Assassin gored your gut." Amy grabbed his right hand with both of hers, intent on making him understand how serious the situation was.

"Yeah, but he threw me so his horn didn't go as deep as it could've. Missed my belly by a good inch. And now we're both here instead of just me. A fair exchange."

"I won the purse," said Amy.

"Well, there you go. The Champ at last!"

Amy beamed. "So . . . do you want to go to Jasper when you get out of here?"

The look of surprise on Gregg's face quickly morphed to pleasure. "Sure! Just let me hail the bartender and get my bill."

Amy laughed. "I don't think you're going anywhere right now, Mister."

"What are you going to tell folks who make fun of the champ bull rider dating a clown?"

Amy blushed scarlet. "I'm going to say, 'A woman can have a relationship *and* be a bull rider. A woman really can have it all.' I'm going to say, 'He's my hero. And he's a bull fighter, buster.'"

Amy got up out of her chair. She kissed Gregg's pale lips as gently as he'd kissed her the first time; she kissed him until his lips were red again. When he made room for her on the bed and raised his sheet, she snuggled in beside him, cuddling as close as she could.

Gregg popped open the buttons on her hot pink top,

and in a moment he had her left breast in his hand. He gently rubbed her little nipple with his thumb. In a moment, the rosy bud hardened. Gregg groaned. "Where you been so long?" He dipped it in his mouth.

It was Amy's turn to groan. She freed her right breast so he'd have more of what he'd been missing. She arched her back to push her tits in his face. "I thought about your mouth," she confessed. Her breath deepened. "Your mouth on mine."

Gregg ran his free hand up between her thighs. He cupped the cotton gusset that covered her pussy. With his middle finger he made a slight furrow between her labia and started a little pulsing beat.

Amy felt that small sensation with what seemed like every nerve in her body. She could not imagine how she'd lived without the electricity of their intimacy for so long.

"I thought about your tongue inside me," she continued, "making me crazy."

He lifted his head from the valley between her tits. "Lie back. I want to eat you."

"Mmm." Amy met his gaze with hers. Now that the barrier of mild flirtation between them had once again been lifted, it was as if she'd been starved for lack of him. She wanted to drink him with thirsty eyes and yes, she wanted that mouth on her pussy, but now just wasn't the time.

She'd have to protect him.

"Better save it for the mountains," she said.

Gregg scratched at the cotton covering her clit.

Amy moaned. Her snatch ached for him. She reached for and found his cock, tenting the front of his hospital gown. She stroked its smooth contours through the thin material, and to her delight he grew even harder.

"We can fuck," she announced. "But it has to be gentle."

"Okay," he agreed. He flashed his sunshiny grin.

Amy shimmied out of her hot pink ensemble and tossed it on the chair. The outfit was followed by her underwear.

"Do you like my fancy clothes?" she asked.

"Yep, and me so plain," replied Gregg, "lacking my finery."

"I get it now and I agree," said Amy.

Gregg gave her a questioning look.

"We don't have to change for anybody," she said. "Not even each other. Unless we want to."

Gregg grinned. "You're pretty smart for a bull rider," he said.

"That's because I'm a lady bull rider," she replied. "I guess I'd better ride you like a not-so-bucking bronc, hmm?"

"Like a mechanical bull set on very, very low," he agreed.

She pushed his gown up so she could see the bandage covering the wound the bull had inflicted. The deep bruising across her midsection clearly indicated where her ribs had cracked. It would be easy to avoid contact with their injuries but more difficult to match body rhythm to body rhythm without pain.

So they didn't get to fuck like they had in Jasper—at least, not that day. This was a gentle fuck, so gentle she thought it might better be called "having sex" or even "making love."

She was wet enough to easily receive his hard-on.

Once he'd filled her with his long cock, she contracted her pelvic floor rhythmically, giving him a Kegel version of the pulsing finger he'd tortured her with earlier.

Gregg ran his hands over the contours of her breasts and belly. "I love your tits, your tummy, your pussy," he murmured.

"Make me come, baby," she said.

She began to rise and fall above him. Amy savored the slight draw of his cock against the walls of her vagina as she slowly shifted so only his tip was inside her. At the same steady pace, Amy lowered herself until once again she was impaled on Gregg's solid cock.

Gregg found her clit with his fingers and circled it in slow motion. His other hand rested on her hip, neither guiding nor resisting her movement, just joining their bodies in a companionable way. This stirred a muscle memory in Amy that got her even hotter.

In no time her slick, satiny tunnel had adapted to his shape and she was riding his cock like a thick, wet pole— in slow mo.

They were lucky not to be disturbed, or perhaps the staff was lucky not to disturb them, because Amy had no intention of stopping, not for anything, and from the look in Gregg's eyes, he felt the same.

Amy knew she'd be back in the arena and she guessed Gregg planned to be, too. It was in their bones and, after all, neither of them had even broken one. There'd be plenty more rodeo thrills. But this! Amy released a guttural groan as her internal pleasure points lit up, so warm and intense she imagined them as little white holiday lights. This was something else.

She leaned forward, her hands on the pillow on

each side of his head. Carefully, she increased her speed. His fingers stayed steady on her clit, his other hand on her thigh. Her pussy contracted suddenly and she gasped.

For a moment she was suspended between flying and falling and, while the flying was fantastic, she was not afraid to fall.

"That's it, baby, show me how much you love having my cock inside you again, all the way, sweetheart, let me fuck you all the way home," coaxed Gregg.

"I'm gonna come," she managed to mutter between gasps. She felt the tension in his hips start to release as he relinquished all self-control.

A split second later she was growling through gritted teeth as one gut-clenching paroxysm followed another.

He thrust up and down, no more than an inch, but it was enough to get him growling, too. His fingers continued making little circles around her clit, triggering wave after wave of pleasure.

Amy held her position, her knees wide apart, her wet pussy gripping and releasing his cock with each contraction.

Gregg jerked and groaned as he climaxed beneath her. His thumb mashed her clit and set off another spark that culminated in another explosion of bliss for Amy. Her pussy gripped his cock, which spurted once more. And so they continued until both were limp.

Amy dismounted gingerly. "Ow," she said. "That was fantastic."

"Ow," Gregg agreed. "It was."

Amy curled up beside him again. He wrapped his arms around her and pulled her as close as he could.

She found she liked the sense of safety she got from being in his arms. It made for a very welcome change.

He nuzzled her earlobe affectionately. "That was no eight seconds," he whispered.

"No, Greggoire," she whispered back. "That was forever."

SEVEN SWEETS
AND SEVEN SOURS

Megan Hart

I have a suitcase packed and ready to go.

It doesn't hold much. A pair of black trousers I took from my brother Jacob's room. One of his white shirts. A pair of socks. I'll wear the pair of hiking boots I bought from the local English department store and have hidden in the suitcase behind the chicken house, where my dat will never find it. My mam might have, if she hadn't passed on last year. She was the reason I hadn't left, but she's gone.

For now, I wear my plain brown dress and the white mesh prayer cap. The ribbons dangle down my back along with my thick braid. My legs and feet are bare. My toes, dirty. When I live among the English, I will never have dirty feet. I will cut my hair short and never wear a dress again.

Hannah's house is dim and cooler than the late August day outside. Today is not baking or wash day. I brace myself for the possibility that her mother-in-law, Rebecca, will be in the kitchen when I come in through the back door, but the room is empty. From upstairs, I can hear the faint singsong of Hannah's lullaby. She must be nursing the baby. He is only four months old and will sleep after she finishes. We will have an hour or two before he wakes.

I'm too eager. I take the stairs two at a time, my bare feet slapping the wood. I've been told too often I talk too loud, run too fast, argue too fiercely. My father scolds that I'm not womanly, and that's the truth. I am not a woman, even if I wear the dress and grow my hair long and do the baking and washing, even if I have managed to learn, sometimes, to bow my head the way a woman should. I have never been a woman.

"Mary," Hannah says as though she's surprised to see me.

I told her I was coming over today. She didn't forget. She always pretends she is surprised when I arrive. I understand why. In case there is someone to overhear us, she needs to be able to pretend she didn't know. She's never told me that, but I understand her. We've been friends since we were infants in our mams' arms. I know her better than anyone ever will, even if Hannah will not admit it.

The baby in her arms falls away from her breast, his small mouth lax in sleep. He suckles the air for a moment before going still. Hannah puts him to her shoulder as she stands from her seat in the rocker in the corner. Her hand rubs along his tiny back until he belches so loud we both laugh, and she hushes me with her eyes alight with glee.

"Don't wake him," she says.

Silently, I stand aside while she settles the baby into the cradle near her side of the bed. He stirs but doesn't wake. She turns to me without a word.

We never speak about the things we do when her husband is away in his woodshop. Hannah, I think, prefers to tell herself that every time is the last time. Even though I know she feels guilty about it and I know she intends that every time should be the last, it has never yet been.

Until today. Today is the last time I will savor her seven sweets and seven sours. I know it. Hannah does not.

When I try to kiss her mouth, she turns her face. Her eyes close. Her head falls back, giving me access to her throat with my tongue, my teeth, my lips. Her throat works with a moan, and I back her up to the bed. She's expecting me to push her onto it, but instead, I pluck at the hook-and-eye closures on her dress.

"What are you doing?" Her eyes wide, Hannah puts a hand over mine to stop me. She says the words in Pennsylvania Dutch.

I answer in English. "I want to see all of you."

Hannah shakes her head, and as I step back and begin to undo all the hooks of my own dress, she averts her eyes. Even when I am naked in front of her, she won't look. I shiver with a feeling of freedom and say her name.

"If Ephraim comes home—"

"He never does."

"Someone else could come," she says.

Like putting the suitcase behind the chicken house, this is a risk I'm willing to take. Once again, I move to tug at the closures on her dress. This time, she lets me. She shakes when she stands naked in front of me, and of course I pull her close. Our bodies align. I'm only a little taller than she is. She can bury her face against the side of my neck. I stroke her naked back. I unpin the thick coil of her hair so that it falls to her hips.

I lay her back on the bed, and she covers her eyes with her hands, but her thighs open for me the way they always have, since that first time so many years ago. It was rumspringa then, our time to run "wild," and we'd been drinking from a bottle of cheap vodka someone's older brother had bought in town. We'd stumbled home to share her sagging bed in the smallest room, covering our giggles with our hands, imagining her parents would not hear us or know what we'd been doing. They'd turn a blind eye to the alcohol. They would not have done the same to what we'd done together in that bed.

"Look at me," I tell her now. My voice is hard and firm and low, rough. It is not a feminine voice of soft murmurs and gentle request. My voice is a command. A man's voice, and Hannah responds as she would to a man who'd spoken.

She pulls her hands away. Her lips are wet from where she's licked them. Her nipples are tight and hard, like my own, but Hannah's breasts are full. Weighty with milk. Her soft belly, rounder than mine, is crisscrossed with stripes from childbirth. I love those marks, the way I love everything about her body.

When I lift her foot to my lips, she gasps and tries to pull it away, but I hold her tight and press a kiss to the sole. I nibble her ankle. Her calf. By the time I make my way to her knee, she is panting softly and rolling her hips upward. I take my time to relish every single inch of her.

"Seven sweets," I say with a tiny, sharper bite to the softness of her inner thigh. "Seven sours. All of your flavors."

It's a reference to the "tradition" of Amish dinners featuring seven sweet and seven sour dishes. It's not a true tradition at all. It was created to promote tourism, but the tourists who flood this area in search of an authentic Amish meal have come to expect it, so it's become common enough for us, too. And it fits here, because Hannah is an entire smorgasbord of flavors, scents, and tastes.

The tangy musk of her center sends a rush of heat through me. I inhale her, again and again, until she wriggles and protests, but with laughter. Her giggles turn breathless when I slide my tongue along her savory folds to find the tight, sweet knot of her pleasure. I close my eyes, drinking her in. The sweets, the sours, everything about her in this moment. My own body tenses, clutching at nothing. On the bed, I grind my pelvis against the plain white sheets as I kiss between her legs, again and again.

Hannah opens for me like a flower that follows the sun. And I'm the bee, sipping at her nectar. She floods my tongue with it. Sweet, slippery fluid drips down her thighs and covers my mouth and chin; I cannot get enough. I lap in slow, steady strokes of my tongue. That little bead of flesh swells between my lips. My tongue dips a little lower, pushing inside. Hannah shudders, but muffles her cry with a pillow over her face. I replace my tongue with three fingers, sliding deep inside her.

The first time we did this, I could only slip a single finger inside her, but time has passed. I don't think about the reasons why her body can accommodate me better, now. To think of that in this moment would make this wrong, and I won't believe it is. No matter what anyone might say, no matter if getting caught means we will be shamed and shunned. What Hannah and I do now is not wrong. It is the best and most pure expression of love I have ever known.

Against the bed, I grind, grind, grind. It's different than how I do it at home when I'm alone. There, I use my fingers to slide between my thighs and find my own pleasure spot. Here, with Hannah, my body wants to move and thrust in time with what I'm doing to her with my mouth and fingers. In my mind, with her, I am complete down there instead of feeling as though this emptiness inside me is echoed by my real and literal opening. With Hannah, I feel more like the person I know I am than any other time, and so I groan into her sweet, hot flesh as I push myself against the bed and imagine what it would be like to push inside her. Not with my fingers, but the way a man would.

The rush of desire takes my breath away. I can't think beyond it. Everything inside me focuses on this, the rising wave of pleasure that builds like a storm. The thunder will crash, the lightning will strike. But first, I want to make Hannah shake and cry out. I want to feel her body clutching the invasion of my fingers. I want that sweet little knot to pulse beneath my tongue. I want her to break apart underneath me. I want us both to shatter, together.

I slide my fingers faster. Twisting. I ease off the pressure of my tongue and lips so I can sip at her honey. Tasting Hannah truly is all the sweets, all the sours. She is tangy and musky and different than the way I taste and smell the times I have lifted my fingertips to my nose after touching myself. I would know her by this scent. By the flavor. In a dark room, with a hundred strangers, I would know Hannah by the in-out hush of her breath.

Her body tenses. Her hips rock. She's begun to make those tiny mewling and desperate sounds in the back of her throat, muffled by the pillow on her face, but I can still hear them. The sharp intake of her breath. The low moan. The sound of her ecstasy pushes me to grind harder against the mattress. I am almost there. So close my body trembles. My rear cheeks clench. My toes are curling. I can't focus on her, not this close to going over the edge myself, so I slow my urgent thrusting.

I want to be able to remember every twitch and clutch of muscles. Every sound she makes. Every second of this has to stay with me forever, because I know this is going to be the last time.

A harsher, guttural groan slips out of her. Hannah claps a hand to the back of my head, holding my mouth against her as she writhes. Her sweet and sticky slipperiness floods my tongue. I can't breathe; I can only breathe. She has never moved this fiercely beneath me before. I almost can't hold on to her. I definitely can no longer hold back myself. As Hannah gives one last, hard thrust upward against my mouth, her body tightens around my fingers. Everything inside her bears down. Clench, release, rapid squeezes. I thrust against the mattress. I shake. I cry out into her fragrant deliciousness and spill over into my own final, writhing desire.

In the aftermath, I want to fall onto the bed next to her and sleep, but we don't have that luxury. The baby is already stirring. We've nearly woken him. Hannah leans over the cradle to check, but so far he's settled back into dreams. She looks at me over her shoulder.

"I need to get dressed. You, too. Hurry."

I don't move, not at first. Then I sit to pull my knees to the side so I can lean close to her. I put a hand on her shoulder. "Not yet."

"Mary, I have to," Hannah mutters. She's back to not looking at me.

I flinch at the sound of that name. When I am away from here, when I've cut my hair and started dressing in men's clothes, I'm going to choose a brand new name. I don't know what it will be, yet. But it will be new the way I will be new.

"Another moment, *bitte*," I say. *Please*.

She doesn't protest when I slide up to her back and press my chin into the curve of her shoulder. My arms go around her to cup her breasts. She sighs and twists to face me as we lie back on the bed. When she pulls my head down to her nipple, I close my eyes and take it in my mouth. After a moment, there is a new flavor. Hot and sweet. If I could lie here forever, both of us naked, if I could live with Hannah this way always, she could nourish me. I would take care of her better than her husband does. He provides for her and for their son, but I would love her better. I already do.

"You can come with me, Hannah."

I shouldn't have said it, but I couldn't stay silent. Hannah twists away from me. Her nipples are dripping, and she stops the flow with a practiced pinch of her thumb and forefinger. She sighs. Her head hangs. Her shoulders slump.

"You want me to leave everything I've ever known. My son?"

"Bring him," I say, although the truth is, I know she never will. What could the two of us do out there in the world with an infant? In all my fantasies over the years, it's always been me and Hannah. I should have asked her before she agreed to become Ephraim Zook's wife.

I should have been brave.

"I love you," I tell her in Pennsylvania Dutch.

Hannah does not say it back. She never has, but I've seen the truth in her eyes and her smile. I've tasted it on her kisses. She hasn't allowed me to kiss her on the mouth since she got married, but I still remember how it felt.

"I love you," I repeat, this time in English. "Come away with me. I'll find work. I'll take care of you."

"You want to be my husband?"

"Yes," I say.

She shakes her head. Her laugh is not cruel, and there is no humor in it. "I thought all of this would go away."

"It won't. I have to leave."

"Why can't you just stay? Take a husband. Obed Yoder's been sweet on you for years."

The thought of it is enough to push me from the bed. I begin to put on my dress. My fingers move without my mind having to think. They fumbled when I tried to put on my brother's trousers, but once they were on, I felt at home. Not as though I've been wearing a costume, the way I've felt for as long as I can remember.

"Mary," Hannah says, stopping me. Her baby wails, and she lifts him to her shoulder.

Her eyes meet mine, and this time, she does not look away. She stands fully naked in front of me, no longer in a rush to cover herself. My hands are shaking, so I close them into fists.

"Stay," Hannah whispers.

"Come with me," comes my reply.

When she does not answer me, I smile because I cannot bear to let her see my pain. I knew she couldn't go with me. She knows I cannot stay. We are both caught.

I don't kiss her one last time. I give her a single nod and leave her in the bedroom. Behind me, the wail of the baby rises up and up, quickly hushed. The last thing I hear before I leave the house through the kitchen door is the sound of Hannah singing to him.

And then, I am free.

BABY DOLL

Sienna Saint-Cyr

Heather thumbed through her messages as she waited at the designated table. The message from Charlie was at the top of her texts. He'd told her to wear her favorite baby-doll clothing, which she'd happily agreed to. She twirled the ribbon on the corner of her soft pink dress as she read the text repeatedly. The silky fabric of her attire lent comfort as she waited with a stomach full of butterflies. She let her hand rise to the tops of her stockings, and she squirmed as she felt the lacy trim. She pictured Charlie playing with her stockings. Her anticipation grew as the minutes ticked by. The longer she waited, the more her stomach turned to knots.

All she could think about was how she'd shared too much . . . told him too much about her PTSD, her anxiety and depression, about her deep need to be Daddy's little baby doll, but she hadn't known what else to do. Too many relationships had already failed because she hadn't communicated her mental state or her need to be cared for early enough on. This time, she'd been determined to change that. But now, these things tore through her head like razors. She'd fucked it up, been too bold. *He wasn't going to show.*

Heather's stomach pinched harder, and she quickly dug through her purse before another pang of pain hit her. She plopped a Xanax into her mouth, letting the pill scratch on the way down. The irritation served as a slight distraction from her anxiety. But the thought, *He's not coming,* refused to leave her mind. The realization made her chest heavy. She picked up her phone again for distraction.

No, she told herself, *you're not going to fuck this up. He's coming. He is.*

Heather opened her camera app and turned it to selfie mode. She was going to get a pic of herself in her beautiful pink dress. Even if he didn't show, she felt good in it. *Right.*

She snapped a couple of pics and pulled one up to look at it. Low-hanging lights had cast a halo over the crown of her head, causing her brown ringlets to fill with warmth. Her cheeks looked rosy, her eyes a little less swollen, lips full. She looked almost like a porcelain doll. If only the rest of the world had dim lighting.

Heather sipped her water, focusing on the wonderful aroma of Thai food around her. She teased out the scent of peanut sauce and something a bit spicier—maybe a red curry—coming from behind her. Her stomach rumbled in a different way now.

She let the noises emanating from the kitchen consume her. She pictured herself back there rather than alone at the table. She wanted to bury her face in her arms and be done. Before she could, the hostess approached.

"Excuse me," she began, then handed Heather a folded piece of paper. "That man at the table in the corner asked me to deliver this to you."

Heather took the paper. "Thanks."

The woman nodded and left.

Before looking at the paper, Heather looked at the corner of the restaurant. There—at a table on the raised portion of the floor—was a tall man with a black blazer and a cowboy hat. He sat with his chest forward, as though filled with confidence. She couldn't make out the details of his face, but she saw that he was smiling.

She looked back to her paper and unfolded it. The paper looked special, expensive maybe, with a slight scent of vanilla to it. Written words filled the note, fancy words. Like calligraphy.

Baby Doll,

You look so adorable over there, watching for me. Waiting so patiently. At first, I thought you'd changed your mind. I've been waiting for over twenty minutes. But then I saw that you too were sitting by a silly cat painting and I realized I had not been stood up.

Please, adorable girl, won't you join me?

Charlie

Heather's heart raced. Was this for real? Had she lost it?

She looked up and saw him waiting, still smiling, patting the seat to his left. Heather squirmed again as heat warmed her inner thighs. The lacy underside of her dress brushed against her bare flesh, causing a rush of desire—*submission*—to move through her body like a wave of gentle release.

After gathering her things, Heather joined the stranger at the table on the platform. She scooted in slowly, as she didn't want her bare thighs to make noise on the seat. She wasn't successful. Her thighs made an annoyingly loud squeak as she scooted in. Heather's cheeks flushed with heat.

"I'm sorry," she mumbled, unable to look at him.

Charlie laughed from deep in his chest. It was a kind laugh. One that suggested he might have enjoyed her noisy thighs and that he wasn't laughing at her.

"Don't be silly, doll," he began. "I love your cheeks pink."

Heather's smile betrayed her, revealing her enjoyment of a little humiliation.

"Have you already decided what you want? I saw you eyeing the Pad Thai as the server walked by you earlier." He smiled.

"Pad Thai would be great . . . " She hesitated as she thought about what to call him. "Sir."

"Pad Thai it is then."

Charlie ordered for both of them, making her breathe a sigh of relief. *So far, so good*, she thought. He was behaving in a manner that lent comfort.

Their food arrived faster than she'd expected, so the two talked through dinner. They spoke so long that her food began to get cold; she was talking far more than eating. They negotiated what they wanted out of a Daddy/baby doll relationship, discussed her mental health and medications, explained their desires with kink, and set limits on what they'd take part in. Everything aligned like the perfect starry night. Then, they moved into an area that made Heather tense.

"You understand, of course, that if I am to be your Daddy, no more of this . . . " Charlie lifted her arm and ran his fingers across her cutting scars. "Daddies help their baby dolls grow and heal. Self-harm is against my rules. I will punish you if I catch you doing this again. Do you understand?"

His tone was firm. It filled Heather's cheeks with a different kind of heat. One that she wasn't sure she liked, yet her cunt filled with moisture at the same moment. Clearly, her body desired what her pride wanted to reject.

"And," he continued, "I want to be in touch with your therapist. You have a lot going on. I won't risk your mental well-being if they feel something isn't safe for you. If you want me to be your Daddy, we're going to do this right. No secrets, no deceptions. We'll do this safely."

Heather both wanted to hug him and run away at that moment. This was what she'd wanted, what she'd asked for, so why was she feeling hesitant? She shuffled in her seat, staring at her half-empty plate.

Charlie reached into a bag to his right. He pulled something plush out, though she couldn't see what it was. He held it behind his back.

"Doll, I'm sure you're nervous right now. This is a lot to take on for me as well. But know that if I take you on, I *will* take care of you." He pulled the item out from behind his back and handed it to her. It was a plush unicorn, just like the one she'd written about on her blog that she'd lost as a child.

"You . . . " she began, but her words caught in her throat. "You read my blog?"

"Every single post."

"Then you know *how* I lost my last one of these?" Slow tears ran down her cheeks.

"Yes, girl. You were forced to burn yours as a child. Something about demons behind the eyes. But I can assure you, there are no demons behind these eyes. I want to protect you, to give you back a piece of your innocence that was so horribly taken from you in your youth."

"I . . . " Heather silently met his eyes. She couldn't say anything more. This was what she wanted. She felt it like fire in her heart, that gentle ache that came with feeling safe, protected, and in his care. Yet he wasn't even her Daddy yet.

"Please," she could hardly get the words out, "be my Daddy?"

"I will be your Daddy, baby doll."

Heather hugged the unicorn tightly. His gesture made her melt inside. He cared . . . paid attention.

She focused on the softness of the plush. The smell of sweetness in the stitching. The texture of the hair mixed with the rougher glitter strands. This was exactly like the one she'd been forced to burn, the one she'd cried over—been called a demon child over.

"Thank you, Daddy."

"You're welcome, baby doll. Now, let's lighten the conversation for a bit and order some dessert. What's your favorite?"

"Mango sorbet." She giggled.

"Mango sorbet it is then."

Daddy's smile warmed her soul. This man was going to change everything.

Months of phone calls, therapy sessions, and getting to know each other had taken place and finally, the night for play had come. Heather could hardly wait for Daddy to arrive. She'd done everything on her list: worn the same lacy stockings, put on her shortest baby-doll dress with no panties, had her hair in ringlets again, and tinted her cheeks with cherry blush. She'd even done the naughtier thing Daddy had instructed her to do, play with her girly bits until they were wet and ready for him.

Heather paced by the front door. Despite sharing so much with him on the phone and during their shared therapy sessions, she still didn't want him seeing her desperate, panicky side, the PTSD, her OCD, or too much of her anxiety. No matter what her therapist had tried, some things just weren't getting any better. *Just don't screw this up, Heather!*

Daddy arrived like clockwork, which settled her pacing. His dark hair and cleanly shaven face popped up just over the window in her door. Her heart raced as she opened it to greet him.

Heather kneeled at his feet, not caring at all if her neighbors saw her being so silly with the door wide open. "Good evening, Daddy. I'm so glad you came."

He chuckled. "Are you going to welcome me in?"

"Oh! Sorry, Daddy!"

Heather stood again and moved out of the way. Once he was inside, she shut the door once, twice, and finally a third time. Then she locked every lock and deadbolt three times before turning to face him again.

"Don't want me escaping, do you?"

"I have to lock every lock so no one . . . " She let her words fade. "Damn it! I did it again! I tried, Daddy. I did!"

"Tried what, baby doll?" He caressed her cheek. "I know you have things you're working on—things we can now work on together—so please, don't stress this. Little girls are under the care of their Daddies. Aren't they?"

"Yes, Daddy." Her chest felt heavy as she looked away from him.

"You can lock all of these locks when I'm not here, but when I am, you get one door lock and one deadbolt. That's all you need. Understand?"

"Yes, Daddy." She said it more like a whimper. She wanted to slink to the ground with embarrassment. Sudden anger built inside her, a rage she couldn't suppress. She dug her fingernails deep into her adjacent hand. "I'm so stupid! Of course I'm safe with you here! Why am I so friggin' mental?"

"Stop!" Daddy's voice was deep, commanding.

His tone snapped Heather from her moment of self-harm. Her mouth fell open. Breath caught.

"What's rule number three?"

She swallowed hard. "No self-harm, Daddy." Guilt filled her chest. Shame too, as she couldn't even make it one in-person day with Daddy before breaking his rules—his *healthy for her* rules. She burst into tears. "I'm sorry, Daddy!"

"Do you remember our conversations about this?"

She nodded, then looked to the floor.

"What's going to happen now?"

"I'm going to be punished, Daddy." Her words left her mouth in a humble manner of sweet surrender.

Daddy stood taller, his chest puffed out as he surveyed her. She could see him from her peripheral vision. He wasn't smiling, but he wasn't frowning either. She couldn't read him at all.

"This *is* our first session together. I'm willing to let this one go *this* time, but not again. Do you prefer not to be punished today, doll?"

His question caught her by surprise. She reluctantly met his eyes again.

"It's your rule, Daddy." Her brows furrowed. Forehead creased. "Why would you ask that?"

"Talking is different than doing, baby doll. Being punished isn't for everyone." Despite the fact that she had broken a rule already and that they were talking about a heavy topic, Daddy's tone was still calm, reassuring.

She surveyed him now. *Was he serious about being her Daddy? Why would he not punish her instantly? She'd broken his rule already.*

The more she thought about it, however, the more she realized how much she *wanted* to be punished. She wanted those boundaries enforced and the safety that went with that.

Heather sucked in a deep breath and let herself open to him. "Please, punish me, Daddy."

"For what, baby doll?"

"Hurting myself. Being unkind to myself. For breaking one of your rules."

Daddy took hold of her wrist and looked around, then led her past the little wooden table by the door, past the egg-white desk with her laptop and straight to the plush, pin-striped couch under the largest window in the house.

He let go of her hand while he closed the giant curtains,

then—like a flash of lightning—sat on the couch and pulled her over his knees. She hadn't been in that position before, though she'd craved it every night since embracing her adolescent side.

Her breathing shifted to deep, long breaths as he slowly pulled her dress up and over her lower back, her bare ass exposed to him. He placed his right hand over her back as everything inside her screamed out at once.

"Please spank me, Daddy!"

"You will count down from ten as I go. Though next time, the number will go up."

His words felt like steel, but safe steel. They sank into her flesh like hooks, embedding themselves deeply in her heart.

Smack. His left hand came down so hard on her bottom that she cried out, "Ten."

Smack.

"Nine."

"Eight."

"Seven."

With each number down, a strange relief filled her, starting in her ass—so full of Daddy's lovely pain—and extending into her arms, legs, fingers, and toes. Everything felt light, loving, *safe,* tingly . . . numb. The burn of Daddy's slaps was washing away her shame, guilt, self-loathing, and self-hatred. With each slap, her pussy grew wetter.

Heather ached for him more with each strike. The sound of his hand on her fleshy ass only made her desire for him to fuck her that much stronger.

"Six."

"Five . . ."

"Four!"

Daddy slipped out from under her, moved her to the back of the couch, then leaned her over it. Once again, he flipped her baby doll dress up and over her lower back. This time, his hand didn't come down as a strike. Instead, he spread her legs.

Cool air rushed her moist cunt. Heather gasped. *Moaned.*

"Is there something you want, baby doll?" His words were calm, smooth. Then she heard his zipper moving.

Heather couldn't hold on any longer. She'd wanted to be a good girl and take her punishment, but she craved him so much she could hardly stand it.

"Please fuck me, Daddy?" Her question was more like a desperate plea, her desire strong as all of the darkness in her seemed to be fading.

"You have three more spankings to go, little girl."

"Please, Daddy? Please spank me—fuck me—please?"

"That's not a very good punishment now, is it?" he said, though his words held a lighter tone.

Heather was about to plead again when she felt his bare flesh up against her, his hard cock rubbing on the outer layers of her ready cunt. Her hips moved side to side as the ache consumed her.

"Please, Daddy!" Her tone so conveyed how desperate she was to feel him inside her that it alarmed even her.

Daddy plunged his cock into her hard, filling every bit of her insides. But he didn't move. Just stood there, in complete control as his hard cock took up the bulk of her insides.

Smack.

"Three!" she shouted.

Heat filled every inch of her, along with lust, passion, desire. She felt his desire for her as his cock pulsed inside her.

Daddy grabbed her hair and pulled her head back with his right hand, then slapped again, so hard this time that the echo moved through her house.

"Two!" she screamed.

Smack.

"One!" Her voice cracked as she cried out again, a raspy tone full of pain, as this was his hardest smack.

He pulled out and thrust hard into her, grabbing her hips as he did so.

Tears rolled from her eyes like she'd never cried before, but these weren't sad tears. They were joyful, pleasurable tears. Tears of love and relief.

He kept pounding into her, filling her with all the goodness that came with being his baby doll, being submissive, being put in her place. Each forceful thrust gave her peace—a quiet calm in a sea of storms—and her eyes began to close. Tears stopped falling. Blood rushed between her legs. The tingles grew as he dug his nails into her flesh. The feeling of him made her burn with a fire she didn't know she possessed. "Please, Daddy . . . "—her words barely left her lips—"please, may I come for you?"

"Not yet, baby doll," he said as he kept pounding into her. "Remember rule one?"

"Yes." She breathed her words. "No coming without permission, Daddy."

"You are still being punished, girl. You will wait."

The heat between her legs continued to grow, the tingles building to a point of pain as she tried to fight her building orgasm. Sensation filled her entire body, her head light as blood rushed between her legs.

"Daddy, please!" she screamed, voice full of desperation as she wasn't sure how much longer she could hold out. "Please let me come for you, Daddy! Please!"

Daddy pulled her hair with one hand now and pinched a nipple with his other. His dominance, the pain in her nipple, the pleasure in her cunt; it all meshed into a delicious mix of intensity. She cried out one last plea for him to allow her release.

"Come!" Daddy yelled, his words filling her entire body as she responded instantly.

Heather cried out as her orgasm raged through her. Fire, *orgasm fire,* consumed her entire body as Daddy kept pounding into her. He cried out himself, letting out a roar of a sound that only made her come harder. He released into her, his cock pulsating as her inner muscles strangled him.

Daddy pulled out slowly and zipped his pants, then helped her to a standing position. He took her by the hand and led her through the house, peering into each room as he passed. She didn't know what he was doing at first because she was so full of euphoria, but he eventually found what he was looking for—her room.

He laid her down on her left side, then grabbed the fleece blanket at the foot of the bed, placing it over her body. He retrieved her stuffed unicorn from the shelf and tucked it into her arms before climbing into the bed behind her.

Daddy scooted close to her and wrapped a leg and arm around her. He leaned in close to her ear.

"You are safe. You are a good girl for taking your punishment so well. You are my baby doll. I will continue to take care of you." He squeezed her tighter. "But you will grow, heal, and be my good girl, won't you?"

Heather felt his words all the way to her core. Her eyes closed, demeanor softened. "Yes, Daddy. This is exactly what I've been wanting, *needing,* for a very long time. Thank you, Daddy."

"For what, baby doll?" He let go of her side and moved the strands of hair sticking to her cheek out of the way.

"For correcting me. For fucking me. For giving me accountability along with compassion. I've needed you for a long time, Daddy. This feels surreal."

Daddy kissed her cheek gently. "It may feel surreal, but I'm here. I'm here for as long as you want me, baby doll. Be a good girl and rest now. I have more fun planned for us tonight."

"What are we doing later, Daddy?" she asked, though her eyes were already heavy with need for a nap.

"It's a surprise, baby doll. But I assure you you're going to love it. Now, let's rest. I'll need my energy for later too. Sleep well, baby doll."

As she lay there, snuggled and safe in Daddy's arms, a new need filled her. She sat up. "I'll be right back, Daddy."

He didn't say anything as she wriggled from him and made her way to the front door. She stood there before the piece of wood that had caused her so much trouble, struggling to reach out to the locks. But she wanted this. She wanted healing. She wanted normalcy. She wanted . . . freedom. So Heather reached up and unlocked every lock but one deadbolt.

She smiled with her entire body.

Heather crawled back in bed with Daddy, snuggling into him again. Just as she was about to fall asleep, he whispered in her ear, "Good girl, baby doll. Daddy is proud of you."

BEAUTIFUL DIRTY WONDERFUL

R. M. Wood

The club is in a part of the city crowded with low cement and brick buildings near the harbor. It's called Casablanca, and I can't decide if it's fitting or ironic considering what goes on inside. The old converted warehouse is right on the water, and when my husband and I step into the lobby on the main floor, I can see the glowing lights of the condos across the bay through the paned windows.

There's a doorman at a large desk, and as he says hello, my heart begins to pulse in time with the insistent beat that forces its way through the ceiling.

"Hi. Um . . . I'm Julie and this is Simon. We're here to . . . to see Danny," I say, my voice shaking. I wouldn't be doing this normally. Taking the lead. Usually it's Simon asking for a table or ordering drinks, but I'm the reason we're here, and I promised myself I wouldn't make him do more than was necessary. I'm still a little surprised he's agreed for this to happen, let alone come along to help.

The doorman checks our names off a printed list in

front of him and then waves us toward a curtained doorway that leads to the stairs.

"Everyone is waiting in room three."

The bass grows louder as we make our way to the second floor. When Simon and I met Danny here a month ago to arrange tonight, I was surprised to find Casablanca looked like any other dance club. There's a bar across from us, and a dance floor and DJ booth in front of thick, shimmering silver curtains that block the view. Taking up a good third of the space are tables and plush chairs. The only things that set it apart are three mattresses on the floor near the back.

There's already a few dozen people here, most of them talking or dancing. But a middle-aged man is thrusting doggie-style into a woman against a table, and immediately to our right a blonde head bobs in the lap of a man sitting in one of the oversized chairs. I try not to stare. To shove away the unconscious reaction that such things are indecent and not to be shared.

These people clearly don't believe that. I shouldn't either—I don't really, but sometimes my brain needs a reminder. Any thoughts of shame are laughable considering what I'll be doing soon enough.

In room three Danny is waiting with a group of guys preparing to fuck me.

It all started six months ago—or maybe it began when I first had such fantasies in my twenties, I don't know. But three months ago was when I decided I needed to put that fantasy into words, to try to make it happen for real.

Simon and I have been together for twenty years, and sex was like pizza night: come home on Friday, pull it out of the freezer, and toss it in the oven for ten minutes.

Sure, it kept us fed, but it was as boring as plain cheese.

It was Simon who first said he wanted to experiment. So we started with the normal things: massage oil, handcuffs, sex toys. It was fun. Wednesdays joined Fridays, and in addition to pizza, we had sushi and chicken carbonara. But the more we did, the more I thought about asking for the one thing I always wanted—the one thought that would send me over the edge when I was struggling to come.

The night I asked Simon, we were in bed. The lights were off, but I could still see his shape from the streetlight shining through the cracks in the blinds. It was a muggy summer night, and the air from a fan licked our toes, its constant hum drowning out any noises from outside.

I stared at the face I'd loved for more than two decades, now with laugh lines near his eyes and gray at his temples, and thought about the worst possibilities: that he'd take it personally, and believe I wasn't satisfied with him; that he would laugh, thinking it was a joke. That he would decide he didn't know who he was married to anymore, and leave. That he'd agree, but it would change everything, and slowly we'd grow to hate each other.

"Simon," I whispered, half hoping he was asleep so I could delay the conversation for longer—maybe even change my mind. But one eye pried itself open, meeting mine across the dim space between us.

"What is it, love?" he asked, his voice laced with sleep.

"I want to ask you something."

He shifted, folding his arms around his pillow and lifting his head overtop so he could look at me directly. He didn't say anything, just waited patiently for me to start talking. He was used to this: me coming to him in the middle of the night with my anxiety-ridden questions.

"I've been enjoying our fun. In bed, I mean. Sex . . . it's been good. Better." I cringed at how inarticulate I sounded. But Simon only smiled and agreed, and his eyes showed a sort of confidence.

"There's a fantasy I want to try. But it . . . " I paused, giving myself a chance to say things clearly. "This isn't something I need, and it doesn't mean anything about anything between us. It's just something I've wanted to do forever, and since we've been more honest and experimenting lately, I thought I would tell you. It doesn't need to go anywhere. If you think it's gross or too much, we can forget I ever brought it up."

"Slow down, you haven't even told me yet." He laughed, only to cut himself off when he noticed I wasn't smiling. He schooled his features into a serious expression, his eyebrows furrowing so a line formed between them. I took a deep breath.

"I want to try a gang bang."

Too scared to see what Simon's reaction was to my admission, I shut my eyes immediately. He said nothing at first. For several long moments, the only sound was the hum of the fan. A strange lightness filled my chest, as if the words left a space where my secret used to be.

Finally, I heard his breath pause, and then a breathy chuckle of discomfort that made me cringe.

"Well, I—wow," he responded. I kept my eyes closed, sure that I'd made a hash of things.

I startled when Simon's fingers brushed my cheek. "Hey, open up," he said seriously. Always unable to ignore that tone, I opened my eyes.

"You want a gang bang?" His voice was laced with disbelief.

"I don't need to do it," I defended myself. "It's crazy, I know." I laughed, but it was the same sort as the chuckle—hollow and anxious—made even less convincing by tears pooling in my eyes. I quickly wiped them away. Simon moved closer, wrapping an arm around my waist, and though I remained stiff, I was relieved.

"It's not crazy," he assured me. "It's . . . unusual, but not crazy. At least, those porn stars seem to like it." His lips lifted at his halfhearted joke.

I twisted my mouth and gave him an innocuous glare, but felt myself relax a little. He didn't hate me.

"You've wanted to do it forever, eh?"

I felt my cheeks burn, but I nodded.

"How many?"

I did not expect him to want details. But I reached for my courage and did my best to answer him. "I don't know. Maybe ten?"

Simon's eyes widened; I knew images of me fucking ten guys were running through his head.

"It doesn't have to be that many," I qualified.

Simon paused, still thinking, then said, "I guess I should have let you sow a few more oats before I proposed." He laughed, more genuinely this time. My fears crowded into my chest like a mob of ghosts, and I shrank back in an effort to escape them.

"Hey, Julie. Hey!" He grabbed my bicep, stopping me from pulling away. "I'm just joking."

He pulled me into his chest, wrapping his strong arms around me. I let him do it reticently, heart once again beating too fast and scared, but eventually his constant warmth drove away the ghosts, and I sank against him.

"I don't know how to talk about this," Simon admitted, his breath tickling my hair. "I'm not sure I can handle it, but we should talk about it, if it's really important to you. Maybe when I'm not half-asleep."

He pulled back just enough to peer into my face.

"Okay," I agreed. Relieved that the conversation was over for now, I buried myself back into his warmth, eager to avoid the sharp edge of anxiety that still gnawed deep in my gut.

"I love you," I said.

"I love you too."

Many conversations followed that night, and then several months of research to locate Danny, who runs Casablanca and agreed to arrange tonight.

When Simon threads his hand into mine and gives it a squeeze, the memories are replaced by the noise of the club. I turn to look at Simon just as the man next to us grunts and comes into the blonde's mouth.

"Not having second thoughts now, are you?" he asks playfully. I shake my head. I'm not about to run away when my fantasy is so close. No matter what.

Next to the bar is a hall with several closed doors that lead to private rooms, and that's where Simon and I head. Danny, wearing black jeans and a leather vest, is in Room Three with seven strangers. There's a mattress and a padded table in the middle of the room, but other than that and a few chairs near the door to the bathroom at the back, the space is empty. The lights seem bright, even with the walls painted dark maroon. The thumping beat from the DJ has been piped in through a pair of speakers hanging from the ceiling. Country. I can't believe I'm going to get gangbanged to country.

"Any way to change the music?" I ask, frowning at the speakers.

"Don't worry, in a little bit you won't even notice the music," replies Danny with a warm smile.

A couple of the men snort in amusement, and once again I'm reminded of their presence. Right.

Everyone is still clothed. We go over the rules before I am introduced to the men I'll be spending the night with. Their ages range from thirty to sixty, and I immediately forget half their names. Will that matter after? I'm not sure.

A man named Bill is the last to greet me. He's got dark hair and dimples when he smiles, and from his confident hello, I guess this isn't his first time.

"Don't worry, we'll treat you good," he assures me.

"You better," I retort, but I'm not worried about that. Danny and Simon will be watching from the sidelines, making sure everyone follows the rules and I'm all right.

"You ready, Julie?" Danny asks from behind me.

"Yes," I say, feeling confident for the first time tonight. This is my fantasy, and I'm going to enjoy it. Excitement overcoming nerves, I strip off my clothes, giving the men their first look at my middle-aged body—belly and stretch marks and all the rest. Simon is staring at me too, and I know he thinks I'm beautiful.

I hand him my clothes, and he gives me a reassuring smile. He doesn't say anything, and I'm glad; I wouldn't know what to say. I give him a chaste kiss and then turn around to face the men, finding them undressing.

Bill is already naked, his cock at half-mast as he eyes me up and down. Then he raises an arm, inviting me toward the table, which is about three feet high and covered in black vinyl. I climb on top and turn around, suddenly unsure what I am going to do with seven men at once. Seven cocks.

I expect them to swarm in like vultures on a kill, but they go slow, Bill taking the lead. As his fingers probe between my legs, I am so struck by the fact someone other than Simon or myself is touching me there. I am oblivious to the two bodies moving near my shoulders until one of them begins palming my breasts.

"Shit," I swear as Bill finds my clit, sending a jolt of pleasure into my groin. Hands are all over me, and I am entirely aware of how real this is. The realization sends a riptide of arousal through my body, makes my skin prickle as if my nerves are reaching out in expectation.

As Bill dips his head to lap at my clit with his tongue, I turn my head to the right and find my first cock. I latch on to it eagerly with my hand, then turn to my left and find another.

It takes me a few minutes to work into a rhythm, but soon enough I have figured it out. In my groin warmth is building like a bubbling spring from Bill's experienced tongue, and I shift, completely aware of how badly I want to be fucked. To have one of the cocks in my hand in my mouth.

I turn my head and open wide, and the owner of the cock in my right hand gets the hint. I peer up and meet his eyes, his half-lidded arousal sparking my own even more. I swirl my tongue around the tip. Take him as deep as I can. Awkwardly, I continue stroking with my other hand as I begin to suck.

I am aware for a moment that Bill's mouth has stopped its sucking, and then I am gasping as I feel his erection searching for my entrance. I moan as he slides inside. My mind chants: *There are two cocks inside me.*

I want more.

Their attention. Their desire. Their release.

Bill's cock banging into my pussy seems to set off a new rhythm. Cocks are traded for cocks. I don't care. I can't, because there're too many, and I can't keep track. My bangers are reduced to body parts, and I think I am too, but instead of feeling gross, it feels like I am bigger, more effervescent than I've ever been before. My insides are exploding and so, so warm, and as soon as fingers find my clit again, I am coming.

The first cock explodes come onto my face, and I grin, deliriously happy that I have made this happen. That between my legs another man is finding his pleasure—and stoking mine.

Danny was right: I have forgotten the music. The only sounds I am conscious of are the slapping of flesh against flesh, the slick sucking sound of spit and lube, the grunts of the men and my own constant moans.

I lose track of time. Of how many cocks I've held in my hands. Of how much sticky come litters my skin, and how many times my own body has responded in kind. All I know is I don't want this brilliant, sloppy, disgusting, wonderful joining of flesh to stop. I am lost in the dream, the reality better than I could have imagined.

I am still raring to go when I notice there are only two men left: one in my mouth, and one thrusting eagerly between my legs. We have moved onto the mattress, where I lie on my back. The others loom over the three of us, watching, but their cocks are spent. I peer up and find it's Bill whose erection I am laving with my tongue.

His dimples appear as our eyes meet, and he rests a hand on top of my head, forcing me into a slow rhythm.

"I told you we'd treat you good," he says, and then he reaches down between my legs, my eyes following to where another middle-aged man continues to pummel me. It takes only a few minutes of this before I'm coming again, and shortly after the man fucking me comes too, hips jerking forward before stopping altogether. Then he's gone. Bill quickly moves to take his place, waving two others over to stand beside me. Their cocks are limp, but I grab them anyway. Mostly they massage my breasts then rub any drying come into my skin.

For an old guy, Bill's stamina is exceptional. His wiry body picks up a blinding rhythm, and soon I am moaning, eyes shut, body rocking on the table. All this sex has made me loose and boneless. I feel like a fluffy cloud being wafted along by the wind.

Bill comes with a loud groan, his hips stilling as he ejects his pleasure for the last time. Then the men are moving away, Bill nodding to Danny and Simon, who I have forgotten about until now. Simon immediately moves next to me, and I feel too drunk off adrenalin and sex to try and read his expression.

As I sit up, I'm tempted to stick my fingers into my pussy, but resist because Simon is handing me a towel. I wipe my face, my breasts, my stomach, and then drop it beside me. There, next to the table, I notice a small wastebasket on the floor for the first time.

It is overflowing with used condoms, a testament to our evening.

Maybe I should feel dirty, but I don't. I feel aroused, and powerful, to have drawn out so much pleasure.

I stand up with Simon's assistance, my knees wobbling as my weight sinks onto my feet for the first time in what must be hours.

"How are you doing?" asks Danny, appearing in front of us.

"Great," I say. I'm sure my grin is stupid and manic, but I can't help it. I still feel as if I am soaring. In the back of my mind, I wish for another dozen guys to walk through the door.

Danny smiles. I don't know if it's because he's pleased it all worked out, or if he believes he's created future business.

I shower at the club, change, and then Simon and I go home. I make sure to thank Bill, who is standing at the bar when we leave. He gives me a wink and wishes me well.

The only thing Simon utters the whole way home is, "Have fun?"

"Mmm," is my hummed reply. But my heart is still pounding, and in my mind the scenes are playing over and over. I barely realize when we pull onto our street.

At home, I feel agitated and aroused as Simon and I brush our teeth and crawl into bed. My legs jump around under the covers. Simon stares at me from his pillow.

"You okay?" he asks. Tentatively, he puts a hand on my arm. The touch ignites something inside me, and I press myself against him. My lips find his throat.

"Julie!" He laughs, clearly surprised.

"Thank you," I say breathlessly. I kiss his neck again. His jaw. His lips.

After a moment, he returns the kiss, mouth opening, our tongues touching. I wonder for a moment if he needs this, or if I do: a reminder that I still want him too.

He lifts the covers and urges me onto my hands and knees. There is no foreplay before he thrusts inside. I am sore but he feels perfect, and I moan as his hips begin to churn. I urge him faster, banging my hips backward against his thrusts. We are panting, quickly rising up the hill toward our climaxes. My left hand moves to dance between my legs.

"Julie," Simon gasps, his hips jerking faster. "Fuck, I'm going to come."

It's the desire in his tone that sends me over the edge, and together we dive over the crest, our moans bouncing off the walls of our master bedroom. Together, we collapse back onto the mattress.

Lying there, I realize I finally feel sated. Tired.

I roll over and burrow myself into Simon's chest, not caring that he's sweaty.

"I love you," I tell him, the feeling an overwhelming pressure in my chest.

"I love you too," he says, making the pressure ease. He wraps an arm around me and tucks my head under his chin.

I know tomorrow could change things. That any of my old worries could appear like haunting ghosts come to life. That wanting tonight could create whole new messes we didn't plan for. But for now I am still floating easily, and so I drift off to dream of Casablanca, six men and Bill and Simon, memories and fantasies spiraling together into beautiful, dirty, wonderful bliss.

ABOUT THE AUTHORS

CALLIOPE BLOOM is a queer writer and editor. She writes fiction, nonfiction, and poetry.

REBECCA CHASE (rebeccahchase.com) is an English rose with a taste for sex and romance. She adores finding story ideas in everyday life and is always looking out for everyone's next book boyfriend. Frequently she can be caught daydreaming in coffee shops or enjoying the spectacle of sportsmen battling with balls.

ALYSSA COLE (alyssacole.com) is an award-winning author of sci-fi, historical, and contemporary romance. When she's not busy writing, traveling, and learning French, she can be found watching anime with her husband, tending to their herd of animals, and finding ways to get around her Twitter-blocking app.

Chicago native **ELIZA DAVID** (elizadavidwrites.com) is an erotic romance author living in Iowa City. She enjoys reading Jackie Collins and indulging in the occasional order of cheese fries. Eliza is also a blogger, serving as a contributing writer for *Real Moms of Eastern Iowa* and *Thirty on Tap*.

JOCELYN DEX (jocelyndex.com) writes paranormal and contemporary romance and erotica that includes humor, lust, love, and four-letter words on the way to a Happily-Ever-After.

PATRICIA ELZIE is a writer (fiction and nonfiction), blogger (kneesockchronicles.com, bookriot.com), librarian, and giver of questionable advice. She lives in Los Angeles, California, with her spouse and hundreds of books.

MEGAN HART (meganhart.com) writes books. Some of them use bad words, but most of the other words are okay. She writes a little bit of everything, although she's best known for writing erotic fiction that sometimes makes you cry.

REGINA KAMMER (kammerotica.com) writes erotica and historical erotic romance. She makes history sexier, whether the era is Roman, Byzantine, Viking, American Revolution, or Victorian. She began writing historical fiction during National Novel Writing Month 2006, switching to erotica when all her characters suddenly demanded to have sex.

MICA KENNEDY (micakennedy.com) writes romantic fiction from the evergreen, ever-damp Pacific Northwest. She is working on her first novel.

ABOUT THE AUTHORS

LOUISE LAGRIS (louiselagris.com) is a writer and editor living in New York City. When she's not reading voraciously, checking out what's new on the big and little screens, or scribbling away for her straight gigs, she slings smutty words online and in print.

TAMARA LUSH (tamaralush.com) is a journalist by day and an erotic romance author at night. Her books have been called "smart smut" by Scandalicious Book Reviews and she finished her most recent novel on a cross-country train trip during an Amtrak Writing Residency.

MADELINE MOORE (moremadelinemoore.blogspot.ca) is an award-winning author of erotica and erotic romance short stories, novels, and novellas. She is also a produced screenwriter and writing tutor. Madeline lives near Toronto.

TAMSEN PARKER (tamsenparker.com) is the *USA Today*–bestselling erotic romance author of the *Compass* series and the *Snow and Ice Games* series. She lives with her family outside of Boston, where she tweets too much, sleeps too little, and is always in the middle of a book.

SOFIA QUINTERO (sofiaquintero.com) has written six novels across multiple genres. You'll find more of her erotica in the anthologies *Juicy Mangos,* edited by Michelle Herrera-Mulligan, and *Dirty Girls,* edited by Rachel Kramer Bussel. Sofia is currently developing a television series based on her novel, *Burn,* written under the pseudonym Black Artemis.

ROSIE BETH RANDALL is a debut author from Southern

California. "Mark" is her first attempt at erotic short-story writing. She is currently crafting her third novel.

SIENNA SAINT-CYR writes erotic and romantic fiction for the *Love Slave* series, *Sexy Little Pages, Melt, Haunt,* and the *Sexual Expression* series. She also writes nonfiction and flash fiction for several websites. Sienna owns SinCyr Publishing, an erotica company with a focus on "shifting rape culture one sexy story at a time."

Editor, writer, American desi, and lifelong geek, **SULEIKHA SNYDER** (suleikhasnyder.com) is an author of sexy contemporary romances like *Bollywood and the Beast* and *Seared*. She lives in Chicago, finding inspiration in genre fiction, soaps, and bacon.

ALESSANDRA TORRE (alessandratorre.com) is a *New York Times*–bestselling author of sixteen novels and the *Bedroom Blogger* for Cosmopolitan.com. In addition to writing, Alessandra is the creator of Alessandra Torre Ink, a community and online school for aspiring authors.

JO HENNY WOLF (johennywolf.org) writes erotic fiction and romance. She lives with her family in the shadow of the Black Forest, where she breathed in fairy tales and myths since childhood. Her writing has been published in anthologies and standalone publications.

R. M. WOOD is a communications professional who lives and works in Victoria, Canada. When not writing, she can be found drinking copious mugs of tea, illustrating comics, or spending time with her husband and two cats.

ABOUT THE EDITOR

RACHEL KRAMER BUSSEL (rachelkramerbussel.com) is a New Jersey–based author, editor, blogger, and writing instructor. She has edited over sixty books of erotica, including *Best Women's Erotica of the Year, Volume 1, 2, and 3*; *Best Bondage Erotica 2011-2015*; *Erotic Teasers*; *Dirty Dates*; *On Fire*; *Come Again: Sex Toy Erotica*; *The Big Book of Orgasms*; *Begging for It*; *The Big Book of Submission*; *Lust in Latex*; *Anything for You: Erotica for Kinky Couples*; *Baby Got Back: Anal Erotica*; *Suite Encounters: Hotel Sex Stories*; *Going Down: Oral Sex Stories*; *Gotta Have It*; *Women in Lust*; *Surrender*; *Orgasmic*; *Cheeky Spanking Stories*; *Bottoms Up*; *Spanked: Red-Cheeked Erotica*; *Fast Girls*; *Do Not Disturb*; *Tasting Him*; *Tasting Her*; *Please, Sir*; *Please, Ma'am*; *He's on Top*; *She's on Top*; and *Crossdressing*. Her anthologies have won eight IPPY (Independent Publisher) Awards, and *Surrender* and *Dirty Dates* won the National Leather Association Samois Anthology Award. Her work has been published

ABOUT THE EDITOR

in over one hundred anthologies, including *Best American Erotica 2004* and *2006*. She wrote the popular "Lusty Lady" column for the *Village Voice*.

Rachel has written for *AVN*, *Bust*, Cleansheets.com, CNN.com, *Cosmopolitan*, *Curve*, The Daily Beast, Elle.com, Fortune.com, TheFrisky.com, *Glamour*, Gothamist, *Harper's Bazaar*, Huffington Post, *Inked*, *Marie Claire*, *Newsday*, *New York Post*, *New York Observer*, *The New York Times*, *O: The Oprah Magazine*, *Penthouse*, Refinery29, Rollingstone.com, The Root, Salon, *San Francisco Chronicle*, Slate, Time.com, Time Out New York, and *Zink*, among others. She has appeared on "The Gayle King Show," "The Martha Stewart Show," "The Berman and Berman Show," NY1, and Showtime's "Family Business." She hosted the popular In the Flesh Erotic Reading Series, featuring readers from Susie Bright to Zane, speaks at conferences, and does readings and teaches erotic writing workshops across the country and online. She blogs at lustylady.blogspot.com and consults about erotica at eroticawriting101.com. Learn more about the *Best Women's Erotica of the Year* series, including writing guidelines, at bweoftheyear.com, and subscribe to Rachel's monthly newsletter with book giveaways at rachelkramerbussel.com.